HUNTERS' LODGE

On the death of her twin brother, divorcee Gillian Sinclair, a career woman bringing up her young daughter Debbie alone, inherits Hunter's Lodge, a country hotel. She is determined not to fail her brother's legacy – no easy task in 1948, restricted by shortages ... As for her ex-husband, for years Gillian has told herself he is out of her life for good. Yet when he reappears suddenly, surely it is not just for Debbie's sake she is prepared to take Stephen back?

HUNTERS' LODGE

Connie Monk

Severn House Large Print
London & New York

This first large print edition published 2010
in Great Britain and the USA by
SEVERN HOUSE PUBLISHERS LTD of
9-15 High Street, Sutton, Surrey, SM1 1DF.
First world regular print edition published 2008 by
Severn House Publishers Ltd., London and New York.

British Library Cataloguing in Publication Data

Monk, Connie.
  Hunters' Lodge.
  1. Inheritance and succession--Fiction. 2. Hotelkeepers--
  Fiction. 3. Single mothers--Fiction. 4. Large type books.
  I. Title
  823.9'14-dc22

  ISBN-13: 978-0-7278-7860-1

Severn House Publishers support The Forest Stewardship Council [FSC],
the leading international forest certification organisation. All our titles that
are printed on Greenpeace-approved FSC-certified paper carry the FSC
logo.

Printed and bound in Great Britain by
MPG Books Ltd, Bodmin, Cornwall.

One

With the receiver of the desk telephone pressed hard against her ear, Gillian listened to the outpouring of jumbled short sentences, each one bringing the threat of hysteria closer. The line was poor, which didn't help.

'What sort of accident? Just start at the beginning, Helen, and tell me calmly what's happened to him.' Her purposefully unemotional tone disguised the irritation she so often felt for her future sister-in-law even though it did nothing to banish her own foreboding. But for Gillian there was no other way of facing whatever she had to hear.

'Gillian, you *will* come, come straight...'

'Stop, Helen! Just calm down and tell me what's happened to David. Was it something in the hotel? Have you sent for help?'

'It was that stupid, beastly, dangerous point-to-point. I *begged* him not to ride, I told him how frightened I was. I *knew* something awful would happen, but he only laughed. Called me a silly girl,' she gulped. 'Said it was pre-marital nerves. But you know how sometimes you just

5

feel things.'

Gillian knew no such thing or, if she did, she would never admit it, even to herself.

'Never mind all that. How can I help if you don't tell me what's wrong?'

Helen took a deep breath, resolving to keep her voice steady. 'I saw it happen, Gillian.' She started speaking more calmly, but her brave intentions were short-lived as the scene came back to her. Her words tumbled out, interspersed with gulps and snorts. 'He was riding Ginger. Well, of course he was, he always rides Ginger. They flew over the first fence, it wasn't the jump that threw him. It happened in a flash, Ginger just fell ... he went down as if he'd been shot. It wasn't even like being thrown, David just went straight down with him.' With self-control lost beyond hope, it was difficult to understand her. 'There go the pips. Wait while I put another shilling in.' A pause that did nothing to calm her near-hysteria. 'So many horses at the first fence, you know how they all come together. He and Ginger were just lying there. Didn't move, not either of them. Some of the other horses stumbled, but no one was hurt. Just David. And Ginger. Ginger had to be lifted off David. I couldn't see, people crowding around, I thought he was dead. So frightened. The St John's people were there. They took him to hospital in Brindley. Come straight away Gillian ... promise me. Don't know what to do.'

'Where are you? Are you still at the point-to-point or have you gone to the hospital?' Gillian

6

marvelled that she could sound so detached, giving no hint that she felt as if her limbs were made of cotton wool. For David's sake she had to hang on to her self-control and support the girl he'd lost his heart to so completely.

'At the District Hospital of course. I had my bike but I was shaking too much to ride. Bill Marchant strapped it on his luggage grid and brought me. Bill told them who I was and they said I was to wait, they said the doctors were looking at him. Bill said Ginger must have had a heart attack. Hateful point-to-point. It needn't have happened. Why couldn't David have just watched the same as I did?'

'Helen...' But it was no use Gillian interrupting the tirade, Helen was beyond hearing her.

'There go the pips again. I've got another shilling ready. Wait, Gillian.' And another pause with just the click of the money being fed into the phone. 'Bill had to leave but when I said I was getting you, he took my bike back to Hunters Lodge. He was ever so kind but I was glad he went. I didn't want him with me trying to keep me talking. Just want to see David, Gillian, it's so awful. Don't know what to do.'

'Helen, you must take a grip of yourself. When they've done with him David's going to need you. He won't want to see you looking red-eyed and blotchy, it'll worry him.' And how true that was. He would never be able to relax if he thought his beloved Helen was tear-stained and miserable. She was his princess. Even

7

though it was a name no one except he would ever use; it stemmed from something little Debbie had said when he had been reading her the story of Sleeping Beauty. The description of the sleeping girl had brought forth an excited giggle from Debbie and, 'Sounds just like Auntie Helen.' And so she had become his princess, and no beauty in a fairy story could have been lovelier. In appearance she was ethereal, slightly built and yet perfect, not a hint of thinness in her delicately slender body. Her finely chiselled features, huge, startlingly blue eyes, honey-fair hair, everything about her added to the impression she created of gentle femininity. All that flashed through Gillian's mind in the second it took her to say, 'He won't want to see you red-eyed and blotchy.'

Whether it was Gillian's sharp tone or the thought that soon David would want her, something appeared to have given Helen's confidence a temporary boost.

'Perhaps he's come round by now. Do you suppose he has?' she said, and momentarily there was an optimistic note in her voice; but it was doomed to be overtaken by panic. 'Perhaps they'll forget to tell him I'm here. Do you think he'll know I'm waiting?'

'Of course they'll tell him as soon as he's ready. And of course he'll know you'll be there for him. We'll get off the telephone now Helen, and I'll go and speak to Mr Merrick.' Over the last few minutes Gillian had given no thought to work, but before she could set out on the drive to Ockbury there were things to be organized.

It seemed that putting her troubles on to Gillian's broad shoulders had restored some of Helen's flagging spirit. 'Perhaps nothing's broken. But they haven't come to tell me anything. We mustn't waste time talking. How quickly can you be here? You will hurry, won't you?'

'I have to explain here what's happened, then get Debbie out of school and call in to tell Mrs Bryant not to collect her at teatime. It's a good two-hour drive. I'll come straight to Accident and Emergency and enquire, but by that time I expect you'll have seen him, and perhaps they might even have told you we can take him home. Tell him I'm on my way when they let you talk to him.'

If Helen had had the situation under control, then Gillian might not have found the will-power to speak in that positive voice. Or perhaps it was all part of her own battle to overcome the fear that threatened to possess her. Into her mind flashed the memory of the strange and unaccountable sensation she'd felt as she'd settled six-year-old Debbie in the front passenger seat of her pre-war Morris Oxford at the start of their morning. 'Sometimes you just *feel* things' came the echo of Helen's voice. Was that the moment Ginger had fallen? There was something unnatural in the awareness between David and herself; surely it was more than the fact that they were twins. A thousand

9

memories tried to push into her mind, but she gave them no chance.

As soon as she put the receiver back on its hook, she went to Ian Merrick's office. Merrick was the senior design engineer at a firm producing farm machinery, and Gillian had been engaged as his secretary about ten years previously. During that time, she had become both secretary and personal assistant. Despite the respect they had for each other, the natural reserve between them had never lessened.

None of those in junior positions envied her, for he was regarded as a difficult man who accepted nothing less than perfection. Indeed, most of the young typists regarded her with respectful awe, seeing no further than the facade of a well-groomed, smart young woman, slim and austere, never a hair out of place, never a button hanging loose on her immaculate business suit, never a chip in her perfectly manicured and painted nails and never a run in her stockings despite the seemingly endless years of clothes rationing, which three years after the end of the war, still held its grip.

But over the years, as she'd fought to find a new purpose in her personal life, determined not to be beaten by a broken marriage and single parenthood, the knowledge that she had become ever more necessary to Ian Merrick and his work had been balm to her confidence. To many women, a situation such as hers would have drawn people close; but not so for Gillian. Her personal life was her own, she shared her worries and hurts with no one – no one except David.

'This is very sudden,' was his comment when Gillian told him she had been sent for.

'Accidents aren't planned,' she snapped, momentarily losing her control. Hearing herself, she saw his expression change even as she mumbled an apology. It occurred to her that she'd never seen him smile, neither had she ever heard him raise his voice in anger.

'I asked for that!' And there was evidence that he really could smile. 'No need for me to say I hope you'll not have to be away long, for my own sake as well as your brother's. He has no other family?' The brief smile having gone, the question implied that he saw her as carrying sisterly affection unusually far.

Gillian shook her head. 'Our parents have been in New Zealand for all our adult lives. David and I are twins.'

'Of course you must go.' It was hard to read his expression; the frown seemed more of sadness than anger. 'I used to have a twin brother myself, an identical twin.' He met her eyes squarely. 'He was lost at Dunkirk.' At Dunkirk! And she must have been working for him and not known. Then, almost as if he were ashamed of exposing even so slender a crack in his armour, 'Off you go, Mrs Sinclair. Leave me to organize someone to do my work. I trust his injuries aren't serious.'

And how could she know the path his thoughts took as he watched her go out of the

11

room, closing the door quietly behind her? Not for the first time he tried, without success, to imagine her outside the familiar setting of the office. He'd heard a rumour that her husband had walked out on her, and, if he had, was that so surprising? Ice cold. And yet it was that very coldness, the never failing courteous efficiency, that was intriguing. Today had thrown her off balance though, no doubt about that. A twin brother. Gillian Sinclair was forgotten as, sitting back in his chair, arms folded and eyes closed, he called up memories buried deep in the past.

'Why've you come to get me, Mum?'

'I'll tell you as we drive. In you hop,' Gillian answered, holding open the door of the front passenger seat.

But the story she gave to Debbie told nothing of Helen's panic nor of her own unacknowledged fear. A fall from a horse might be no more than a minor incident; she and David had had many a fall when they were children. But David was no longer a child with the ability to bounce back as easily as a rubber ball, he was a man of thirty-two. That was as far as Gillian let her mind go. She wouldn't allow herself to remember Helen's terror; wouldn't let herself remember and yet couldn't get from her mind the images those hysterical words had created. No, don't let it be, she pleaded silently. Helen was frightened, she gets frightened over every silly little thing. Don't let him be – but even

12

silently she couldn't let herself put her fear into words. Probably Helen had exaggerated because she was upset. And another thought before loyalty to David pushed it away: Helen had no backbone. Bruises, even a broken bone, but – no, no, please, no.

With her foot pressed hard on the accelerator, she forced the elderly car forward. She had put her name on the waiting list for a new car, a Flying Standard, taking pride in the fact that she had managed to save the money to pay as soon as the garage let her know it had arrived. This old Morris she had bought second hand as soon as she had learnt to drive in the mid 1930s. Like so many vehicles still on the road, it had seen better days and the seven years of "imposed rest" due to petrol only being available for essential use had done nothing to rejuvenate it.

When she stopped at a garage, the lad who came out to fill the tank seemed to have no idea of urgency, he strolled off with her money and kept her waiting for what seemed like ages before he reappeared with her change. Then she was on her way again. Until David knew she was there, he would be worried about how Helen was coping. Then that other thought that had to be crushed before it had a chance to air itself: he treated his beloved Helen as though she were made of cotton wool, so did Gillian's irritation with the younger woman stem from jealousy? Jealousy of David's near-worship of the girl he was to marry? Jealousy of Helen's natural loveliness that nothing could change, so

13

unlike her own well-groomed and hard-fought-for appearance? She pushed the question away unanswered and let her mind go back to David. Once he knew she had arrived he would be free to think just about himself and about getting better.

Yet when she came to her journey's end at the Accident and Emergency Department of the hospital, she took one look at Helen's face and knew there was no way of escaping the truth.

'You've taken ages. I thought you'd never get here.' Unashamedly Helen sobbed while the other few people waiting on the benches tried to look engrossed with something, anything, rather than appear to hear her. 'Such a long time. It's not true, Gillian, it can't be true.' Then giving her nose what was supposed to be a restorative blow on her tear-drenched hanker-chief, she made a supreme effort. 'They let me see him ... he didn't even know I was there ... I kept talking to him ... was with him when he ... it can't be real, can't be true.' It was almost impossible to understand what she was saying.

Irritation and fear got the better of Gillian's good intentions to be kind. 'Shut up, Helen. Just tell me where he is.' Anything but face Helen's distraught outburst. 'It can't be real, it can't be true.' The words echoed and re-echoed. She felt sick with fright, sick with misery, expressions she'd heard but until that moment had never realized the truth of.

'Just told you. Don't shout at me, Gillian. Please don't shout at me. It's not the same for you. There won't be a wedding. Everything we'd planned, everything we'd dreamed of, now there's nothing. *Nothing*. Dead. I told you. I was there. Never seen anyone before...' But that one word, "dead", was all that Gillian seemed to hear.

'Mum?' Debbie tugged at her hand. 'Mum?' Frightened by Helen's show of grief that made a stranger of her, the little girl needed reassurance. "Dead", that's what Auntie Helen had said, but being dead was what happened when people got very old, like Mrs Hamlyn had been in the flat across the landing from where she and Mum lived. But Uncle David was exactly the same age as Mum so surely poor crying Aunt Helen must have made a mistake. If he was old enough to die ... she shied away from the thought that was forming in her mind and gripped Gillian's hand tight.

'Debbie,' Gillian said, returning the grip and marvelling that while her heart was pounding and her stomach churning, while her mouth felt as though it were full of sawdust and her legs as though they hadn't the strength to hold her up, she could sound so controlled, 'Debbie darling, Uncle David was hurt quite badly when he fell.'

'Why don't you listen?' Helen blubbered, while others in the waiting room stared at the out-of-date and well-thumbed magazines with increased concentration. 'I told you, he's *dead*.' Then, making another supreme effort, 'I told the Sister you were on your way and she said she wanted to see you as soon as you got here.

15

Me? I'm nothing, nobody. I'm just the girl he was going to marry. It's you who they think is important.'

'I'll go and find her. Debbie darling, you wait here with Auntie Helen until I come back.'

'Can't I come Mum? I'm important too.'

She was not given to shows of emotion, yet in that second Gillian needed reassurance every bit as much as Debbie did. Taking them both by surprise, she lifted the slightly-built child and held her in a bearlike hug.

'Yes, sweetheart, you're important. But this is just something we have to do for Uncle David. And Debbie, for *him* I want you to stay with Auntie Helen and take care of her. I'll be as quick as I can.'

Responsibility helped to take away some of Debbie's uncertainty. She just wished Helen was like she always had been: happy, Uncle David's princess, smiling, pretty and lots of fun. But she mustn't let her mother down, so she nodded, gave her a squeeze to show she wasn't a baby and she understood, then wriggled to the ground.

'Shall we sit down over there, Auntie Helen? I don't expect Mum'll be long.' There now, she was sounding like quite a grown-up.

It seemed that Gillian's words had had their effect on Helen too; David would want her to be strong, so she told herself it was for him that she made the effort. In truth it was partly the effect of Debbie's solicitous tone. Just for a moment she found herself seeing beyond the cruel blow fate had dealt her, and she recognized frightened uncertainty in the little girl's eyes.

'Yes,' she agreed, taking Debbie's hand, 'let's go to those seats by the wall next to the vending machines. We'll see what we can buy, shall we? A bar of chocolate or a can of fizzy drink? You choose.'

Almost visibly, Debbie relaxed. This was more like the Helen she had fun with when she and her mother came to Hunters' Lodge at the weekends. She called her "Auntie" but it was really only a pretend name because she would not be a proper aunt until after the wedding. Debbie pictured the bridesmaid's outfit hanging in her wardrobe and for a second felt herself standing taller. Then back came the thing she had been trying not to remember: they said Uncle David was dead. There wouldn't be a wedding. She'd like to be able to ask what would happen to her beautiful dress and the flowers for her hair, but instinct warned her against it. So she gave Helen a reassuring smile and resolved to make the new, less miserable mood last.

'Let's have chocolate,' she suggested. 'It's hard to share a can of drink and we can break the choc into squares. You know what Mum says? If I fall over and bleed, anything bad like that, then she always finds me two squares of chocolate – one to stop me thinking about being hurt and one to give feeling better a good start. Shall we try that?'

17

Helen nodded, frightened to trust her voice. It was soon clear to Debbie that even two squares weren't having the desired effect. 'It's not going to happen,' Helen croaked through a mouthful of chocolate, 'my beautiful wedding dress, and your bridesmaid one too, Debbie, we won't be able to wear them.' Somehow it helped to put it into words, to see the child's solemn nod and feel the small hand slipped into her own. It made her feel less alone. 'If only I'd put it on so that he could have seen. Too late now. He's dead Debbie, dead, dead, dead.' Over and over she said that one word just as if she were talking to herself.

Debbie dug deep in her mind to think of a way to stop Helen slipping back into all that misery that made her keep on crying.

'Mum bought a beautiful hat. Auntie Helen. Listen, I know a plan.' As she spoke she held up her index finger as if to command obedient attention. 'When Bobtail died – you remember Bobtail, the bunny Uncle David let me keep at his place – well I cried like anything. And he said to me that if I was so sad it would upset Bobtail, 'cause even though I couldn't see *him*, he would know how I felt because he had really loved me. And I know that was true, 'cause he used to be pleased as anything when I came to Hunters' Lodge. So Uncle David said that if I wanted to keep Bobtail happy, I had to be happy. 'strordinary, 'cause he didn't know about me when I was home with Mum and he was alive. But that's what Uncle David said,

18

and so it must be right.'

So far it seemed her words had done little to cheer Helen for, although she no longer blubbered out loud as she had earlier, still she was biting hard on the corners of her mouth while tears rolled down her face. 'So listen, Auntie – I shall still call you that 'cause you can't suddenly not be my auntie can you? – I have this plan. We'll all get dressed up in our pretty things, you in your white dress and me in my gorgeous pink one – and Mum, Mum in her new suit and her hat. If Bobtail could see me, then Uncle David's sure to see *us*. Look, two squares left. Open wide and I'll pop yours in.'

She'd been so sure that the scheme would cheer Helen but apparantly she was wrong. As pretty as a fairy princess, yet Debbie saw her as someone who, although she was an aunt, still loved having fun; someone who skipped better than anyone she knew and who loved games like hide and seek or rolling down the hill on the downs near Hunters' Lodge just as if she weren't a grown up at all. Given the responsibility of taking care of her, the little girl looked round helplessly as if for inspiration then, when it wasn't to be found, she tightened her grip on Helen's hand, hoping that would give the message that she cared. All her excitement about an unexpected visit to Hunters' Lodge had vanished.

'Don't know what I'm going to do, Debbie,' Helen wept quietly, thankful to voice her fears to someone young and unworldly. 'The children I taught gave me cards when I left at the end of last term, the staff collected for a present, everyone knew about David and me getting married. Mrs Harper where I live has found someone else to take my rooms because I was going to move my things before the wedding, bring everything to David's. Only it wouldn't have been just David's, it would have been *mine* too. Don't know what to do, Debbie. All our dreams, everything, gone. Was going to be so perfect, the wedding, then he was going to teach me about running the hotel. Nothing now, Debbie.'

Debbie nodded sagely, digging deep in her vocabulary to find words that might bring some sort of solace. Relief came in the form of her mother.

'You said Bill was taking your bike back to Hunters' Lodge, Helen?' There was a sharp note in Gillian's voice, a note that defied any show of emotion. 'We'll go back there together.' Then, feeling a small hand in hers, 'I expect your poor tummy thinks we've forgotten to give it any lunch, Debbie. We'll soon be home.'

'Home at Uncle David's?' The words slipped out before they could be stopped. 'Well, it is his, isn't it, Mum?'

'Yes sweetie, it's Uncle David's.' Stop it, *stop it*, she told herself, frightened by the chink that had appeared in her armour.

'Umph,' Debbie's grunt told of her satisfaction. But she did wish Auntie Helen would stop sniffing. She betted one thing, she betted that just because they had been going to get married, that didn't make her as special to him as Mum. "Two sides of the same penny" that's what he had said twins were, so no one could be more special than that.

During the six mile drive from the hospital to Hunters' Lodge, the hotel that stood just outside Ockbury village, the only sound was Helen's pitiful sniffing punctuated by an occasional snort. This time Debbie was travelling in the back of the car. She looked at the two in front of her, her mother sitting so erect and staring straight ahead as she drove, Helen unnaturally hunched and mopping her face with the sodden handkerchief. Standing up and forcing her head between the two of them, Debbie tapped the bent shoulder.

'Think about Bobtail, Auntie Helen.'

Glancing in the driver's mirror she could see her mother's quick frown. If only she wouldn't look so cross, perhaps Auntie Helen would stop crying. Usually her face was pretty, but today it was all swollen looking so that her eyes were nearly closed up.

Once they were back at the hotel and out of the car, just for a moment there was something about her mother's expression she wasn't used to, and the way she gripped the car door handle as if she were frightened of falling over.

'Mum?'

'There are things Helen and I have to do, things to do for David. Run and play on the swing.'

21

'I can't go in there,' Helen whimpered, nodding her head in the direction of the hotel building while she kept her face shielded by her hands.

'Helen, you've got to pull yourself together. Do you imagine this is easy for any of us?'

Debbie was glad to go. Swinging all by herself didn't tempt her, so instead she made for the stables where she could talk to Mike who looked after the horses.

'It's not the same for you,' Helen turned to Gillian with something like anger. 'I wanted our marriage to be perfect. And it would have been.' She paused, her eyes closed. 'David loved me.' The three words 'David loved me' at least temporarily dispelled Gillian's irritation at Helen's behaviour. Memory took her back two years to the time David had made a special journey to talk to her. The two of them in the sitting room of her flat, he telling her so earnestly about the girl he'd fallen in love with.

That's when she'd learnt about Helen's background. Born of middle-aged parents and orphaned at a year old when they were killed in a motoring accident, she had been put into a foster home. There had followed years of being shifted from one place to another. 'David loved me', three words that told Gillian so much. For a moment she felt compassion for the girl so different from herself. But it evaporated as Helen went on, 'Marriage was the most important thing to me – not like a career or making money or any of those things. I never had casual boyfriends, I hated all that sort of thing, but I would have been everything David wanted. Being married, belonging, knowing that for as long as we lived we would be together. When David and I got married everything was going to be for the first time, right and perfect because I was his wife. You lived with Stephen Sinclair before you married him. I know you did because David told me about you and Stephen and tried to persuade me that it could be like that for us too. And when you did get married, look what happened. It didn't last and that's because you never loved each other enough to wait for the time that being together – like *that* – was – was honourable. He saw everything you did as right. But I wouldn't let us make love, I wanted it to be perfect.'

'Stop it, Helen. That was between you and David, it's nothing to do with me.'

'I said no – and now it's too late. I just thought of the chattering and sniggering there would have been amongst the staff making it seem – seem smutty, cheap and beastly. I wanted it to be perfect and because he loved me, *me* for myself, not just as someone to take to bed. Now it's too late, it'll never happen.'

'Don't, Helen. That's nothing to do with me.'

'Nothing to do with you! You say that! You, all the time it was you, you, *you*. Everything you did was right. "Gillian did this ... Gillian did that ... Gillian thinks this ... Gillian says that", as if he hadn't got a life of his own. But it was *me* he was going to marry; it was me he loved, loved more than he ever did you. I was going to help him run the hotel, the staff would look up to me and respect me.'

Numb with misery, Gillian was helpless to quell the hysterical outburst. She told herself it was natural for Helen to be so full of resentment, losing the happiness she had been sure was soon to be hers, who could blame her? With their back towards the building of Hunters' Lodge, they walked across the wide lawn to the summer house. Gillian even held her arm around the girl's slender shoulders. She assumed it was a good sign that the wild crying had given way to silence. So Helen's next words came as a shock.

'I gave up my job when term ended in July,' she said, this time speaking more calmly, 'and my rooms have been let from when I was leaving to get married. David would have taught me the things I didn't know about looking after the hotel.' Then, sitting on a wicker chair, she looked up at Gillian, her whole manner very different from the broken reed she had been half an hour before or the wild-eyed creature who had lashed out only moments ago. For a moment she seemed to have found new strength and seen a way ahead. It was as if her mind had quite suddenly gone back into focus.

'Yes,' she said, and was it relief Gillian detected in her tone? 'Yes, he went to Gregory and Tufnell's last week. Did he tell you that? David always took care of me, and so he will have now.' Listening to her, Gillian felt lonely and alone. David was gone from her life, never again would she laugh with him, never again would she bring him her troubles and know he'd understand.

Helen was still talking. 'When he told me how much he owed – perhaps you didn't know how much he'd borrowed on this place – each month his outgoings were enormous. But when he told me, I wasn't frightened, I had faith in all he did. And through the summer this year the hotel was doing quite well. Even though it didn't do much more than cover the expenses, he was sure he could repay his debts and our future would be secure. We even dreamed of a time when he could sell out and we'd have enough money to start a new life.'

Her tone suggested that she had wept herself dry and found her confidence not completely drowned in tears. 'In the beginning he knew if he put it on the market he'd never get back what he owed. Now that people can use their cars again, they come from miles around to have dinner here, the place has a good reputation, and the bedrooms are well filled. It will cover its debts and more when it's put on the market.'

'Sell Hunters' Lodge? But David wouldn't have sold!'

'One day we would have. One day we were going to find somewhere new, a place just for ourselves and our children, somewhere in the sunshine. Just a dream, now it can never happen.'

Gillian didn't want to hear. With her back to

Helen she looked out of the summer house window across the swathe of lawn to the hotel, an L-shaped stone building that had stood for nearly 300 years, most of them as a farm house and labourers' cottages. David had bought it as little more than a neglected wreck and had put everything he'd possessed and all he could borrow into transforming it into a hotel. She remembered the look of pride on his face as, with the internal transformation completed, he had watched the thatchers at work on the new roof. 'Like putting the icing on the cake, Gilly,' he had said. Gazing at it now, Gillian could almost hear his voice.

'David gone. Now there's nothing, nothing.' Helen's ominous croak cut across her thoughts. Then, holding her chin higher, she spoke firmly, even though she couldn't look directly at Gillian. 'David was making a fresh Will because I was to be his wife. He told me so. Yes, I shall put it on the market, Gillian. David, if he can know, will expect that I should. He would understand that I couldn't possibly run Hunters' Lodge without him.'

Gillian didn't want to listen. She felt empty and sick. 'We haven't been inside yet. We must talk to the staff – and the guests.'

'*I* can't talk to them. You can't expect me to do it! At the hospital it was *you* who was important, now you expect me to go in there and tell them – tell them...'

Gillian knew she was being cruel when she said, 'Don't you think David might expect you

26

to do it?'

'No. No, I know he wouldn't. That just shows how little you understand. David wouldn't want me to have to do it. Look at me! How can you expect me to go in there and tell everyone that it's all gone, all the dreams, all the plans. I can't, Gillian.'

Without answering, Gillian left her never-to-be sister-in-law sitting hunched miserably in the summer house and, head high, retraced her steps across the green sward, then round to the side of the building to the staff entrance. She found her salvation in taking responsibility.

'Sarah,' she greeted the receptionist cum any other job that came her way, 'I want you to hunt up all the staff – everyone – and tell them to wait for me in the office.'

'Is something wrong? Someone brought Miss Murdock's bike, just leant it against the front and called out would someone take it to the shed. Now you've come. What's happened?' The young girl had been watching out of the window, so she was sure something was definitely wrong. And why had David's sister come without warning on a Wednesday?

Ignoring the question, or shelving what had to be told, Gillian asked, 'Are any guests here other than the Crosbie sisters?'

Sarah Wright shook her head. 'Just them. They said they were going for a walk before the daylight fades, but I bet they've changed their minds. They're in the lounge. Shall I get them into the office too?'

'No. Round up the others. First though, put the bolt on the front door and take the telephone receiver off the hook so that we aren't disturbed. Then give me five minutes with the Crosbie sisters.'

Margaret and Jane Crosbie had lived at Hunters' Lodge since the first week it opened. At one time they had both been teachers, but had long since retired and had been contemplating finding a comfortable "Twilight Home" where they would be looked after. Then they'd read the account in the local paper of the hotel opening on the outskirts of Ockbury village and had decided to have a week or two there while they made enquiries about somewhere more permanent. Once they met David and settled into their comfortable room overlooking the garden they decided not to hurry. Gradually weeks had turned to months, one year had gone by, then another, and they knew that Hunters' Lodge would be where they would stay. They doted on David, and although even to each other they never put it into words, they each saw him as the son (or more accurately grandson) they'd never had. Of course Gillian was well acquainted with them, she'd been aware of how fond they were of David, yet even after so long she and the elderly sisters had never moved beyond the stage of polite courtesy.

Coming into the visitors' lounge, Gillian found them sitting by the fire David had instructed should be lit for their benefit and knitting as if it were second nature and required no attention. It was as if the scene imprinted itself on her; she dreaded what must come next.

'Why! It's Mrs Sinclair. Oh dear, did David know you were coming? He's out riding; pleased as punch he was about it when he talked to us last night. But he didn't mention that you were expected.' That from Margaret, the younger but more dominant of the pair.

'No. Helen sent for me.' The knitting needles were suddenly still; the room was silent. It took all Gillian's courage to say what had to be said.

'Sit down, Mrs Sinclair, my dear.' Jane's kindly voice could so easily have been Gillian's undoing. It took every bit of willpower she could muster to speak calmly – indeed to speak at all – as she sat very straight-backed on the sofa.

'He was riding in the point-to-point.'

'That's it. He told us about it last night.' Margaret was talking for the sake of talking. Dear Helen wouldn't have sent for Mrs Sinclair for nothing.

'He's had a fall? The dear boy's hurt?' Jane prompted. 'I expect it frightened poor Helen. She went to watch, you know. Not badly hurt? Such a splendid rider. Did his horse throw him?'

'He wasn't thrown...' Gillian heard the way she stressed the words. 'David was an excellent rider. Ginger must have had a heart attack; he went down as though he'd been shot. That's what Helen said. David came off and Ginger rolled on him.' Words, just words, spoken as

29

though she were reciting a part. She tried not to look at the two elderly ladies who had so loved David. She must be strong ... she had things to do ... for David she must be strong...

'Is he hurt very badly? Oh, my dear, if only we could do something for the dear boy.'

'It's too late. We can none of us do anything. He died without regaining consciousness.' There! She'd said it. She marvelled at the unemotional tone of her voice. How could she speak at all when her mouth seemed full of sawdust and she felt hollow and sick?

Margaret and Jane Crosbie were weeping. One after another they spoke, neither listening to the other, neither expecting a reply.

'And here we are, old and useless. That poor dear boy with his life ahead of him. Where's the justice?'

'And little Helen, poor child, poor dear child. How can she bear it?'

How can Helen bear it, they'd said. Gillian turned away, frightened they might show sympathy to *her* when their thoughts moved on from Helen.

'She'll have no choice,' she heard herself answer coldly, and then hated herself that she could take that tone about the girl David had loved so much. 'I have to talk to the staff.' Brisk, efficient, cold, heartless, make of her what they would, she could face the next hours no other way. 'But I know David would want you to hear it from one of us separately. I'll send something in for you, a small brandy will

30

buck you up.' To be honest, she didn't care whether or not it would buck them up, but with the image of David before her she knew that to see they were cared for was just one of the things she would do for him.

Crossing the foyer, she could hear voices in the small office and knew those of the staff on duty were waiting. Before she joined them she went into the bar and poured two brandies, then took them herself to the sisters. They looked old and frail, their knitting untouched in their laps. Perhaps it was that affinity she had always had with David, that in that moment she felt real affection for them.

'Drink it up for David. He was very fond of you two.'

It was an un-Gillian-like thing to say and before either of them replied she had put down the tray and retreated.

In the office, she stood in front of the gathered assembly. Still wearing the protective armour of formality and with no trace of emotion, she told them the morning's story. By then it was already mid-afternoon, lunches were finished and in the normal course of events the kitchen staff, even the head chef, would be going off duty. The two lunchtime waitresses had only just finished laying up ready for the evening, so those gathered were Norman Bicton the chef, his two young assistants, Maud Hume who did the washing up, two waitresses, Sarah Wright the receptionist and Mike who looked after the stables.

'Gawd help us, can't believe it could 'appen.' Maud wiped eyes and nose with her already well-splashed apron. 'The best boss I ever worked for and that's the truth.'

Sarah felt it ought to be up to her to say something, seeing herself as senior member of the staff despite being one of the youngest. But what could she say? She'd never worked for anyone else and from the day she'd come to Hunters' Lodge, David had been an object of hero worship.

'So awful.' She tried without success to attract Gillian's glance so that her grief could be appreciated. 'We are all sorry, dreadfully sorry. Oh dear, and poor Helen. Is she coping all right, Mrs Sinclair? Can we do anything for her?'

'I think not, thank you, Sarah, but I'll give her your message. I think that's all I can tell you at the moment, any of you. Sarah, will you type a notice to put on the desk – no, give me the paper and I'll word it myself. It would be embarrassing for any of David's regular clients not to know what's happened.'

Those gathered were looking uncomfortably from one to another. It was Norman Bicton who voiced what was in everyone's mind.

'We'll be closing this evening, of course. Then what about the days until after ... after the...' He looked uncomfortable. Even though he had to get his instructions, he felt it wasn't right to talk about a funeral when the best boss he'd ever worked for wasn't even cold.

'We shall be open this evening as normal. No

good can be done by closing. We have a duty to keep things going. Closing would do David no good ... and he wouldn't want it. If you'll give me a sheet of paper, Sarah, I'll type that notice.' Then, to the assembly at large and with a dismissive nod of her head, 'That's all I can tell you for the present. When I know anything more you will be told.'

'Hard-nosed bitch.' Norman forgot his seniority and voiced his thoughts aloud as they made their way back through the restaurant.

Left alone, Gillian put a sheet of paper into the typewriter and stared blankly at the keys, dreading the stark finality of the words she must print. First, though, she had a telephone call to make. Their parents must be told. They had seldom spoken over the years; calls had been major events reserved for birthdays or Christmas. But distance had put no barrier between them and it would take all her courage to hang on to her own control while she gave them news that even from the other side of the world would cloud their lives. But it had to be done, so closing her eyes as if that would cut her off from the misery that swamped her, and completely disregarding the difference in the time zones, she lifted the telephone receiver.

'Number please,' came the impersonal voice of the operator at Brindley exchange.

'I want a call to New Zealand.'

'New Zealand did you say? And what's your number?' Then when she had both numbers

33

satisfactorily recorded, 'I'll call you back as soon as I can get a connection.'

Alone in the summer house, Helen physically ached with misery, her swollen eyelids stung, she felt sick. She was frightened to rekindle memories of the early months after she had met David, months when she had first known there was someone she could trust completely, someone who was her real and total friend. Now, leaning back against the wooden side of the summer house. she closed her aching eyes; memory wouldn't be denied. Walking with him across the downs ... the time he had first taken her hand in his ... his teaching her to ride (something she wasn't good at and secretly had hated, but to please him she had hidden her fear and tried hard to do as he wanted) ... that day when he lifted her down from the saddle and just looked at her, his hands on her shoulders, his eyes willing her not to look away. That was the day she realized he loved her, a deep-into-his-soul love that had nothing to do with the sort of romances you read of in magazine stories.

And from that day on, her life had been changed. No longer had she seen herself as being alone and important to no one; even though he hadn't put it into words until much later, she had known she was the centre of David's existence. Neither of them had spoken of love, but their lives had become more and more entwined. And then there had been little Debbie, she must have been about four then, her visits and the childish fun they had had with her had enriched their lives.

Only hours before, the future had been secure and wonderful. Now she was nothing, nobody. But David had loved her; he would want her to do whatever was right with Hunters' Lodge. And so she would. She would make herself be strong and she would put it on the market. Even then the future was no more that a blanket of fog. The only thing that gave her any hint of satisfaction was the knowledge that what happened would be up to *her* and not to so-sure-of-herself Gillian.

Much later, the news carried to the other side of the world and a typed notice on the reception desk bringing a less than festive atmosphere to the dining room, the day was finally over. Debbie had accepted the changes just as she would have accepted any other in the lives of those around her. She knew about people dying, but her experience hadn't yet stretched to the endless void of death. Her much-loved uncle had gone and there was a strange sort of hush about the hotel, but beyond that she had no conception of the finality of his going. She was glad that Helen had stopped that horrid crying enough to cycle away from Hunters' Lodge back to where she lived.

The day over, there was nowhere for Gillian to hide from the misery that wasn't just for her own loss but David's too. He had so loved life. The hotel had been both a challenge and an adventure, yet in the beginning, a free man thankful to have come safely through more than six wartime years of flying in the Royal Air Force, logic should have told him that the cards were stacked against him. In a land of austerity, who in his right mind would have been confident of a successful future for a country hotel?

But David had looked beyond the hurdles, nothing had deterred him as he'd applied for planning permission for the alterations, watched the project take shape, obtained furniture dockets for what had to be bought new, and scoured salerooms for suitable pieces to sit comfortably in the old house. And his faith was being repaid. By those last months of 1948 there were plenty who could afford to take a trip into the country and dine at Hunters' Lodge. Food rationing persisted, but for those who could afford it, what better than to eat out? Now that the hotel was becoming established, his heart given so utterly to Helen and their wedding only weeks away, where was the justice that his happiness should be snatched from him?

Over the last hours it had been action that had been Gillian's armour, action and the fact that both Debbie and Helen depended on her. With the day over, she felt alone and lost. Brothers and sisters are often close, but the bond between David and her had been something integral to their lives. Was it always like that for twins? She'd accepted it without thought; only

36

now did she feel a loss that went beyond grief. His presence was all around her, something so natural that until now she'd not thought about it. She and David had needed no words. Ghosts from their past filled her head. Quite clearly she remembered the pushchair where they had sat side by side, she could still imagine the motion of it as it was bumped down the kerb, eased up the kerb, the two of them tightly strapped in and sitting so close that their shoulders touched. Memories flooded back of incidents buried deep in the past, things she'd not thought of for years: first day at kindergarten; sharing a pair of roller skates she had had for her birthday (such a tactless thing for someone to do, to give roller skates to one and a fishing rod to the other); sharing the fishing rod too; day-long outings for just the two of them in school holidays; long cycle rides and the time her chain had broken and they'd taken turns to ride his bike while the other had run by the side pushing hers.

On this night, comfort was out of reach, but those were the memories that made the building bricks of her confidence to face the things she had to do, to do for *him*, her other self. Lying in the darkness, it was something rarer and more precious than loving companionship that crowded her mind. Surely nothing, *nothing* could destroy the closeness that had bound them – had and always would. Don't let me lose him, please, I beg let his spirit stay close. Sometimes we haven't seen each other for months, but it never made a difference. He's part of me, like I'm part of him.

Remember when I met Stephen. I'd had boyfriends, but I'd never been in love until then. I was frightened to believe that Stephen could have cared about me; that's why I didn't talk about him to anyone, not even David. The first man I made love with – the *only* man – was Stephen. Remember how it was – a hot Sunday afternoon, I felt I'd lived all my life for that moment, I believed it was like a glimpse of paradise, I was even naïve enough to think it was the same for him. What a fool I was! We were still lying there, not wanting to move, the sun warm on our bodies, when the phone rang. 'Don't answer it, stay here with me,' that's what Stephen said. But I knew I must, I *knew* it was David. 'Something's happened, I know it has. Gillian, Gillian, are you all right? Someone ... I just know.' It wasn't a question; he was stating a fact. 'Yes, there is someone. Nothing has ever been so right, David. You've got to know him. It's important.' That had been in the spring of 1939. Now, all these years later lying there in the dark bedroom she felt utterly alone, Stephen gone, David gone.

When war came, David immediately volunteered for the Air Force. She could still recall her shame that she could have been so wildly happy while he was being trained to fight in the sky. Yet, she had been.

Even though as a roving reporter Stephen had been away from London far more than he was there, when he came back it was always to her

38

flat – their flat as she had thought of it. Let the whispering neighbours think what they liked, she'd cared for nothing but the happiness he brought to her. As her mind rushed out of control to those months and years, she had no power to shut out memories she had repressed for so long: days on the Thames, visits to the theatre, dining and dancing, and always their happiness finding its culmination in the joy of love making.

Through the early months of the war he'd travelled far and wide in Britain, France, the Netherlands, anywhere where he could send home to his paper in New York articles building a picture of life for civilians in war-torn Europe. Towards the end of 1940 they were married and, with what was to become known as the Battle of Britain fought and won in the skies over England, David had had leave to be with them. Surely that must have been the most purely joyous period of all. And through all that time, wherever they went, Stephen took his camera. Back in "their" flat was the album, which she had never had the courage to destroy: pictures of her, pictures of him, and pictures of the two of them taken by waiters in restaurants or even casual passers by. She could almost hear Stephen's voice, 'Pardon me, marm, but would you take a picture of me and my girl-friend?' or later '...me and my wife.' So handsome, so charming and with that American friendliness, no one could resist him.

Gillian pulled her mind up short. David, it

was David she wanted to think of, it was David's never failing understanding she craved. All their lives there had been times when he had known things without her having to tell him. At that period, he seldom saw her and her letters gave no suggestion that some of the sparkle had gone out of her marriage. Why should she and Stephen have been so happy when he'd spent every moment he could with her before marriage, and yet so soon things had started to change? After France fell, he spent more time in England and surely that should have brought them closer; instead an invisible barrier had seemed to stand between them. Even though her letters told David none of this, he had *known* she was unhappy and had known the reason why.

Tonight of all nights, Gillian didn't want to think of Stephen, tonight she wanted nothing but David. But memories came to mind uninvited. The last time Stephen had been with her, 9th December 1941, arriving from Edinburgh a day before she'd expected, he had found her curled on the sofa in front of the gas fire reading, having had an early bath but being more comfortable where she was than going to a cold bed. After more than seven years, nothing dimmed her feeling of angry humiliation as she remembered the intensity of her joy in seeing him, her excitement that she was alluringly perfumed and wearing nothing except a dressing gown.

He'd seemed quiet but she'd assumed he was

tired; lately he'd often come home listless and weary after a journey, something it was easy to understand in view of cancellations in trains, overcrowded compartments dimly lit and airless. But she'd been keen to wake him, to arouse a desire as keen as her own. Whatever his intentions may have been, physically he'd followed her lead. Not for the first time, they hadn't waited to go to the cold bedroom. Looking back (something she had been resolved not to do) she recognized that his love making had lacked tenderness, but at the time the roughness in his touch had heightened her excitement. In minutes it had been over and she'd sunk into those first moments of satisfied contentment. On that evening, though, contentment had lasted but seconds.

Now, lying alone in the dark bedroom at Hunters' Lodge, she closed her eyes and tried to close her mind. But the echo of his voice could not be shut out: 'God!' he'd panted, exhausted and angry. 'Oh God,' and then with a change of tone, his voice cold, distant, 'I never meant that to happen, it's not what I came for.' Then, pushing her from him, 'It's no use Gillian; it's all over for us. I've known for months. What those swine have done at Pearl Harbour has brought it home to me. What in hell's name am I doing over here? This isn't my country. I'm going home, back where I belong. There's nothing to keep me here. My heart's back home with my own sort of folk. How much has it meant to you that those swine have bombed the American

41

fleet? Nothing. My country is in trouble, deep trouble.'

'But we could both go.' Why had she said it? Surely his tone had told her that he wanted to close the door on the lives they'd shared.

'It's over, Gillian. OK, we've had some good times, but how much have we really shared? Sex, that's about the lot. A few snatched hours that hardly interrupt the way we spend our real lives. You have yours, I have mine. But what's happening back there is *real*. My own country is where I belong, offering myself to the Army.' There had been no shame that he'd decided to walk away from a marriage as casually as though he were changing his job. His words came back to her, as did the sound of the clock on the mantelpiece chiming the half hour, half past nine. Even now she shied away from her own reply, her accusation that that was all he'd ever used her for, spite making her lash out at him in her pain.

This night belonged to David, her beloved David, her second self. And yet there was no way of shutting out those other memories. 'I came here tonight to talk to you,' Stephen had told her. 'In the time since I headed north, my country has gone to war. And what do you care? The only interest you have in me is getting me fired up so I'll lay you. Well, you got what you wanted. Chuck me my things from the chair and get something on. We can't talk like this.'

Lying in the dark bedroom, she closed her eyes, but there was no escaping. He might have been talking to a stranger as he'd told her that he wanted a divorce. She should sue for desertion and he wouldn't contest the case. Not that he'd be around; he planned to cross on the first sailing he could find. If she gave him the name and address of her solicitor he would contact him and say he had no intention of living with her again.

As she'd heard the lift carrying him down to the vestibule, she'd picked up the apartment keys he had left on the table just as the clock on the mantelpiece had chimed and struck the hour. Ten o'clock. In half an hour her world had fallen apart.

Later that night as she'd lain awake in the small hours, she'd heard a ring at the door buzzer. No one would come at that hour of the night – no one except *him*. He must have come back.

'Stephen,' she'd called into the intercom as she pressed the button to release the latch of the front door of the Edwardian house that had been converted into flats. Tears of joy had threatened to rob her of the power of speech, 'Steph...'

'Gillian, it's me.' David had come and with him had come sanity. A minute later she'd been held in his familiar bear-like hug. He had known her despair; he had felt her misery. And so it had always been.

In the silent bedroom Gillian called on the spirit that had never failed her. Whilst she lived, David would never be gone. She had believed the night ahead would be filled with wakeful hours, but almost within minutes sleep had overtaken her. It wasn't a deep, refreshing sleep, but one full of dreams: she was with David, on a beach, which with no warning became a high hill where ponies grazed. Briefly Debbie was there and then inexplicably she was gone to be replaced by Stephen; the hill vanished and they were in a busy street amidst jostling crowds, her arms linked through his and David's as they moved effortlessly through the throng. Such is the way with dreams. In a changed scene she was alone on a small boat, being tossed by a storm. She tried to cry out but could make no sound. Stephen was in the wild and angry water and she was trying to haul him aboard, his arms tight around her neck. Panting, she woke. Rain was lashing against the window; a flash of lightning followed almost instantly by thunder lit the room.

'Mum ... don't like it, Mum.' The dream receded, the arms that held her were Debbie's and reality took over as they tightened their hold.

'I love storms,' Gillian said, something that was an exaggeration of the truth but said in an effort to drive away Debbie's fright. 'Hop in with me, we'll lie and listen to it together.'

Cuddling the little girl, she tried to recapture the spirit of contentment she'd felt as she'd walked through that throng with David and Stephen. But there is nothing more elusive than a dream. David, whose life had been so entwined with hers, was gone forever. And so, just as surely, was Stephen. Now she was alone. No, never that! She held Debbie's warm little body close.

'Not so noisy now, Mum,' came the sleepy voice of contentment. 'Can I stay? I can, can't I?'

'Just for tonight.' Whose need was greater, her own or the child's? As the thunder grew more distant, Debbie's even breathing, interspersed with an odd grunt, told Gillian that she slept. The first purple of morning touched the eastern sky, the day ahead already rushing to meet her.

Two

'I'm so thankful you're here to see to things. You're so calm; you seem untouched. Me? Oh Gillian, even talking about it and I feel like cotton wool. Honestly, I do try to be strong but I feel lost. Frightened.' Helen's mouth quivered out of control. 'I'm not like you. You're so capable.'

'Hobson's choice, I fear,' Gillian answered briskly. 'I've made a list of all the things I have to do this morning. So Helen, you're sure you're OK with Debbie? Why don't the two of you go for a ride? She's getting on well and would be fine on Lyndy.'

'I couldn't. I'll *never* ride again. Not without David.'

Ignoring the break in Helen's voice, Gillian answered, 'Maybe you could walk her on Lyndy then.' David had driven to the New Forest to buy Lyndy at the pony auction the previous autumn and had brought her home in his horse trailer as a surprise for his adored niece. Bought for a song and named because she had been rounded up in the Lyndhurst area of the forest, docile Lyndy had proved to be the perfect first mount, and the highlights of the little girl's life were the weekend visits to Hunters' Lodge.

'I shall never ride again; I only felt safe because David was with me. I tried to look as if I enjoyed it to please him. I was so frightened – except that I trusted him and knew if I was with him it would be all right. But I don't mind watching if Mike has time to put her through her paces in the paddock. If he hasn't, I'll walk with the leading rein.'

'She'd love to work with Mike if he's not too busy. She was so proud of herself last weekend. David put the jumps out – only on the lowest rung, hardly off the ground but she saw herself as almost ready to join him out hunting.'

'Don't! If you'd been at the point-to-point like I was you'd not want even to imagine jumps. I begged David to give up hunting and point-to-pointing and I truly believe that after we were married he would have agreed rather

46

than see me so frightened. Everything was different in the summer when he just rode out to exercise Ginger. If only he'd listened to me he would still have been here.'

'Of course you couldn't have expected him to give up. He loved it.'

'I mustn't talk about him. Don't want to get upset, not again. Got to pull myself together.'

'We *must* talk about him, Helen. He's no less important to us now than he was before the fall. I won't let him be shut out.'

'It's easy for you. He was only a brother. Now he's gone and I – I...' She what? She didn't finish her sentence, but there was no need. Briefly Gillian was moved with pity for the girl who so often irritated her. Perhaps Helen sensed it and drew strength. When she spoke again her voice held a note of determination. 'Gillian, what we were talking about yesterday, about Hunters' Lodge...' She made a supreme effort to sound in control. 'David told me he was making a new Will before the wedding. He went to see his solicitor last week. Promise me you won't let me down while I'm waiting for a buyer, that you'll help me with all the business side. If only a company with a hotel chain would take it on straight away. If I have to look after it, perhaps for weeks or even months, before it sells, Gillian you *must* help me. Promise you won't let me down.'

'I have a living to earn, Helen. But I'm always at the other end of the phone and Debbie and I will come down every weekend.' The rare burst of compassion faded as Gillian, putting an end to the conversation, picked up her car keys. 'Debbie's on the swing. She's dressed ready for riding.'

'Aren't you going to say goodbye to her?' Helen had long held the unspoken view that Gillian treated her daughter too casually.

'She knows I'm out for most of the morning and you're in charge,' Gillian answered, confirming the opinion.

So, as the car drove away, Helen collected her charge, who seemed quite happy to accept her mother's departure without the hug Helen considered she deserved, and together they went to the stables.

Perhaps with the trust of the very young, it was the memory of Bobtail that dulled Debbie's feeling of loss that this time it was Mike, not David, who set up the jump and called out to her alternating instructions, encouragement and praise. There would be plenty of times in the future when she would know overwhelming sadness at the finality of David's going, but on that morning, only twenty-four hours since the event, she smiled a secret smile as Mike called, 'Well done, now round again. Then I'll saddle Bella and if your Mum's out for the morning we'll have a proper ride.' She sat tall in her saddle. Uncle David would be seeing how well she was doing and would be proud of her!

Gillian's morning had less reality than the vivid dream of the night that had gone before it.

Following the helpful instructions she had gleaned from the doctor who had signed the death certificate, she attended to the necessary formalities, ending at the office of Gregory and Tufnell, David's solicitors on Church Hill in Ockbury. She expected the visit to be brief.

'Mrs Sinclair,' the suave-looking over-groomed man greeted her from the open doorway of his office, hearing her introduce herself to the girl in the outer room who guarded his privacy. 'Come straight through. It's all right, Evelyn,' to his loyal typist who preferred to call herself his "assistant", 'and if I have any calls while Mrs Sinclair is here, don't put them through to me.'

He drew a chair forward for Gillian then returned to the seat on the other side of the desk.

'Firstly let me express my deepest condolences.' He sounded as pompous as he looked, but Gillian knew it to be a facade; in fact he and David had been good friends.

'You've heard about David? That's why I'm here, I came to tell you and, of course, to give you copies of the certificate.' Somehow the fact that the news had travelled ahead of her was unnerving.

'My sister-in-law was at the point-to-point and of course I made enquiries afterwards. A most tragic accident – and especially so with his wedding only weeks away.'

'Yes,' she murmured, her face expressionless and her back as straight as a ramrod as she

49

passed him copies of the death certificate. 'I don't know how many you need,' she explained, glad to say something while she pulled herself back on track.

'I was about to dictate a letter to you, Mrs Sinclair. Your brother may have discussed his affairs with you, but it is customary to have these things in writing. He called here one day last week but unfortunately I was away from the office so an appointment was made for him to come again – to come today, in fact.'

'He was having a new Will to be prepared before he was married. Helen told me.'

'Ah, his fiancée.' It seemed he, too, was filling the gap with unnecessary words.

'She is very upset, Mr Tufnell, as you can imagine. She is frightened of letting him down. He'd built Hunters' Lodge up into a good business – but *I know* the risk he took when he borrowed so heavily to convert the old farm and set the place up. It's enough to frighten her.'

'Say no more, Mrs Sinclair. The letter I was about to dictate would have told you the facts. Somewhere amongst your brother's papers at Hunters' Lodge there is a copy of the valid Will. This that I have here is the original, the legal document at the time of his demise. Whilst I have a word with my secretary, I will leave you to read it.'

And so Gillian read ... read it once ... read it again. David's entire estate was hers, the Will being dated when he had joined the Air Force at the beginning of 1940. But there must be a

50

mistake. At that time David had had no thought of getting married, he had had no one except *her.* That was Gillian's first thought, anxious for James Tufnell to come back so that she could talk to him about the possibility of doing what David would have done on that visit last week if only there had been someone to see him.

After a few minutes he returned.

'But of course he wanted to replace this, that's why he came here last week,' she said as she put the document back on his desk. 'David signed this one years ago, before he started flying in the Air Force, before he even envisaged Hunters' Lodge, let alone the thought of having a wife.'

The solicitor, who was only a few years her senior for all this old-world dignity, ran his hand over his liberally brilliantined hair, then touched his spotted bow tie and matching breast-pocket handkerchief, the action an attempt to restore his confidence in the situation. Under different circumstances, Gillian would have enjoyed the sight of a country solicitor so brimming with pseudo-sophistication. Instead she barely noticed as she waited for his reply.

'When he called last week and found I wasn't here, he borrowed stationery and wrote this letter, leaving it unsealed and with a further note that I should read it.' Still he didn't pass the envelope to her; instead he gazed at her, unable to disguise his unease. 'It's uncanny. He was a strong, fit man, a man with everything to

51

look forward to, yet could he have had a premonition of tragedy? The note he left is addressed to you, Mrs Sinclair, and this one to me.' He held out a single sheet on which David had written, 'James, unnecessary I know, but in the unlikely circumstances of my hanging up my saddle between now and the time I'm able to sign a new Will, can you read the enclosed note and then see it is given to Gillian. Call me a fool – it's purely a belt and braces precaution. I shall see you next week. David.'

James cleared his throat and carefully moved the position of his fountain pen a fraction of an inch on the desk as if it were imperative that it be parallel with the blotting paper pad. Then, sitting back in his chair, he folded his arms and faced her.

'I knew about the forthcoming wedding – indeed I had already accepted an invitation for my wife and myself. This is a most sad business. Mrs Sinclair, you have my heartfelt sympathy.'

'Thank you. But – the Will. Surely it's enough for you to go on that you know what his intentions were?'

Ignoring the question, indeed he might not even have heard it if his expression counted for anything, he started to talk.

'Under these sad circumstances I believe it right that I should speak to you with complete frankness.' There! He's made his decision and taken the plunge. 'I haven't met your brother's fiancée, but he talked of her quite freely, yes,

52

most freely, so much so that I have a clear picture in my mind. Correct me if I misconstrued what he said. He and I had come to know each other very well and for this reason I shall speak to you with equal frankness. When he talked of you, his sister, indeed his twin, it was with pride and confidence, that and affection. He said that you and he were on the same wavelength – his expression – and he always knew that whatever you undertook would be done, and done well.'

'But that's nonsense.'

'I have no opinion; I'm merely repeating what he said. Then, more recently, he talked of Miss Murdock. Helen. This is not easy to put into words and if I were speaking to anyone but you – I recall he described you as his "twin spirit" – I wouldn't even try. When he said her name, "Helen", I could sense that the deep affection he felt for her was protective. He said you were strong just as he was, but she needed to be loved and shielded. He said that his fiancée had plans for the two of them looking after the hotel together, but from the way he said it I knew exactly how it would be, just as he knew it himself: he would be the organizer, the planner, the worker, but would do it in such a way that she felt jointly involved. He described her as gentle, delicate, on one occasion even as "a happy child". But one thing was crystal clear, and that was how deeply he cared for her. So this letter to you, Mrs Sinclair, is a request that you involve her and care for her in the unforeseen

53

event of his demise while the terms of the original Will stood. And now, sadly, we are faced with exactly that.' At that point he passed Gillian the envelope.

'Gillian,' she read, 'I've trusted you all our lives and I know I can trust you over this. If I'm not there to do it, promise me you'll take care of Helen for me. Don't let her be hurt, don't let her be sad. And even though everything I leave behind is yours (profits and debts alike!!) with that "everything" comes this heartfelt plea: let Helen be part of it all, don't let her feel alone. Your other half, David.'

Slowly Gillian's numb mind was coming back to life. If only she could be like Helen: release the safety valve and find relief in tears. Instead she looked for defence in the only way known to her.

'I have a home in London and a job that's important to me. I have a daughter. Even today there are people arriving to stay at Hunters' Lodge. There will be bookings. David was the perfect host for a hotel of that sort. But me...'

'I understand your concern. The last thing you want to do is to let Hunters' Lodge fail. I can see that.' Then, almost without a pause, 'There is the alternative, and perhaps you will consider this the wise thing to do. You could put it on the market as a growing concern – for that's what it has shown itself to be. Nothing can take from Miss Murdock the grief she must be feeling, but at least if you handed the business over to experienced hands you could ensure that she came away with money enough to see she has something to help her over the time of readjustment. That, surely, would satisfy the request David makes of you.'

So far, his impression of Gillian had been that she was either devoid of feeling (which he believed unlikely remembering how her brother had spoken of her) or else adept at hiding her emotions. Only now did he see a change.

'Sell David's hotel and take the money? That I most certainly *won't* do. I won't let him down. He knows I won't.'

The die was cast.

Leaving Ockbury and driving back up the long hill to Hunters' Lodge, Gillian made herself face the outcome of her talk with James Tufnell and to compare it with what she had naturally assumed would have been David's wishes for the future of those left without him. But then none of them (and surely not *him* despite the "belt and braces" note he'd left for her) had imagined that he wouldn't have had years of married life ahead of him.

But suppose last week's visit to Gregory and Tufnell had been for him to sign the Will he intended James Tufnell to prepare, leaving everything to Helen; Gillian shied away from the images it conjured up, both that of Hunters' Lodge being sold and that of herself back in her apartment in London, just Debbie and her, no David, no second home waiting ready to welcome them whenever she was free. But was the

55

true situation any easier? For all her efficient handling of the immediate outcome of the tragedy, face to face with what it meant, her brave front disappeared. Squaring her shoulders, she prepared for something she dreaded: Helen must be told; not only told but made to feel part of the future they would build just as David had wanted.

'Trust me, David,' she whispered as she drew the car to a halt. Then, speaking to she knew not whom, 'Help me, help me find a way to make it work.'

It seemed to Helen the whole world contrived to add to her misery.

'How you must be laughing! I was frightened; frightened I'd get in a mess while I waited for it to sell. Yes, it's funny to think I begged you to help me.' But there was more hysteria than humour in her tone.

'Here,' Gillian took the folded sheet of paper from her handbag and passed it to Helen. 'James Tufnell wasn't there when David called last week, so he made an appointment. He planned to go this afternoon. But Helen, while he was there the other day he wrote this and left it to be given to me if ... if ... No one expected I'd ever have to be given it, but read it. It'll help.'

Perhaps in the end it did help but, reading it, Helen was blinded by tears.

'He loved me, he really did. You've always had someone, you can't know.'

Was it for Helen's sake or for David's that

Gillian found herself taking Helen in her arms? 'And he still does love you,' she heard herself say, 'he always will. And when we look after this place together you'll do your part for his sake.'

'Just words,' Helen blubbered. 'What help would I be here? You're efficient, you aren't afraid of making decisions. Got no job, got no home, no family, nothing. David was giving me all the things I'd never had, because he loved me and that gave me everything. It's different for you, you're never frightened.'

Gillian wanted to shake her, to tell her to grow up and show herself to be worthy of David's undoubted adoration. Instead she made herself keep her arm around the narrow, shaking shoulders. She had found Helen in the summer house, where she had retreated once Debbie had been left safely in Mike's care in the stables, so now she closed the door to ensure privacy and opened the casement window and then, with more gentleness than she felt, pushed the object of her "second self's" devotion into one of the two Lloyd Loom chairs and sat in the other herself.

'You should have come with me this morning,' she said. 'Then you would have heard all this direct from James Tufnell.'

'Oh yes, throw it in my face that I was too upset to face the things that had to be done. Anyway, he wouldn't have talked to you confidentially if I'd been there too; I'm an outsider. You don't know what it's like to lose someone

57

you love. He was just your brother, not the person you expected to share the rest of your life with. It's cruel and wicked ... why did it have to happen?' Helen blew her nose with a gusto not a bit in keeping with her delicate loveliness. 'You say you don't know anything about running a hotel, so even you must know in your heart that the only sane thing is to sell up. If you insist on hanging on to it, we can be certain what'll happen: all David strived for over the years will be lost. A hotel keeper has to be smiling and welcoming, no one will want a return visit with a hard-nosed business woman in charge.'

'I'm certainly not *that,*' Gillian answered, trying not to snap.

'It's how you seem,' Helen answered, sounding more like a sulky child. 'And you probably don't know as much about this place as I do even. The people I meet here always like me, I know they do. Just look at you, smart enough to be in a fashion mag with your high heels and your posh suit. Hunters' Lodge is a country hotel – you look as if you ought to be at a board meeting.'

'I came straight from work when you phoned...'

'Never mind that,' Helen interrupted. 'Just listen to *me* for once. You treat me as if I'm stupid, but it's me who has the common sense. Sell Hunters' Lodge now while the bookings are good, let someone take it who knows how to run it. If David wanted to be sure I'm looked after, then that's the only way to do it. If he could know how things would be, it's what he'd want.' Poles apart as they were, Gillian had gone out of her way to show friendship to Helen because she was the girl David loved. Gentle, delicate, full of loving kindness, always ready with a smile, that's the impression she'd always given – always until now. Helen said again, 'You'll let the place go downhill and then have to sell it anyway.'

She couldn't be sure what Gillian was thinking and was never to find out, for at that moment Debbie rushed across the grass towards the summer house.

'Mum!' she yelled as she saw the figures through the glass of the door. 'I've been looking for you, Mum. Mike said you were home, he saw your car. He put the jump up to the next notch, that's what he called it. Lyndy and me went over it – like a bird, that's what Mike said. Mum, do you expect Uncle David knew how high I jumped? I bet he did, 'cause if Bobtail knew things, *he'd* be sure to 'cause he's a proper person.'

Her childlike trust found a weak spot in Gillian's armour so that it took all her willpower to reply in the voice Debbie expected.

'I bet he was thrilled to bits,' she answered, ashamed that she took delight in seeing Helen's disapproving expession.

'Think about what I said.' Helen tried to push the conversation back to where it had been before Debbie's excited shout had interrupted and brought Gillian to her feet. 'If you believe he knows what's going on, then you must know he would want you to listen to me, not to ignore me as if I'm nobody.'

Gillian opened the door of the summer house so that Debbie could come in. From the doorway she looked across the sloping sward, her vision taking in the building, a hotel now but with a long history before that, the wide expanse of grass leading to the tennis court and the trees beyond. Hunters' Lodge, she mused, David's dream, a dream he'd turned into reality from the hopeless looking wreck of a farmhouse and outbuildings he had brought her to see. He'd been so *sure,* so *proud.*

'Run back and tell Mike to leave the jump up,' she told Debbie. 'I want to come and watch.' Then, as the child ran off, full of her own importance at the success of her feat, 'Yes, Helen, I do believe he knows and perhaps he is trying to tell each of us something. He wrote that note to me to cover just these circumstances. Perhaps we're all like Debbie, perhaps we each have our hurdle to jump. I must go and watch her and then I have phone calls to make.'

Leaving Helen, she followed the child towards the stables and the paddock where the jumps were set up, but just as she came to the gravelled parking area a car drew up. If the occupant was someone coming to the hotel, then Sarah would attend to her, yet something made Gillian hesitate and turn towards the stranger.

'You're David's sister,' her visitor announced, a statement, not a question.

For a second Gillian shied from what must follow; here was someone who'd known David and would expect him still to be here.

'That's right, Gillian Sinclair,' she answered, holding out her hand to be taken into a firm grasp.

'My dear, I had to come when I heard. You probably would rather be left alone, but – silly I dare say – it's for *his* sake that I felt I must tell you how sad the news has made us.'

'David was very special. I can't seem to take it in that he's gone.' Gillian heard her answer, saying what she hadn't said to another soul.

The visitor nodded.

'Kathleen Harriday,' she introduced herself, 'and I knew immediately that you must be the sister he spoke of with such – oh, hark at me, blathering on as if you need to be told these things.'

Gillian found herself smiling, feeling in tune with her visitor, who clearly had been fond of David. A tall woman, slim and yet giving the impression of strength. No longer young, but still handsome, her iron grey hair worn in a bun in the nape of her rather scraggy neck, her light blue eyes giving the impression that she could see into the far distance, her face naked of make-up except for a hint of lipstick. In her ears she wore small pearl stud earrings and on her capable-looking hands no jewellery except a wide gold wedding ring on her long finger.

'You live in the village?' Gillian found herself genuinely interested.

'No. Over yonder that way, in Streatham Manor. Like many more in the area, I was very fond of David; I dare say he may have spoken of my daughter and me.' It wasn't a question, so Gillian let it pass that David had never mentioned them. 'He was always so kind to Ella – my daughter – and he often used to look in on us. Yes, a dear soul. I dare say I needed a young man around the place and perhaps he needed a mother figure to talk to.'

'How did you hear about David's accident?' Gillian wasn't really interested, it was merely something to fill the gap.

'My dear, you live in London. You don't know the efficiency of the country grapevine. Word spreads quicker than a forest fire. What a mercy you came so quickly. That young lady he was about to marry would have been like a rudderless ship on her own. And you have a little girl, I believe.'

Gillian laughed, the first spontaneous laugh since that fatal phone call from Helen.

'The country grapevine does you proud,' she said. 'Yes, Debbie is six. She's waiting for me over in the paddock, she wants to show off her jumping. Why don't you walk across with me?'

And so began her friendship with Kathleen Harriday, a woman more than thirty years her senior.

Debbie was put through her paces, praised and encouraged and all the right things said. It was after she'd run off to ask Helen to come and help her get out of her riding gear and into a jumper and skirt, that the two women strolled back towards the car.

'It was a lucky day for Hunters' Lodge when Mike Trelawney booked in. Do you believe there's a pattern set for the way lives work out? That's what I thought when David told me about the Irish-Canadian guest and the outcome of his stay.'

'I'd forgotten Mike came to the hotel as a guest. I know he and David got on well, but I've hardly seen him. When I came at weekends David always brought the horses round to the front before we went out. I wonder why he agreed to take Jim's place, he's hardly the usual stable lad.'

'What did you make of that plan the two of them had lined up?'

Gillian looked puzzled. 'Jim and Mike? Did they know each other? I thought Jim had already left and David had been looking after the horses.'

'David and Mike, I mean. Surely David must have talked about it to you? Of course that was the reason Mike took over looking after the stables.' Then, seeing that Gillian didn't understand, 'When David told me about it, he was over the moon. But after that one occasion, not a word. Something stopped me questioning him. It was no business of mine; he would have come to talk about it if he wanted.'

'You've left me behind, Mrs Harriday. I know

63

nothing of any scheme.'

'Then David must have changed his mind about it before he saw you or he would have told you.' Did she hesitate for a second or was that in Gillian's imagination? 'More likely he had his mind changed for him. Would he have been happy tied to such a wishy-washy creature?'

'He adored her.'

'Ah, so he did. Well, here we are, we've talked ourselves full circle, back to the eternal question: is the pattern of our lives set for us? And what now for Hunters' Lodge?'

Kathleen Harriday was a stranger, yet reserved Gillian found herself telling her of the outcome of the visit to David's solicitor.

'Well, my dear, for David's sake I am thankful the pattern is to have a bright thread woven into it. Indeed, a thread akin to his own. But you, how do you feel about running a hotel?'

Gillian hesitated, wanting to answer truthfully. 'That's a question I have been avoiding. How do I feel? At present I just feel numb about the whole thing. One thing I promise you, Mrs Harriday...'

'I'd prefer to be just Kathleen, if you would.'

Gillian smiled as she repeated the name, 'Kathleen, yes that's nice. One thing I promise you, I'm not going to let it beat me. I shall try and do everything as David would have wanted. And, pattern or no, I *do* believe that by working hard and doing my best I shall find some sort of satisfaction.'

'You're just as I knew you would be, as strong as David. But if he has asked you to take young Helen under your wing, don't let her get the upper hand.' By that time they'd reached her waiting car. 'Give a girl the gift of beauty – and no one can deny she is certainly an exquisite creature to look at – and she can twist the strongest of men around her finger.'

'She loved David,' Gillian defended. 'She expected their future to be certain.'

'Ah, very likely she did love him, poor child. Now I must shoot off, Ella will be watching out for me. My daughter, don't you know. And I have a son. Paul, he was a golden boy, every-thing he did – everything he still does – is a success. He's a writer, calls himself Paul Streat-ham and writes about a detective by the name of Hicks, Inspector Hicks.'

'But I've heard of him, of course I have. Although I admit I don't read detective stories.'

'Nor me, my dear. Life gives us enough tangles to sort out without finding relaxtion in other people's. Anyway, Paul moved away from home even before he went off to the war. He's single and as far as I know, heart-free and un-attached. But I was saying, I had the two, first Paul and then too many years later, I had Ella. It took me by surprise, I was well in my forties – forty-nine when she was born – and Sydney would never see sixty-five again. Poor child. It's not right, you know, not healthy to bring children into the world when nature's clock has slowed down. Right from the first we knew

65

something was wrong with the poor weakly mite. Her legs needed support with horrid heavy irons – still do, but with those and a pair of crutches she gets around, although she propels herself much more quickly in a wheel-chair. Each time I look at the poor little darling I feel ashamed – not of her, oh never that. Fate plays some rotten tricks, don't you know. I've never had a day's illness and yet I produce a child whose life is blighted. Though she has talents not given to most of us. Her paintings are quite exquisite. In the morning, Miss Henderson comes and helps her to bathe and gets her dressed and settled. But by now she'll be gone and life is so restricted when mobility is a challenge.'

'How sad. I'm sorry.'

'Sorry, yes. But never let Ella think you pity her. Each life finds its comfortable pace and Ella gives so much to those of us who love her. Sometimes I think because she is so confined she can see things more clearly; there's something uncanny in her understanding.' For a moment she hesitated and Gillian waited, expecting her to continue on the same lines. Instead, she said, 'That scheme David and Mike had in mind, I believe David was keen. In fact I *know* he was; when I met him in the village and he told me about it, he was over the moon. Then, as I say, not a word more. Maybe it was to do with the investment that would have been needed. But, more likely that flibbertigibbit fiancée bent his will to hers. How strange it is, the call of one spirit to another. Who would have expected he could have lost his heart to such a – such a *wet lettuce leaf.*'

Gillian laughed aloud before loyalty to David made her ashamed.

By that time Kathleen was getting back into her car and when she was asked about the scheme David had had in mind the engine was already running.

'Ask *her* about it. I must fly. When you get settled into a routine here, my dear, come over to the Manor. Drop in and surprise me. And Ella would so enjoy meeting you.' And with that she was gone.

Gillian found Helen pushing Debbie on the swing.

'Did Debbie tell you Mrs Harriday just called?' she said as she joined them.

'I'm glad I wasn't the one to see her. People mean to be kind, but I can't bear the thought of listening to their condolences. I'd try to be polite, but...' She gave up speaking. What a pathetic sight she was, clenching her closed lips between her teeth and trying to stop her face crumpling as her eyes swam with hot tears.

Gillian pretended not to notice. 'Hold tight Debs, here comes a huge push,' she called, matching action to words and giving Helen a few seconds to recover. How anyone could turn the taps on and off so easily she couldn't imagine, and of one thing she was determined: for her, the tap must remain stoically turned off.

'She mentioned some plan David and Mike

had in mind for Hunters' Lodge. She couldn't stay to tell me about it, said I should ask you.'

'I suppose she blames me that David refused. Well, I don't care if she does. I was right. That stable man Mike wanted to invest money in Hunters' Lodge. As if we needed an outsider muscling in! He wanted them to build more stabling, buy more horses and take on extra labour. He had some stupid idea that the hotel ought to concentrate on riding holidays or even take raw beginners and teach them enough to stay on a horse and be taken trekking. Something like that, anyway. I didn't take too much notice because from the moment David told me about it I knew it would be *wrong*. We get nice people staying here – not that I'd been able to be here all that much until the end of last term when I left my job at the school. But the idea of filling the place with a lot of horsey people was so horrid. David could see it upset me.'

'Was he keen, then?' Yes, of course he would have been keen. There would have been nothing he would have liked better than to have "filled the place with horsey people".

'Not when he saw how upset I was. Like I said to him, we had such wonderful plans and if that's what he did, they would all be spoilt.'

'A bit unfair, Helen, if it was what David wanted.'

'That's unkind. Hunters' Lodge is what David made of it. That's how I wanted it to stay, not have everything different because some interfering outsider butted in.'

68

The swing had slowed down almost to a standstill.

'Come on, push me!' Debbie yelled.

'A "please" might not go amiss,' her mother corrected her.

Helen scowled. Gillian really was mean, she considered, and had no idea about children.

'Hop off a second,' she told a scowling Debbie, 'and I'll show you how you can work the swing yourself. That way you can go as high as you like. Now watch. Lean back, legs stretched out in front; lean forward, legs tucked under the seat; then back again, now forward...' Helen worked the swing so that it went higher and higher while Debbie stood watching and jumping with excitement.

Gillian left them. What she had learnt that morning from James Tufnell not only altered the shape of her future, but of the present too. There were things she had to do. Five minutes later, in David's office behind Reception, Gillian dialled the familiar London number and took her next decisive step. She was ready for Ian Merrick to put hurdles in the way of her leaving without working the period of her notice; what she was unprepared for was his understanding and sympathy.

'I shall continue to use the secretarial agency for, let us say, three months,' he told her as they were about to ring off, 'after that you understand I shall have to advertise for someone to fill your place unless you've had a change of heart. Three months will give you long enough

69

to know whether you want to come back. We have worked together very well, very comfortably.' Then, he said what he never would have had they been face to face, 'It's not the same without you.'

Gillian felt an unexpected rush of affection for the poker-faced man she had worked with for so long.

'We are used to each other, Mr Merrick. But I feel compelled to do what I am doing. The hotel meant so much to David.'

'Indeed, yes. But should you have a change of heart...'

'I won't let it fail, I swear I won't.'

'And I know your capabilities well enough to believe you. I simply want you to bear in mind what I have said.'

And so they said goodbye and she replaced the receiver with a feeling of nostalgia. Sitting at David's kneehole desk in the little office, she felt overwhelmed by a future that had no shape. Diffidently, she opened the drawer to her right, as if she were prying into his things. 'Help me, David,' she cried silently. 'There's no time for me to get used to things, work goes on all the time. Salaries, income tax, paying suppliers – I don't know anything. Help me. I must stay calm and take it step by step.'

So she opened the cupboard on the lefthand side of the desk and took out the account book on the first shelf. After years in a job where she knew she was appreciated for her competency, she suddenly felt more frightened than she would let herself acknowledge. But the hours were slipping by, at Hunters' Lodge there was no time to stand still and take stock; the hotel staff would need paying, each day would bring fresh clients, fresh problems. For a moment she buried her head in her hands, fear combining with grief. What went on in her head and heart in those seconds as she made that plea to David only she knew. But a minute later she sat straight, pulled the chair nearer the desk, lifted out two more ledgers and set to work reading her way into some sort of understanding.

Three

Gillian suspected David's popularity in the district to be behind Debbie's immediate admission to the primary school in Ockbury. Perhaps she was right or perhaps that was the way the system worked here in the country. Either way, the morning after she'd made her decision to run the hotel herself and to build on what David had started, she visited the school. The outcome of that visit was that when the bell rang at one forty-five for the start of afternoon lessons, Debbie was in line with the other six-year-olds.

'Was she all right about being left?' asked an anxious Helen, who had been watching out for Gillian's return.

'Debbie doesn't know what it is to be shy. She marched off as pleased as Punch. Now I've an hour and a half to get more acquainted with those ledgers. Don't worry about her, Helen, honestly she was fine.'

'I was thinking, watching you go off with her and knowing how busy you are, would it be a good idea if I made it my job to take and fetch her? Taking her today was different, they wouldn't expect her to be handed over for the first time by an outsider.'

'If you would, that would be great,' Gillian answered, ignoring the hint of self-pity. 'They have such short hours and I have a thousand and one things to learn. Tomorrow especially, I'll be grateful if you'll look after her. You see, I have to do something about my flat. I shall drive up to town and see the agent in the morning. I'd like to sell it really, but it might be wiser to let it furnished. That way it would bring in a bit of income.'

'Of course I'll look after Debbie, I'd love to. Then you needn't rush home, I can see she is bathed and sent to bed.'

'I shall be back by half past six. Remember, I have a bar to look after in the evening.'

Helen frowned. 'It's not the place for you to be. It was different for David to do it, he was a *man* and he had such a friendly way with people.' She shook her head miserably. 'It's so unfair.'

'A habit life has,' was Gillian's quick retort. 'So I can escape to the office and forget about meeting Debbie? Thanks, Helen. I really am grateful.'

And escape she did, giving the next two hours to sorting out the staff wages and discovering the mysteries of deducting Pay As You Earn income tax. She escaped in a very real sense, for by immersing herself in the challenge that had been forced on her she tried to keep her mind occupied.

That evening when there was a lull in the bar, Helen approached with an unusually purposeful air. 'Gillian, I know we can't go tomorrow because you'll be in London but after that there's only one more day before ... before...' she couldn't finish the sentence. 'We must go cithcr to Oxford or Reading – which do you think? – to buy some black to wear.'

'Black? David would hate it.'

'Of course we must wear black. It's the last thing we can do for him. The last...' Her voice died as a sob caught in her throat.

'No! It may be right for you Helen. You may do it and feel it is for *him*. Not me.'

'You are going to the service in your business suit? Oh Gillian you can't. It looks as though you don't care.'

'I don't give a damn what it looks like to other people. And no, I shan't wear my business suit, I shall wear what I know David likes.'

Miserably, Helen started to turn away; there was never any point in arguing with Gillian. 'The Crosbie sisters have given me their clothing coupon books to use.' Then, more hopefully as the thought struck her, 'Perhaps I'll suggest to them that they come with me. We could get a cab to Ockbury Halt and go in by train. They'd like that. And I'd get home in time to collect Debbie.' Already she was looking more cheerful. 'Poor darlings, they are so sad. I could try and see they have a nice few hours out.'

In that moment Gillian felt a rare and half-acknowledged affection for her.

Next morning, leaving Helen in charge right from the start, Gillian was on the road to London soon after seven. The outcome of the day ahead would draw a final line under her past: how proud she had been when her salary had been raised sufficiently that she could afford to move from her bedsitting room to the flat on the western outskirts of London which had become home to her for more than ten years. A Georgian house which, from being home to a comfortably well-shod family, had changed with the times into four self-contained apartments.

Her first vision was of the early years, the excitement and joy of falling in love. Determinedly she moved her mind forward to the war years, the companionship that had developed between the residents as they had congregated in the basement shelter armed with thermos flasks (or a feeding bottle in Debbie's case), blankets, torches, gas masks and a pack of cards. A wind-up gramophone had been kept down there with a pile of scratchy records and a tin of needles. It was like looking back at another world, but there was no way of holding back the images of those years as she followed the A4 towards London.

First she called at the estate agent's office, and was delighted when he agreed to accompany her to the flat straight away. He assured her that he could let it furnished immediately, and with the shortage of housing in the capital that was no more than she had expected. The rent would more than pay the mortgage and leave her with the security of knowing that come what may, she still had a home.

She set to work and through the day sorted every drawer and cupboard, boxing items a tenant wouldn't want and taking them to the depot for the Salvation Army to distribute. Clearing her wardrobe, she made two piles, one to be taken to Hunters' Lodge and the other for a second trip to the depot. Through years of shortage and austerity, clothes had to last long beyond their natural lifetime and some brought back memories she thrust from her mind.

Then there were the things to be thrown away, items that had grown old without her noticing. Most of her books she gave to the secondhand bookshop on the corner, but there was one on the shelf that despite her strong intentions she found herself turning each page with no power to stop herself. An album of photos, each one of them stirring a memory of a time when the future had seemed cloudless. She and Stephen on the beach, herself on Hampstead Heath, Stephen on Hampstead Heath, picture after picture, memory after memory.

'Pardon me, sir,' she could almost hear his voice and imagine him waylaying some passer-by as he had so often, the casual charm of his tone as much evidence of his roots as his American accent, 'Would you do a snap of me and my lady together?' How could he have said they shared nothing, their lives running on separate lines and brought together only by sex? It wasn't true! There had been such joy in being alive, in being together. Or had she always been blind to the truth? Surely sex had been glorious because they loved each other. Now, after all these years, had he forgotten, had he put her out of his life as if none of it had ever happened? And the war, his war? What had that done for him? Thousands of lives lost – but not Stephen, please not Stephen. She turned the pages, feeling more alone with every second. He had grown bored with her. It had been fun while it lasted, he'd said on that final evening, when all his passion had been centred on returning to serve his own country.

'Damn him, damn him,' she whispered, feeling the scalding tears sting her eyes. She slammed the book closed and added it to the pile to be taken to the dustbin. Perhaps he'd been right, perhaps all the time it had been sex that held them together. She knelt on the sheepskin rug, the scene of their last encounter, and every nerve in her body ached with desire, desire that he had awoken and from which there was no escape. 'Damn him,' she said again. *I was happy before I met him*, she thought, *before he showed me what love was all about – love, sex, whatever it is that makes me feel like this. So lonely. Lonely for him. No, no, that's not true, I won't let it be true. I don't need him, I don't want any man. Couldn't bear to be touched by any other man. I wish I'd never met him. No, no never that. He gave me Debbie.*

Here alone in the flat there was nowhere she could hide from the torment of her longing. Over the empty years she had trained herself to keep busy, to keep her thoughts centred on her work, on running her home, on caring for Debbie. Only in the silent watches of the night did she lose her battle. Now with her arms folded and her hands cupping her breasts she knelt, bending over as if she were racked with pain. When her body yearned for love, always it was the same: it was *his* body she wanted. All we had was sex, his voice echoed. And now she had nothing.

The clock on the mantelpiece struck. Already it was two o'clock. Holding her jaw firm, she stood up and collected the pile for the dustbin, the photo album stuffed into a carrier bag with rubbish, old shoes, half-used toothpaste, a mop head and last weekend's newspaper. Could it have been only last weekend that this had been home to Debbie and her? Resolutely she went down in the lift and dumped it all in the bin.

When at last her farewells had been said to loyal Sally Bryant and the other flat owners and she was driving back to Hunters' Lodge, her foremost feeling was relief – she wouldn't give

77

an inch to any other emotion. She had fought and won her battle, said goodbye to her past. Surely that would lay the ghost.

Looking back afterwards on those days between David's accident and the funeral Gillian saw everything through a haze of grief, grief that, in truth, was mixed with fear. Helen referred to her as capable and efficient, but deep in her torn soul she was aware of how much she didn't know about the task she was setting herself. These days belonged to David, to picking up the gauntlet he had thrown to her. The staff were good, and although she meant to take on all the duties that had been David's, in those few days before the funeral the chef sent a kitchen helper to collect supplies from the local tradespeople; at least those who worked there had become familiar with the permitted meagre allowances of rationed items available even more than two years after the end of the war. Milk, butter, bread, meat, cheese, sugar: the list was long and, the country over, tested the imagination of chefs who strived to produce fare that gave a festive feeling to eating in their dining rooms.

Even years later, the day of the funeral was one so painful that Gillian tried to force it to the back of her mind. There was just one moment though, in which anguish and hope combined. It was as the coffin slid out of sight and she stood like an expressionless statue while by her side Helen tried to suppress her uncontrollable snorts as she wept. As the curtains were closed and the coffin vanished from view and the congregation started to sing David's favourite hymn, *I Vow to Thee My Country*, Gillian felt rather than saw Helen's hostility, for she had argued that it wasn't suitable. But Gillian had been adamant and in those seconds as she stood weighed down by silent misery, unable to add her own voice, suddenly and without warning she had felt David's presence very close. She had seemed to see him give that intimate wink that meant they shared a secret and she had known how glad he was that she'd remembered and chosen it for him. With her head high, she had been ready for the second verse. For David, she had sung.

Gillian had been mulling over in her mind what she had learnt about the scheme for enlarging the stables. So, a few days later, beginning to feel less uncertain about her new routine, she went in search of Mike Trelawney, tracking him down in the tack room.

'Mike, I thought it time we got to know each other better. I ought to have come before, but I've been a bit overwhelmed with everything these last few days and when I used to come at weekends I didn't come to the stables.' To her own ears it sounded a clumsy introduction.

'David often spoke of you, Mrs Sinclair,' he said, his words as stilted as her own. Then, turning from what he was doing and giving her his full attention, 'David was a great guy. That's

79

what made me take this job. I hear that you intend to carry on. I wish you well – but, say, it's quite a thing for a lady to take on.' He smiled broadly, showing his white and even teeth. 'And from what I gather, you are a real townie.'

'Then you gather wrong,' she answered sharply. 'But yes, I intend to do as David requested and carry on at the hotel. To my mind, gender makes no difference when it comes to capability.'

'Say, Marm, I wasn't meaning to sound offensive. If you'd heard the way David used to crack on about you, you would have known I wasn't doubting your capability. I guess I just feel bitter. He and I had great plans. Then his lady knocks them on the head. Not that he told me that was what changed his mind, but no one will ever make me believe different.'

'Yes, it was Helen. She told me about it.'

'Now we have to think of the future and that's why I'm glad you've looked in, Mrs Sinclair.'

'If David was David and you're Mike, then I'd rather you called me Gillian.'

'Sure I will. Gillian. Nice name. I was saying about being glad you looked in here. I wanted to talk to you...'

'About the plans you and David had?' She felt a surge of excitement, an emotion that had been drowned in shock, doubt and misery.

While they'd talked she had been studying him closely. He was certainly no stable lad. A man she guessed to be in his late thirties, tall, broad-shouldered and strong, a man not to be argued with. His wiry, light brown hair wanted to curl, his complexion spoke of a lifetime in the fresh air, his strong hands were surprisingly well groomed, his breeches were worn and his pullover had leather patches on the elbows, but there was nothing unusual in that, leather patches gave new life to many a garment that had otherwise come to the end of the road. And his accent? Neither Irish nor Canadian, but somehow a combination of the two. All that flashed through her mind in the few seconds it took to look at him.

She hoisted herself to sit on the wooden bench.

'I won't let you down until you get fixed first with someone else,' he was saying 'but, like I said, we have to look to the future and things are bound to be different.'

'But they mustn't be. I want to carry on just as David would have.'

A quick smile lightened his expression. 'You know this idea David and I had had been knocked on the head, so I guess I would have been saying the same thing if it had been David himself here with me. I ought to have moved on before, but I hoped that once they were married he might have persuaded her to see the logic of what we wanted to do.'

She shrugged her shoulders as she answered, 'I doubt that marriage would have altered any-thing.' Then, looking at him very directly and willing him to make an honest answer, she said,

'If you want to move on and put all this behind you, then I can't blame you. But from what I could drag out of Helen the plan sounds to me the most exciting thing that could happen to Hunters' Lodge. You may be thinking like Helen is, that we ought to sell the hotel before I run it into the ground. But I swear I won't let that happen. For David's sake, I believe the staff will give me a fair trial. I don't even know yet how I'll be financially. I know he had a whacking mortgage on this place and no leeway in the beginning, but already trade was picking up.'

'Listen, Gillian, I'll tell you what our idea was and you see what you think. We wanted to enlarge the stable block, make stabling for a dozen more horses. Then we said we would look for suitable mounts – not filling them all, because part of the draw would be that folk could bring their own. The paddock where we put the jumps out for Debbie, we figured that could be made into a covered arena where we could teach. Are you still with me?'

Gillian nodded. 'No wonder David was keen. Maybe he had something of the sort in his mind right from the beginning when he called the hotel Hunters' Lodge.'

'Yep. That wouldn't surprise me. Now look, it's nearly a quarter past two. How about you get your kit on and I get the horses ready and we talk as we ride. Seems to me after these last days what you need is some clear air to blow the cobwebs away.'

82

'I'll be as quick as I can.' Already she was on her feet.

Ten minutes later, hurrying back to the stables, she met Helen standing aimlessly and gazing at the front of the building.

'I'm just off with Mike, we're exercising the horses,' Gillian said, hardly slowing her pace. 'I can leave Debbie to you, can't I?' she added unnecessarily.

'Meeting Debbie is my favourite time of the day, and I know she enjoys it when we come back together,' Helen replied.

Gillian told herself there was no reason to feel guilty; Debbie loved being with Helen. Putting it out of her mind and, with it, that green-eyed monster jealousy that threatened to rear its head as she hurried on towards the stables. If only it were David waiting there for her ... no, don't let your mind go down that track ... he'll never be waiting, but always, *always* his spirit would be here at Hunters' Lodge.

Mike had Brutus by the mounting block, holding the reins of Bella, a chestnut mare, in his other hand.

'Did you go with David to buy Bella?' she asked as she settled into the saddle.

'She's mine. Where I go, she goes. I bought her over in Ireland. If you'd ever been across to the stables on your weekend visits you would have made her acquaintance before. It was because there was stabling for her here that I checked in at the hotel in the first place. Now, to the downs.'

Setting off from Hunters' Lodge, they turned up the lane, then along a bridleway towards the open downs. For a while they rode in silence, then she said, 'I wish David had talked to me about you and about what you had in mind for Hunters' Lodge.'

'He had such loyalty to Helen. But I would guess your mind is going in the same direction as his and mine.'

'Of course you're right. But, don't get me wrong, I'm not suggesting that it's possible now, not with me being so inexperienced and the future of the hotel having to prove itself for the second time round. I'm sure David would have had to raise another loan, and no right-minded bank manager is going to advance anything to me until I prove myself.'

He didn't answer immediately, clearly mulling over what she'd said.

'Tell me when the time comes that you're ready, Gillian,' he said after a minute. 'I spoke to you about moving on, but I guess I'll be happy to hang around until you make your mind up. I have absolute faith in your ability.' It sounded formal, businesslike.

What sort of a man was he? She knew nothing of him. Perhaps he wasn't even honest, perhaps David hadn't been sure enough of him and that was why he hadn't forced the issue with Helen. Where was the logic in what he and David had suggested? Here was Mike, doing a job that had been done by a semi-educated eighteen-year-old and talking of buying himself into the ownership of Hunters' Lodge. As suspicion forced itself into her mind, she felt utterly alone and vulnerable. It would be so easy to trust him, and yet...

By now they had come to the open downland, and for a while they continued to ride side by side and in silence. Misery, touched by fear, filled her as she put her horse into a gallop, pulling ahead of Mike.

'Race you to down to the stream,' she shouted back to him. Perhaps he could have overtaken her, but purposely he stayed a few yards behind, watching her and seeming to see her anew. David had been right when he'd said she was a fine horsewoman. Perhaps out here in the open country, now that those cobwebs were blown away, he was seeing the real woman. 'Last one to the stream's a sissy,' she yelled, just as she had so many times to David.

They arrived at the bottom of the grassy hill at the same time, reining in so that they were alongside each other.

Mike heard the stifled sob in her throat and reached to put his hand on her shoulder; the gentle, sympathetic movement was her undoing. The floodgates she'd kept resolutely closed for so long were open. There was nothing dignified or restrained in her crying. For years she'd kept her emotions in check while the ice grew ever more solid around her heart. Now as it melted she was defeated and present misery flowed into past misery; her hard-won battle to repress all feeling was lost as she sank to the depths. She must have realized that he dismounted; automatically she moved to do the same, as if by climbing from her saddle she would regain her lost control. But when he lifted her down, her will to fight had gone as he held her trembling body in his arms.

'Good girl ... that's it, honey,' he whispered just as he might have soothed a frightened horse. 'Let it all come out. Good girl.'

She fought to take a breath. She wanted to cry until her strength was gone, but crying such as hers racked her body. Her head was throbbing, already her eyelids so swollen she could scarcely open them. She knew she looked ugly and in some perverse way she was glad. When she heard herself belch, it seemed to confirm to her just how low she had sunk. Then came a second uncontrollable belch as she tried to speak.

' ...sick,'

'Okay Gillian, I've got you,' for as she turned away she seemed to have no power to stand.

'No!' She pulled free and stumbled from him, 'going to be...' She didn't finish the sentence and if Mike hadn't been right behind her to hold her steady she would have fallen to the ground as she retched. She was at rock bottom, all self-respect gone, all control gone, her body shaking as, giving way to his support, she vomited. In those seconds she knew nothing except her physical misery. Then she realized she was leaning all her weight against him.

'Ashamed,' she whispered, for she had breath for no more than a single whispered word.

86

Digging in the pocket of her jodhpurs, she found her handkerchief and with a trembling hand scrubbed her face with it, then wiped vomit from the sleeve of her jacket.

'Better?' he asked gently.

She nodded. 'Don't know what happened. Haven't cried – not for years.'

'Then it was overdue. Now then, let's give you a wash in that stream, eh?'

She nodded, letting him guide her back to where the horses were nibbling at the grass at the water's edge, unperturbed by the afternoon's drama.

Mike pulled off his yellow neckerchief and, kneeling by the stream, thoroughly soaked it.

'Face first,' he instructed, handing the dripping material to her. 'Give it a good wetting – there's nothing like really cold water for putting you back on track.'

Like an obedient child, she did as he said and could feel the stingingly cold spring water restoring her.

'Don't dry it off; leave it to nature. Just throw it back to me and take off your jacket. We'll get you home as good as new.'

'Don't be too kind to me, Mike, or I might start blubbing again.'

But she did as he said and watched while he rubbed the offending stain from the sleeve of her riding jacket. That done, he stood up, gave the coat a shake and then attempted to rub it dry with his own handkerchief, which looked as though it doubled up for a duster.

'Mike ... Mike I don't know what to say. I'm so sorry. So ashamed.'

'Then you ought not to be. There's nothing sissy in crying, but there would be something sick if you lost David and carried on as if part of your heart hadn't gone with him. I'm proud that I was the one to be with you.'

Gillian nodded, suddenly afraid to trust her voice.

'I've *got* to make it work, Mike,' she said, and they both knew she was referring to the hotel. 'Am I crazy? Helen thinks it ought to be on the market now while the bookings are still there.'

'That dame's frightened of her own shadow.' The remark was spontaneous and spoken before he could hold it back. 'Sorry, there's me speaking out of turn again. David pretty well worshipped the ground she trod. Sometimes, you know, I wonder whether there's any pattern to the way things turn out. Plenty of people who've notched up long lives, with nothing left to live for and no wish to carry on, but can they hang up their saddles? Not a chance. Yet there was David, fit, full of life, everything ahead of him.'

'Less than a month and they would have been married,' she said, her mind still on Helen.

'Just thank the good Lord that David passed the responsibility to you and not to her, besotted with her though he was. Could he have had a premonition, do you reckon? From what I knew of him, that would seem out of character.'

'No, I'm sure he didn't. But I think Helen had

made him conscious of dangers he wouldn't have considered.' And so she told him about the letter David had left at the solicitor's office the previous week. 'So, you see, even though on paper the responsibility is mine, I really do have a duty to share it with Helen, to try to build her confidence. It's what he would have done, so now it has to be up to *me*.'

Mike didn't answer. She assumed he'd accepted what she'd told him and agreed that she had no alternative but to act as she intended. Sitting side by side on a tree stump by the stream, Gillian felt David's presence all around. So many times they'd ridden here together, so many times they'd sat just as she and Mike were sitting now. In an attempt to keep emotion out of the conversation, she asked him what had brought him to Hunters' Lodge.

'It's a long story. I'm Canadian born, as you'll have gathered, but like plenty more I was over here during the war waiting to be sent overseas. When I had leave, I looked up a great uncle in Ireland. Great uncle Archie, a grand old boy. Any leave I got while I was based in England, even a seventy-two hour pass, that's where I went. Maybe only had long enough there to spend a night, but he and I jelled real well. After Italy I had a whole fourteen days with him and later an embarkation seven before D-Day. When the war ended and I got shipped home and demobbed – sounds crazy, but honest to God, Gillian, it's the truth – I couldn't get the thought of the dear old boy out of my head. If you'd seen the place you would understand.

'It must have been a grand house when his grandfather, Jesse Trelawney, wed the daughter. Now great uncle Arch was the last of the line. What a sad end to his days, alone with old Paddy, who'd looked after him for years, the place full of ghosts. Our roots are Cornish.'

Gillian sensed that his long story was aimed at giving her time to recover and thought he was going off at a tangent, until he went on, 'It's more than a century ago my great-great-grandfather – no, I guess great-great-great – went over to Ireland, young and fancy-free. But he got beguiled by an Irish colleen, married her and that was the start. Mighty tough time they had from what I can make of it, bringing up two sons.

'Then when the boys were somewhere around thirteen, maybe fifteen, she died of some fever or other. That's when he upped sticks and went to Canada to make a fresh start. One son went with him, the other stayed back in Ireland.'

Whatever his reason for telling her the family history, she found herself interested. 'Horses were the lad's great love and he got himself a job after the fashion of the one I've got at Hunters' Lodge, but he was at a place called Dalgooney, a pretty smart estate in those days, so I believe. From the lowest of the low, he worked his way until he was looking after a whole bunch of real fine horses. It was a profitable stable with a good line of racers; the stock could change hands for what must have seemed

90

a king's ransom in those days. I know that's true, I've seen the original account books he used to keep. Quite a slice of history. You know, Gillian, for the first time in my life I felt a real link with the past – those were my own people.'

'How did anyone alive today have the account books from this place – Dalgooney did you call it? – from all those years before?'

'The one-time stable lad fell in love with the boss's daughter. They were married, she was an only child and when her parents died she inherited – which meant in effect that he inherited. Dalgooney was in the hands of the Trelawneys. Groom and heiress, you might think they would have had a rocky time, but from what Uncle Archie had always heard, they were incredibly happy together. Anyway, when I got back home Dalgooney tugged at my heart-strings, the old house and Uncle Arch about as decrepit as each other. So I got a shipping and came back. He was on his last legs poor old guy but, Jeez, Gillian I could have wept with thank-fulness that I was there for him, he was so glad. Glad? Relieved? Sort of at peace. I'd been there about three months when he died and I found that I was heir to everything, everything bar a bit he'd left to Paddy. The Will was old, dated back in the days before we even met. It must have been to do with the pictures my grand-mother used to send of the Canadian bunch and the fact that I looked so much like he used to back when he was young.' Then, with a change of tone that somehow made her suspect that his reminiscences had been no more than thinking aloud, he said, 'So there you have it. That's how the Trelawneys became heirs to Dalgooney and that's how it is that I am able to invest in Hunters' Lodge.'

'Dalgooney. You've sold it?' For how else could he have the money?

'I guess I haven't figured out whether to sell it or not. Somehow I feel I want to hang on to it. A wise man might let it go – although in its present state it might be hard to shift. But there's something about the place, the row of empty stables, the roof that leaks, the godawful plumbing, the rotting window ledges, that sort of tugs at my heart strings. But, hey, Gilly don't worry on that account. I told you, I got left everything he had, everything bar something for Paddy. I can afford to sink some of it into Hunters' Lodge. So, seeing you think like David did until *she* twisted his arm, I'll hang around until you feel the time is right to get some plans drawn up. And, I tell you one thing I've found out while I've been getting to know the folk roundabout: the Humphreys, the couple who run the market garden along the lane from the hotel, are ready to pack up work. At the right price I'm pretty sure they would sell to us. We need grazing land, somewhere with space enough to fence it into three plots so that the horses can be moved around while the grass recovers. Their set-up would be ideal. We could even grow some of our own vegetables for the hotel and the bungalow could be used to accommodate staff.' Then, with a laugh, 'That's the way I've been planning things even after David said it was no go. Just kept hoping that once she had that ring on her finger she might stop fussing the poor guy.'

'But you said earlier that it was time you moved on.'

'That was before we talked about the project, before I knew you liked the idea. I can put up the money we should need for the work. Honest to God, I'm straight. But there's no reason why you should take my word for it. I'll get a letter from Uncle Arch's solicitor, he'll vouch for me.'

While they'd talked, they had stood up and started to lead the horses away from the stream, and now he helped her into the saddle before he mounted Bella.

'I don't need to see a letter, Mike.' Was she a fool? A silent voice whispered that perhaps he had only made the suggestion that he'd get the solicitor to vouch for him believing it would make her see him as "honest to God straight". Let the silent voice warn her all it might, she wouldn't listen. 'I make my own decisions,' she told him.

Through the next few weeks, learning to step into David's shoes took every hour of her day: getting to know the suppliers, learning about deducting PAYE income tax from the staff when she prepared the weekly pay packets, visiting the bank where James Tufnell had arranged for the account to be transferred into her name, collecting daily supplies and learning the mysteries of catering to a high standard when supplies were dictated by rations which could vary from month to month and according to a system of points. She knew John Griffiths from Ridgeway Farm had been friendly with David and she assumed it was because of that that he and his wife were always welcoming and sometimes with an exagerrated, 'Ssh ... ask no questions', added a slab of golden butter or a gammon ham to her order. Without her realizing it was happening, Gillian was finding a place for herself in Ockbury.

But even though her concentration had to be on her new role, at the back of her mind was suppressed eagerness at the thought of the work that must be carried out if the plan she and Mike had in mind was to take shape in time for the following summer. Together they drew up a rough sketch which they took to Ockbury's one and only architect. The first move taken, it was out of their hands as the official plan was drawn up and submitted to the Planning Office. Fortunately, Clive Burrell, the architect, was a personal friend of the Planning Officer, and even more fortunately, the venture appealed to him.

But over the weeks when those things were taking place, except for an hour or so a day exercising Brutus with Mike, the daily tasks of the hotel became her life, or so she thought until a morning when something happened to throw her off course.

She came through from the kitchen having collected the morning supplies, then through the dining room and into the hotel foyer.

'I just took a booking for the last double for tonight, so all we have now is Number 3, the little single at the end of the corridor. And in the dining room all the tables are taken,' Sarah greeted her.

'That's good, Sarah, but the dining room ought to be full at this time of year – we've got works' parties nearly every night.' Her words were drowned by the shrill bell of the phone.

Something made her wait while Sarah answered it. Clearly another booking. Yes, a single was all that was wanted.

'What name is it?' Sarah was asking. 'Sinclair. Mr S. Sinclair. London,' she repeated as she wrote.

Gillian seemed to have lost the power of movement. S. Sinclair. Well, what of that? There must be lots of S. Sinclairs in London. Stephen had gone back to his homeland. He had finished with London, it had been good while it lasted, it was over, there had been nothing to hold him.

'That's the lot gone now,' Sarah said as she replaced the received. 'Same name as you, Sinclair. But it can't be anyone you would know, this one sounded to be a Yankee.'

Gillian crossed the foyer and went through the bar to the door marked 'Private'. Beyond that were the rooms where she and Debbie lived: a living room, a tiny kitchenette, a bathroom, one large bedroom (hers) and one too small to be worthy of the name (Debbie's). Once in her room, she carefully creamed away any remaining traces of the morning's make up. As she stared at herself in the mirror, her will-power took another nose-dive and she found herself comparing the Gillian of today with that of seven years ago. No sign yet of any lines on her face, but no one would look at her and warm to her as they did to Helen, no one would see her as anything other than a thirty-something who had schooled herself to stand up against the knocks of life. She appeared cold, aloof, unemotional. If only it were true, she screamed silently. She closed her eyes as if she were frightened of what she might read in their reflection, shutting the lids like pushing the cork back into a bottle of fizzy drink. Then with calm determination, she started to re-apply her make-up, resolved to put the last few minutes behind her.

For all her good intentions, that name in the reservation book haunted her. Reason told her it couldn't be Stephen, pride told her she didn't care one way or the other. For seven years he'd been out of her life and out of her mind. If only it were true, if only memories weren't always waiting to catch her unawares.

'I'll collect Debbie from school today,' she said when she tracked down Helen playing Scrabble with Jane and Margaret Crosbie in front of the log fire in the residents' lounge. 'I have to be in the village.'

'What a good idea,' Jane Crosbie said. 'Helen has had such a nasty fit of sneezing as ever I heard. I believe this poor child is getting a cold.'

Helen smiled affectionately at the two old ladies.

'Truly I'm not, Miss Crosbie,' she assured them. 'It was when Jane came in to put that large log on the fire, you remember how hard she raked the ashes, she sent them flying everywhere and they tickled my nose. You ought to tell her not to let it make so much dust, Gillian. It was that that made me sneeze.'

'Silly girl she is, she ought to have been more careful,' Margaret tutted, as devoted as her sister to sweet Helen, who was bearing her sadness so bravely.

'Is there anything I can bring any of you from the village?' Gillian offered. Her manner was friendly but brisk. The elderly sisters had seen her come and go to the hotel from the start of their stay there. They had been conscious that their dear David had been fond of her, yet they shared the opinion that there was a hard streak about the young woman. That dear little girl Debbie, she was a real treasure and poor little soul having no father. But that was today's world for you, they'd heard of one or two cases even in a quiet little village like Ockbury, where couples had split up. Such things used not to happen. It was all the fault of that dreadful war, women working as though they were men, couples living separately. Like a lot of those silly film stars the young people put on pedestals, they saw no wrong in breaking their vows as easily as they changed their socks and the poor little children were the ones to suffer for it. Now, dear Helen, how different she would have been if only David hadn't been taken from them all so cruelly.

'What about a nice tub of Turkish Delight? Would you get that for me if it's not a trouble, Mrs Sinclair? Here, I've got my sweet coupons in my purse. Take them, if you don't mind popping into Mrs Hooper's sweetie shop for me. I haven't used any this month, so get as large a tub as she can give you. And here's the money. You'd like that wouldn't you, Helen dear? We remember they're your favourite.'

Right on cue, Helen's blue eyes were swimming.

'You are so kind,' she spoke with sincerity, then to Gillian, 'They know Turkish Delight is what David used to buy for me. He never used his ration on himself, he always spent it on me.' Then, pulling her mind into line, 'But, Gillian, Debbie doesn't come out until half past three. It's not two o'clock yet.'

'I want to see if I can get my hair done.'

'On a Thursday? But Monday's your hair day.' Helen looked puzzled, she liked an orderly routine.

'It looks a mess.'

'It always looks very nice, dear,' Margaret Crosbie ventured, surprised at herself that she should make such a personal comment to starchy Mrs Sinclair.

'Well, anyway, I shall call in at the hair-dressers and see if I can be fitted in.' It was quite stupid, Gillian told herself, that she should feel embarrassed by an extra hair appointment and have an urge to escape before Helen commented that she had changed out of her work-a-day skirt and everyday overcoat. What was so special about wearing a good tweed skirt and the sheepskin coat she had gone without so much else for and even then added some of Debbie's coupons to her own so that she could buy it the previous winter? *Anyway*, she added silently, *what I do is my own affair.*

No wonder as they watched her go they all shared the unspoken feeling that she was a cold woman, efficient but with her head full of business.

It seemed the ladies of Ockbury were saving themselves until Friday or Saturday to be smartened up for the weekend, so the assistant shampooed her hair immediately and when it was done, Delia, the owner, took over to set it herself and fix it in its customary sleek page-boy style. Then, the Turkish Delight bought, Gillian took up her position near, but not too near, the group waiting at the school gate. If Helen had been waiting there, she would have stood with the others as she always did, chattering as easily as any of them.

Gillian was rewarded by Debbie's expression of excited surprise, although her, 'Where's Auntie Helen, Mum? Why did you come to get

99

me instead?' took the edge off her pleasure. 'Did you have to do shopping or something?'

'I came just to meet you. Aren't you pleased?'

'Course I am, I can tell you all about what I've been doing, 'cause I know you won't have time to listen when we get back home. But Mum, Auntie Helen's OK isn't she?'

'Helen's fine. She was by the fire playing Scrabble with the old ladies.'

'Miss Margaret and Miss Jane, that's what they said I was to call them. Sounds more friendly than saying Miss Crosbie all the time, and anyway they can't both be called the same. It was Auntie Helen's idea and they were really chuffed.'

Gillian just stopped herself from saying that she would rather Debbie had said they'd been delighted, agreeable, pleased, all proper words, rather than chuffed. But an inner voice warned her it was better to let her chatter naturally. A few months previously there had been no Helen on hand to usurp her place in the little girl's routine, so that miserable green-eyed monster hadn't had the need to rear its ugly head. And yet was that true? Right from baby day, Debbie had been left with Sally Bryant while Gillian worked, so what was the difference? The difference was that the highlight of the little girl's day had been when her mother fetched her and took her back to the home that was their own. Now nothing was *just* their own and it was Helen who listened to the after-school chatter and who managed to make the walk home fun;

it was Helen who made sure bath time was fun too and that there was a story or a game of I Spy or Grandfather's Cat before tucking her in for the night. The ritual never varied and to Debbie it brought continuity and security.

Gillian's evenings were always busy. Just as it had to David, so it fell to her to oversee the restaurant and to look after the bar, where she was often held in long conversation with some solitary guest. Willingly, Helen saw Debbie to bed and, without knowing quite why, they both knew it was better not to talk about those end-of-day precious moments. Helen, like most of those at the hotel, saw Gillian as fair-minded and hard-working, but with no ability truly and unselfishly to love. Wasn't her broken marriage evidence enough?

Even though loyalty didn't allow Debbie to let the thought take shape in her mind, she knew that an outing with her mother was never the fun it always had been with David and Helen. Now that Helen was settling at the hotel and being so nice to the people there and everyone liking her, some of her old sparkle was back and, because there were times when she and Debbie would play together like they had in the past, the little girl learnt to understand and accept all her wailing and crying when she'd been so miserable. Laughing and crying were all part of being a proper person in Debbie's opinion, but it was an opinion that got stamped on almost before it took form in her mind. She loved her mother dearly, of course she did, and she would hate to see her cry; even to imagine it made her feel uncomfortable. But why was it she didn't sometimes laugh, *really* laugh, not just smile?

On that early December afternoon, as they walked up the long hill to the hotel and Gillian listened to Debbie's chatter, there was a feeling of comfortable companionship between them. Perhaps it had to do with the unacknowledged anticipation that refused to be repressed. Arriving at Hunters' Lodge, Gillian instinctively checked the parked cars for any new arrival. Yes, there were two that hadn't been there the previous night, one Triumph Renown and one Flying Standard. The Renown had a towing attachment on the back, it must belong to a couple who were bringing their horses and staying right over the weekend. The Standard ... she pulled her imagination into line. It wasn't the style of car she would have expected Stephen to drive – she had imagined him arriving in something sporty, something with a deep throbbing engine. But like most things, cars were still in short supply, so he had probably been glad to take whatever he could. Stop it! She pulled her thoughts up short. Even to imagine it was tempting fate. Anyway, she added for the hundredth time, it's nothing to me where he is or what he's doing.

'Can I go and tell Auntie Helen I'm home? She'll be waiting for me. We're going to pin up the paper chains we've made for my bedroom.'

'May I,' Gillian corrected automatically. 'Off

you go.'

Just for a moment Debbie hesitated, feeling guilty and yet not sure why.

'Sorry. *May* I? We knew you'd be busy, you see, Mum. It wasn't that we wanted to do it without you.' She sounded uncertain. Would her mother think they had more fun without her?

'True enough, I shall be busy,' Gillian replied. 'Take the drawing pins out of my desk drawer.'

Reassured that no feelings had been hurt, Debbie dashed off completely unaware of the surge of emotions chasing themselves through Gillian. Could it be him? Perhaps at this very minute he was watching her out of his bedroom window. At the thought, she stood a little taller as she went through the front door.

'I see some of tonight's guests have arrived already,' she said to Sarah, her voice purposely casual. 'The trailer is round at the stables I suppose?' Remarks she might have made on any day and aimed at disguising her internal turmoil. But it was senseless to feel like this, she told herself ... if he'd wanted to find her he'd always known where she was. In any case, he belonged to the past; she had a full life and he played no part in it. Those were the thoughts she pushed to the front of her mind as she waited for Sarah's reply.

'I suppose it must be,' the girl answered, her own thoughts having travelled no further than the whereabouts of the horse trailer. 'Mr and Mrs Jackson checked in a while back, and that

Mr Sinclair too. The Jacksons are probably still round at the stables, but the other one asked for tea, so he's in the lounge.'

Gillian nodded, making sure the action gave the impression of disinterest, then she went through into her own part of the house where she examined the hairdresser's handiwork and made sure her make-up disguised the ravages of seven years of living. Satisfied, or as near satisfied as possible, having matured from a carefree young woman believing life would leave her untouched to a single parent with no such illusion, she returned to the public area and wandered casually through the restaurant and foyer and into the lounge, carrying the tub of Turkish Delight even though she was sure that by this time the Crosbie sisters would have gone for their walk.

Four

At the sight of the newly arrived guest, Gillian's spirit fell to rock bottom, there and below. She was angry at herself and, quite unreasonably, at the stranger too. What a fool she was! A portly man of late middle age, there was something unmistakably un-English about his appearance. He was dressed in a navy blue suit with wide pinstripes, his jacket was unbuttoned and his

104

gawdy pink and purple tie was knotted loosely which, in her unfairly critical view, gave an immediate impression of untidiness. Even the top two buttons of his waistcoat – or vest as he would have termed it – were unfastened and the heavy gold watchchain strained across his plump stomach. Nothing about him was co-ordinated. Or was her silent criticism based on disappointment she wasn't prepared to acknowledge?

At the sight of Gillian, he pushed the small table to one side and stood up.

'Good afternoon,' he geeted her, his voice sure evidence of his roots. 'I guess, like me, you've arrived with a long wait before they start serving meals. You've asked them to rustle up some tea for you?'

'You're Mr Sinclair, I believe,' her answer spoken in a voice he heard as more English than the English. 'Don't let me disturb you. No, I'm not a guest, I'm the owner of Hunters' Lodge. I was just making sure you have everything you need.'

'A pleasure to meet you. But, say, I only heard when I checked in that there had been a change of hands here. Say, but what a dreadful business it was – the accident I mean with the previous owner. This is my first visit here. Maybe you can tell, I come from across the pond although I have every intention of staying in your country. Married an English girl when I was over here during the war but she pined for home and her own folk, so we've come to make our future back here. With all the lads home from the war I reckon I was lucky to get work so soon.'

Jovial Stanley Sinclair was content to ramble on, oblivious of the fact Gillian was giving him no encouragement. 'I'm working in the cloth trade, visiting tailoring shops. Not that folk can buy new suits too often over here. It's been my line back home ever since I finished high school, except for those few years in the war. And you, have you been in the hotel trade for long?' Mercifully he didn't wait for an answer. 'I was looking forward to making the acquaintance of the late owner. My predecessor used to stay here and he left a glowing report of the hospitality he found.' Gillian bowed her head briefly in agreement. 'And I don't mind telling you, lady, I was curious to meet the owner on another count too. I'd heard this hotel mentioned in the family, you see. You might almost say I had a connection with the late owner, loosely speaking. David, I've heard my aunt call him. Mind you – and this is just between ourselves – I don't boast about any connection with that son of hers. A trouble in the family and always was.'

'David was my twin brother,' Gillian cut in, not prepared to hear this stranger maligning Stephen and yet surprised at herself that she could feel his words were a personal slight.

'For all the saints! You must be – oh, I say – why didn't you shut me up quicker? Well at least you may be in no doubt of my feelings towards that philandering cousin of mine. One

106

can't choose one's relatives. I haven't set eyes on him since – since just before he joined up. And as far as I'm concerned that's the way I like it. Never was any good, but you don't need me to tell you. You must be the poor wife who was left in the lurch.'

'I didn't see it like that, Mr Sinclair.' True or false, she found herself defending Stephen.

'I commend your loyalty. But facts are facts, Gillie. See, I even remember your name. You got your freedom from him because he'd deserted his responsibility, need I say more? We are a close-knit family or, to be more accurate, the rest of us are. And it's just the same, even with Alice and me being this side of the water nowadays. Letters every week – and sometimes we arrange for a word on the telephone too. Nothing like hearing a familiar voice. Sad to say, Stephen's mother is no longer with us, so it's seldom news filters through of your ex-husband. But time was when the family was all in the same small town, all of us having to bear the shame of the scandal the young bounder brought on the family name right from his high school days.'

Gillian wanted to escape but could hardly walk out and leave him talking, and there seemed no stopping him. It was obvious that her frosty tone had gone right over his head. 'Yes indeed, the gossip there was about him when at no more than sixteen years old he seduced the minister's spinster daughter, a respectable lady twice his age and there they were caught in the very act down by the riverside. Poor dear lady, it blighted her life, of that I am certain.'

'Mr Sinclair,' and this time her firm voice penetrated even *his* thick skin. 'Stephen's youthful escapades don't concern me. And as for the break-up of my marriage, we can't go through life blaming others for things that go wrong. We are masters of our own destiny. Now, if you have everything you want, I'll leave you to enjoy your tea.'

With a courtly bow of his head, out of keeping with his chubby, rosy-cheeked face, Stanley watched her go, poured a second cup of tea, then settled down to enjoy the first edition of the evening paper. But he couldn't put Gillian from his mind so easily, and it amazed him that a young man with Stephen's record could have come to tie himself up to such an iceberg. Miss Frigid indeed. A handsome enough woman in a hard sort of way, but Jimminy Cricket, it would take a brave man to put his hand up *her* skirt. Oh well, none of his business, just be glad for the family's sake that Stephen had shifted away. And, with that, Stanley took out his pen and prepared to do the crossword. Now that he'd been given this region to cover it might be best if he stayed somewhere else next time he was in the area; the last thing he wanted was to get tied up with Stephen and his affairs.

That evening, in her role as hostess, Helen welcomed him as she did all the guests and when, on hearing that she dined in the restaurant, he suggested that rather than sit at separate single tables she might join him for the meal, she agreed with obvious pleasure. He proved to be a willing listener. She shed a tear or two, even though she tried hard to be brave, but how could she help it as she explained how it was that she and Gillian were "sharing the responsibility" left by her beloved David and told him of all the plans she and David had had for their future.

'I say we share, but it's not true,' she said, her lovely eyes filled with sadness. 'I don't think I even want it to be true. Running a business is a foreign land to me. She is clever, she is a proper business woman. Me? I love people, I try and see that the guests feel that each one of them matters. And the one thing I do which I know Gillian – Mrs Sinclair, that's Gillian, the same name as yours – I know she depends on, is that I spend so much time with little Debbie, her daughter.'

'There's a child?' Stanley asked casually. 'So she has a husband?'

'They were divorced before Debbie was born, poor little darling. Gillian is so efficient, I doubt if many single parents have done as well as she has. In London she held down a good job, had a nice apartment. But of course the child got dumped on a neighbour each day. Now we're all here together and Debbie has really given me a purpose. David and I always loved her and now, looking after her, I somehow feel that he is watching over us.'

'Is she a baby still?' He made sure his interest

was casual.

'Gracious me, no. She's six. She was three, almost four, when I first saw her, but I suppose because Gillian is her mother there never was much of the baby about her. A very adult little person, no baby talk or anything. I used to long to cuddle her and baby her, but I knew Gillian wouldn't approve.'

'A cold woman, your David's sister?' Stanley was trying to piece the jigsaw together and make a picture.

'I honestly don't know. And that's sad. David couldn't have cared for her like he did if she'd been as hard as she appears. Of course she loves Debbie. But I'm so glad I'm there for the little mite. Every child needs time for fun, time for hugs, time for a story before being tucked up. I bet your children have all that.'

'They surely do.' My word, but what a wicked thing that this enchanting creature's marriage to Miss Frigid's brother hadn't come to pass; he'd never seen a young woman more cut out to be a loving wife and mother (apart from his Alice, of course).

As Gillian moved amongst the tables, making sure the guests were all attended to and satisfied with their meal, she saw the two of them talking earnestly. Not for the first time, she envied Helen her gift for overcoming barriers and relaxing even the most withdrawn of guests – not that rosy and rotund S. Sinclair from across the water came into that category.

Stanley had booked into Hunters' Lodge from

Thursday until Sunday because his work took him to tailoring businesses and upper class meanwear shops, both of which would be open until late on Saturday afternoon, after which he wanted to write up his orders, have an early night and drive back to London the following morning. However, a devoted family man, he made a point of telephoning his Alice each evening. So as soon as he left the dinner table he drove into the village to the call box. What he wanted to say was better said away from the hotel. Alice heard the story, contributing no more than, 'How sad. So, is the hotel closed?' when she heard about David; 'Poor little lass,' when the story moved on to Helen, and ''Struth, Stan honey, what sort of a woman would stand up for the way that rotter had treated her?' about Gillian – or Miss Frigid.

'I agree, sweetie, it sure did beat me. But wait for the rest of the tale, Ali, here comes the best bit. Do you known what that rotten bastard did? He walked out and left her when she was carrying his child. It seems there's a little girl, six years old. There go the pips again. Better go, honey ... yes, yes of course you can call home and tell the others. I'd like to be able to hear what they all have to say about the young devil. Hope you can get through. Goodnight sweetheart.'

An hour later, a trans-Atlantic call made, word was already travelling through the small mid-American township where most of the Sinclairs still lived.

For the rest of his stay Gillian saw very little of Stanley, but having him there was unsettling, bringing the past to intrude on the new life she was making. On the Saturday morning of his visit she drove to Streatham Manor for one of her unannounced visits to Kathleen.

'My dear, what a lovely surprise,' Kathleen greeted her, holding the heavy front door wide to welcome her in. 'We're in the kitchen. It's the warmest place,' she said, leading the way down the flagstone passage to what used to be the servants' quarters. 'You're the breath of fresh air Ella and I were needing.' It was said with a smile that included the gloomy faced girl in her wheelchair.

'With the ground so icy there's no hunting today. But I'm hardly a breath of fresh air in anybody's book. To be honest, I've come over to see you two by way of escape.' Gillian, too, was careful to include Ella.

'Helen?' It was Ella who suggested it, looking more cheerful by the second as she anticipated David's beloved Helen was to be the subject of general criticism.

'No. This has gone right over Helen's head and I'm certainly not going to rake over dead ashes talking about it to her.' Then Gillian laughed, realizing what she'd said. 'See. You're doing me good already. Talking about it is what's brought me here. It must be my fault, you know, but I couldn't possible talk about any of it to Helen.'

'Sit down, my dear. There's coffee waiting in

the Cona still, we'll all have a cup and you start at the beginning and tell us all about it.'

So that's what Gillian did, using Kathleen as her safety valve. The only part of the story she omitted was her visit to the hairdresser and the donning of her better clothes.

Ella took it all in and as is so often the way with those who are onlookers in life's merry-go-round, she recognized even more certainly than did her mother that seven years without Stephen had done nothing to extinguish the flame in the candle Gillian carried for him. The morning took on a brighter hue; Ella lived for romance.

'Of course it raked the ashes,' Kathleen said at the end of the tale of the meeting with Stephen's chubby cousin, 'memories good and bad alike. But there is one thing that has come out of his visit: you know now that Stephen came through the war. Don't you think it is partly the fact that you didn't know what had happened to him that has made it impossible for you to find closure? I dare say dreadful possibilities have niggled the back of your mind, but now you can draw a line. Now that you know he is safe and no doubt, like you, building a new life, you can let yourself think of the unhappiness he caused you and hate him for it with an easy conscience. Yes, and remember the good times too – of which there were many I am sure. Life goes on, my dear, and one thing to be thankful for is the greatest gift he gave you – an enchanting daughter.'

'Coming here always does me good,' Gillian said. 'What are you two doing today?'

'I have to go to Oxford after an early lunch. My dentist is preparing to give me a beastly afternoon.'

'And what about you?' Gillian asked Ella.

Ella shrugged. 'I'll chunter around. Maybe do some painting, maybe read.' Then, her earlier aggression threatening, 'I don't need a carer, I'm OK on my own.'

'Glad to get rid of me for a few hours I dare say,' Kathleen laughed, trying to restore the girl's humour.

'I was just thinking ... how does it appeal to you to come home with me, Ella? We can fold your chair and take it along. Mr Murphy the builder is coming this afternoon, about two o'clock he said. He wants to measure the land so that as soon as permission comes through he can start the men working on the foundations. Would you be interested in seeing what we have in mind?' It was said in a momentary feeling of sympathy for the girl. Imagine being not quite twenty years old and having a life so narrow.

Ella's childishly pretty face flushed with pleasure.

'Can I really come? I went once with David. I did some drawings of the horses. And I did one of David too.' At the way Ella said it, Gillian's sympathy took firmer hold. Had the girl imagined herself in love with David? 'He and I got on well – didn't we, Mumsie?'

'Of course you did, dear.'

114

'Not *her* though,' Ella pouted. 'If Mumsie and I ever went for lunch when *she* was there, he was different. Don't like *her*.'

'Go and comb your hair and get your coat off the hook.' Kathleen purposely ignored the outburst. It was only after the wheelchair had trundled off along the flagstone floor of the passage from the kitchen where, in an effort to economize on the strictly rationed fuel, she and Ella spent most of their time, that she told Gillian: 'I dare say you put two and two together. Poor little Ella, her head is full of dreams. I know her so well I can read her every thought. She believed she was in love with David and, bless him, he was so good to her.' She shook her head, her handsome face suddenly looking old and careworn. 'It's no life for the poor child. Dreams – we've all had them. But what chance has she of ever turning them into reality?'

'She'll make a life, Kathleen. Think of that pattern we've talked about before: none of us know what's around the corner. Ella does so many things better than the rest of us – look at her paintings, listen to her on the piano.'

'I know, yes, I know. But what when I'm not here for her? She's not even twenty, and here am I only months away from my seventieth birthday. It haunts me, Gillian. I tell myself we are as God made us – but where was the justice?'

Gillian raised her finger, pointing it towards the passage and the sound of the returning

115

wheelchair.

'Sure you'll be OK at the dentist without me there to hold your hand?' enquired a laughing Ella as she joined them.

'I'll cope. Up you get, poppet, Gillian will give you a hand while I put your coat on for you.'

'I'm better than I used to be. If I have a chair or something heavy to pull on, I can get out of Wheelie Willie all by myself,' Ella said as Gillian took her weight and held her while Kathleen got her into her thick coat. As she settled back into the chair she raised her face for inspection. 'Did you think I was ages? I put lipstick on. Just matches my jumper.' Then, with a laugh that showed nothing was going to destroy her excitement at the prospect of an outing to Hunters' Lodge, 'Now I've got my coat on it doesn't even show. Are we off? Bye Mumsie, hope he doesn't hurt you. Will you fetch me when you get back?'

'Of course. I thought I'd take the opportunity of doing some shopping while I'm in Oxford.' She looked enquiringly at Gillian.

'Don't rush. Ella will be fine at the hotel,' Gillian said. But what must it be like for the young woman having to be left in someone else's care as if she were a child? 'You'll be doing me a favour if you don't collect her too soon, I was intending to do some stocktaking in the bar, it'll make light work of it if we do it together.'

On the drive to the hotel, Ella's chatter was

116

almost non-stop; certainly it tested Gillian's good intentions. Once there, she left her guest with the cutlery, napkins and place mats to be put on the table in her own living room and went to the hotel kitchen in search of something for their lunch. Unlike Helen, Gillian never ate in the restaurant.

'You know what would make this day really perfect?' Ella greeted her when she came back with a tray of food, and from the look on her face as she said it her day was pretty well perfect already.

'Tell me and we'll see if we can do anything about it.'

'I'd like to see the horses. After Mr Murphy finishes, will there be time before we start doing the stocktaking?'

'We'll make time, Ella. And if we don't get the stocktaking done today, perhaps you can come and give me a hand tomorrow.' In truth the stocktaking task was one she'd pulled out of the air to give Ella the feeling of doing something useful and she was more than rewarded by the look of pleasure on Ella's face. But, even so, she had plenty of other things demanding her time, so her own friendly offer took her by surprise.

After they'd eaten their meal, Ella offered to wash their plates.

'I'm pretty useless, but that's one thing I *can* do. Let me, Gillian, go on, let me, *please,* Gillian, say I can.' Her tone reminded Gillian of a pestering child she had heard in the sweet shop

117

when she'd been buying the Turkish Delight on Thursday afternoon. 'Let me have it, Mum, please, please Mum, I want one, Mum. Let me, *let me...*' a "scene" threatening more certainly with each word. Gillian had left the shop without seeing the outcome but sure that the mother would give in, as sure of it as the child herself had been. A spoilt child – and yet Ella sounded so much the same. 'Let me', 'I want'. But surely she wasn't to be compared with an over-indulged and badly behaved child, poor Ella who begged for a chance to wash dishes.

'Do you mind? Thanks Ella,' she said. 'And while you do it, I'll slip over to the stables and remind Mike that Mr Murphy is coming. He ought to be there to see him too.'

With Ella installed by the sink in the tiny kitchen, the plates stacked and the hot water run, Gillian went in search of Mike.

'You're early,' he greeted her. 'Murphy isn't due for half an hour. Is everything OK?'

'Everything's fine.' So why had she needed to escape, to make an excuse to come and speak to him? 'I brought Ella home for lunch. She's coming over with me to see what we're planning with Mr Murphy.' She had an uncomfortable feeling that he was laughing at her.

'So?'

'Well, I just thought I'd come and tell you. I didn't want you to look surprised that she should be there. When he's gone, I told her she could see the horses.' Then, with a sudden burst of honesty, 'To be truthful I just needed to

118

escape. I'm not used to being so considerate of people, I needed a breath of fresh air.'

'That's my girl.' And this time he didn't hide his laugh, nor the affection it held as he looked at her. 'You know what I remember David saying when he brought her over here? He said how rotten it must be to always look up to everyone from a chair. I'd never really thought of it before. You know what would be good for her? To sit on a horse, to look down on the rest of us. Let's see what she thinks of the idea when Murphy is gone, eh?'

Just after two o'clock, Ella sat in the stable yard watching. With the plans secured to the mounting block with two large stones, the builder measured the land and drove in stakes to mark it out. The planning meeting was that evening and being on friendly terms with the chief architect, he had every reason to believe that official approval would be in the post the following day. By twenty to three, the sound of the van bearing the words Rodney Murphy the Reliable Builder was growing fainter as he descended the hill to the village.

There was no stocktaking that afternoon. When Mike suggested to Ella that he could lift her into the saddle and lead Bella, she looked at him as she might have some religious vision. A few months ago David had been her secret love. In those seconds as she listened to Mike's suggestion her hero worship found a new outlet.

'My things will be too big for you, Ella, but just for once that won't matter,' Gillian said. 'If

119

you enjoy it we'll have to get you kitted out in things of your own. I'll ask around to see if anyone has something second-hand to get rid of. You can't use coupons on new. Let's see how we get on with mine for today.'

Sitting in her chair, Ella couldn't keep the smile from her face even though she tried to prepare herself for disappointment.

'You're so slim,' she said. 'I'm quite porky. Sitting gives you a big bottom, that's the trouble.'

It was in more than her bottom that there were differences. The waistband was inches too small and, of course, the legs too long. But a baggy sweater covered the yawning gap between button and buttonhole and the legs were turned up at the bottom. When Gillian found a hacking jacket that had been David's, Ella's happiness was complete.

That afternoon saw the beginning of a new life for her. It wasn't that she came every day to Hunters' Lodge, usually not more than once or twice a week, depending on when either Gillian or Mike could collect her. As close a friend to Gillian as Kathleen felt herself to be, she never brought Ella to the stables uninvited. But the hours that she spent there were her highlights. True to her word, Gillian asked around amongst her hunting acquaintances and managed to acquire a pair of well-worn but still usable jodhpurs; as for a jacket, what could be more perfect than that the one Ella wore had once been David's? Always a dreamer, there was

120

something comforting in carrying the past with her as her imagination looked into a future into which she weaved a new romance. This time it was Mike, with his attractive, gently spoken Canadian drawl, with his strength as he lifted her into the saddle and his easy conversation as he walked Bella. Kathleen recognized the signs, but so she should, she had seen it happen on many occasions since Ella's first stirrings of adolescence and had inwardly grieved.

There had been the lad who used to work in the garden until he was old enough for the Army; next had been an Italian prisoner of war, one of a batch who had come from their camp in a lorry each day to work at the neighbouring farm. A sweet boy with huge dark eyes, he'd managed to spend more time than he should talking in his limited English to Ella by the gate in the lane. Soon after the end of the war, the prisoners had gone back to their own country and she had fixed her dreams on the next. Perhaps that's the way with imaginary romances; no hearts are broken. Then had come David, David who saw nothing beyond Helen. But that made no difference as far as Ella was concerned. So, with him gone, she was ready to weave a secret romance with the next while Mike, ever friendly, was unaware.

'She changes her mind like shifting sand,' Helen said in an unusually unkind tone. 'Not long ago she was casting sheep's eyes at my David.'

With the coming of spring and with planning

permission granted, the building work started. Originally, stabling had been for seven horses; now it was to be for a further twelve, six on each side of the originals and built at right angles, so that the entire block would form three sides of a square around the stable yard. True to his word, Rodney Murphy, Reliable Builder, put a team straight on to the work and by early summer the brickwork and roofing were finished, and water, drainage and lighting installed. Once all that remained was inside work, even a spell of wet weather didn't cause a delay. By the end of June, Gillian and Mike were ready to look for stock to fill the new accommodation. Their idea was to find seven mounts, some suitable for experienced riders but one or two of the "plodding" variety. The rest of the stables were to be left empty, ready for horses brought by guests who wanted a riding holiday.

The Humphreys had agreed to move out of the market garden at the end of the summer season.

'Where they've been growing their vegetables will have to be put down to turf,' Mike said. 'Seed would be useless. Tough turf isn't easy to find.' He spoke the truth, for at the onset of war every spare foot of pastureland had been ploughed and converted to arable use in the battle to keep the nation fed. And while rationing lasted, that battle continued.

But nothing could destroy Gillian's confidence; so far everything had gone so well, she wasn't going to be beaten for the lack of turf. And that's when Rodney Murphy turned out to be more than simply a reliable builder.

'I've always taken a real interest in the future of Hunters' Lodge, right from when that brother of yours first took it on,' he told Gillian, when by chance she met him in the village High Street. 'Did a lot of work on it when he got "change of use" permission for the old farm buildings. By gum, but what he set out to do took more guts than most of us can muster, that's for sure. I'd like to think I was able to help out a bit. I'll keep my ears open for turf. No good getting the sort you'd want for a garden lawn.'

Gillian warmed towards him; he had been David's friend and she felt that he was hers. Even so, she didn't put much confidence in the hope that he might come up with a suggestion for the amount of turf they would need for an erstwhile market garden. However, she was proved wrong, for not a week after her meeting him she saw his van drive into the stable yard.

'Mrs Sinclair, you and Mike both here, that's what I hoped. Harking back to what we were talking about the other day, that turf you'll be needing. I didn't mention it when we spoke – call me a fool, but I've never liked to tempt fate. And that's about what I would have been doing if I'd counted my chickens too soon.'

'Have you heard where we can get our hands on some, then?' Mike prompted.

But the good-natured builder wasn't to be

hurried, he'd tell his story in his own good time.

'You'll have read in the local rag about the houses the council are set to have built on the old site where the "Ities" had the POW camp. Well, like many another, I put in my tender to get the work. A fair offer I made, but you know how it can be with the big boys, always ready to cut out the little man. That's how it was I didn't tell you what I had in mind. Had in mind? Frightened to give it a chance to get into my mind, if I tell the truth. Like I say, the best thing is always to do your costing fairly, put in a tender and then forget. Any road, this morning I got the letter from the council.'

He took off his cap as he spoke, ran his hand through his thinning hair and rammed it back on again. 'The job's mine. Rodney Murphy and Co. are to build the lot, six semis and a pair of maisonettes. Nice site too. Lucky young folk who get taken off the housing list to be put in there, and no mistake. But, now then – the turf. Put your mind on that site and you'll see that it's your lucky day as well as mine. I'll be putting the diggers in within the next fortnight, and in the normal way of things it would have just been dug out with the rest of the earth. No good for the gardens, like I said. But just right for your nags to trample on, that's for sure.'

'Mr Murphy, you're a saint,' Gillian told him.

'Saint I'm not. But this new enterprise you two are going into takes a lot of guts. I said so to David when he came over to see me back last summer. Full of it, he was, that morning.

Couldn't talk about anything else. To tell the truth, when he said no more about it I thought perhaps the hotel wasn't doing that well and he was cautious about taking the risk. And risk it will be. There's not a lot of spare money around for folk to splash out on riding holidays and things of that sort.'

'Reckon you're right,' Mike said. 'So far as the folk in the village are concerned. Back home where I grew up things were different from here. I never came across the sort of layers of society you find here. Kids didn't get kitted out for sitting on a horse just so long as they had a pair of old trousers. Maybe it was different in towns, but where I come from it was just a way of life. Here though, those with money enough to indulge their kids take it for granted they might want to join the pony club. Oh yes, there's money around if you cast your net in the right water, and I'd bet my last cent that once we get going a steady flow of that money will come to Hunters' Lodge. And now what's your price for putting down the turf, Mr Murphy?'

'Let's walk over and take a look at the area, then we'll work out the figure,' answered Rodney the businessman.

Although Gillian and Mike were partners, she purposely kept out of the negotiations. Any financial outlay at this stage had to be his. It was half an hour or so later as, side-by-side, they watched the van carrying Rodney Murphy the Reliable Builder drive off, back to his yard. Mike took her hand in a firm grasp.

125

'Our lucky day, Gill. Hey, but it's great the way things are working out.'

She nodded, her dark eyes bright with hope as she turned to him.

'How soon can we get the turf laid? The Humphreys said they would move out at the end of the summer cropping.'

'We'll talk to them. They're moving up north, buying a place with their son.'

'But that might take ages.' Her bubble of excitement showed signs of bursting.

'Not the way I see it. They have a place lined up – once they get their money they'll be off.'

'They have to sell their summer crops.' She was less optimistic.

'We'll go and talk to them, the two of us together.'

Gillian had never been more aware of her inadequacies. What a moment for her to imagine Helen: gentle, understanding, compassionate, that's how everyone saw her, and loved her for it. It was the echo of Helen's voice that taunted her with words like "efficient", "hard-headed", "more at home in the boardroom".

'You go on your own, Mike. They don't even know me – and anyway...'

'Anyway nothing,' he replied, tightening the grip on her hand and, she suspected, reading her mind. 'We're in this together, Gillian my friend – my very dear friend.' There was something unfamiliar in the way he spoke those last words, making her feel even more unsure of herself. 'We'll go and talk to them now before you have

126

time to get cold feet. Hey, but Gill, this is going to be one hell of a fine set-up by the time you and I have got it sorted. Come on, I can't be doing with a chicken for a partner.'

She found herself laughing as, without being aware of it, she left her hand in his as they turned out of the stable yard and along the lane to the elderly couple's bungalow.

At the beginning of July the furniture van chugged through Ockbury carrying all Ernie and Kate Humphreys' possessions while, keen not to waste time, Mike was already busy fixing electric fencing so that the area of recently turfed land was divided into three plots.

Watching from her chair on the gravel patch just behind the bungalow sat Ella. Since Mike had first hoisted her onto Bella, her life had taken on a new dimension. She had believed herself in love before, but never had the dreams she concocted been touched with reality like this. She started each day with hope; would she be going to Hunters' Lodge? Would Mike take her for a ride and talk to her like he did about ordinary things – the horses, the advertisements he and Gillian had put into county magazines as they spread their net for horse-loving guests, the purchase of new tack, a journey he and Gillian had made and the mare they had bought – everyday things in his life, just as though she were the same as everyone else.

Each time she sat astride Bella, seeing the world from a new angle as, holding the leading rein, Mike walked by her side, there was something new to tell her, something that made her feel part of the venture. She had never been so happy. But as is often the way with those who allow imagination to take precedence over reality, if Mike had given any hint that his feelings were on a par with hers, her confidence would have evaporated and, with it, her dream. On that July day as she sat watching him hammering in the supporting posts and attaching the electric fencing, she was busy drawing. Her pad would be firmly closed by the time he came over to collect her for her ride.

'Poor child,' Kathleen muttered more to herself than to Gillian, as the two of them walked across the tough grass to join Mike.

'Perhaps we could push her,' Gillian offered hesitantly, imagining how difficult it would be over the newly-laid pasture.

'No, no, I didn't mean that. She's happy where she is. Twenty years old and yet still a child in so many ways. She can't go on like that forever. She needs love, not just mine or yours either. She is a normal woman – except that she is chained to that chair and can't live a normal life.' They had slowed their pace and finally stopped walking, still only halfway towards Mike. 'Physically she is like any other woman. And, damn it, Gillian, is there a woman born who doesn't need, crave, the physical love of a man? Since Adam and Eve, isn't that nature's way? Oh, there are those who are different, but that's an act of God.'

'There must be more to love than that.' As if it had been only yesterday she seemed to hear Stephen's voice, 'All we share is sex...' 'She's young. There will be someone – in that pattern we talk about, Kathleen. Sex isn't everything; without companionship it's not enough.'

Not for the first time, Kathleen wondered what had broken Gillian's marriage. Was she as ice cold as she tried to appear? An unnecessary question, and one that was discounted as the thought formed; Kathleen knew well her friend's warm and generous nature hidden behind the austere and solemn facade. They started to walk on.

'Of course you're right, sex isn't everything,' Kathleen said, casting a glance across the field towards Ella. 'But I know her so well, better than she realizes, and I know that even though companionship without sex might feed her dreams now, the time will come when that won't be enough. She could have children, you know. Please God one day it will happen, please God someone will see beyond a girl in a wheel-chair and her thread of the pattern will bring her the fulfilment that deep in her heart she yearns for.' Then, standing a little straighter, 'Now then, let's go and admire Mike's handiwork.'

When Gillian had become the owner of Hunters' Lodge, it had been out of loyalty to David that the staff had decided to give her their support for a few months, by which time they expected the hotel would be on the market or perhaps already taken over by someone experienced. There had been only one person who had foreseen success and that person had been Gillian herself, simply because she would envisage nothing less.

Time soon proved the staff wrong as they gave her their grudging respect, although she was still held at arm's length. If she walked into the dining room where the girls were chattering together as they did their last job of the day, laying up the tables for breakfast, they would immediately stop talking or, even worse, smile politely and say 'We're almost done Mrs Sinclair,' as if she belonged on another planet. And Gillian was incapable of making some friendly, casual remark that would have relaxed them. She was "Mrs Sinclair"; she represented authority.

Just as she had earned respect from the staff, so she had from the local traders and as the months had gone on, without her realizing it, she had become confident in her new role. She marvelled that she could find time to drive miles with Mike as they selected suitable horses. The outings were a happy mixture of good companionship and serious business, all served with a healthy smattering of fun. She couldn't remember any time when she'd felt so carefree. Had she been with anyone but Mike she might have felt she was being disloyal to David, whose spirit seemed ever close. She never voiced that thought, yet she felt sure without it being said that his feeling was akin to her own.

Then dawned the all-important day, the date they had worked towards. 'As from 1st November 1949...' had commenced the advertisements spreading the word of the new enterprise at Hunters' Lodge. Not quite a year since David's fatal accident, it was a day when no less than eleven riders checked in, seven bringing their own mounts, four riding those belonging to the establishment, all of them keen to be there at the onset. Planned to coincide with Hunters' Lodge's new role, the opening meet was to be held at the hotel. Mike and Gillian were regular members of the Downland Hunt, but on that morning they were joined by the eleven hotel guests, whose fee for riding on that day was part of the deal at the hotel. The gods smiled on them. As the two young waitresses carried trays bearing the "stirrup cup", Mike and Gillian looked at each other with a silent message – 'We did it!' – then raising their glasses, drank to the future. It was a perfect autumn day, the first red-gold appearing on the leaves, the air filled with the combination of so many scents, autumn fruitfulness, decaying leaves, bonfires. Gillian felt it had never been more beautiful.

'Hey, but what a day.' Mike spoke quietly, his words just for her ears, as he walked Bella sideways to come close to Gillian.

'Magic,' she answered in the same vein.

Helen, watching resentfully from the window, saw it differently. For nearly a year she had found some sort of comfort in seeing the hotel

131

much as it had been when David had been there. But on that morning it wasn't just the "hotel full of horsey people" that gave her such a miserable, empty feeling in the pit of her stomach; it was the knowledge that deep in his heart, this was what David, too, would have wanted. If the departed are able to watch those they've loved (and that was the belief she had clung to), then this morning his spirit wouldn't be with her, watching from the window, it would be out there with the riders. She felt lost and alone as she heard the huntsman's horn and saw them move off down the drive, the sound of their hooves accompanied by the excited barking of the hounds.

But for the rest of them the day progressed in the spirit it had started. The hounds lost the scent and the fox went to ground somewhere near Milbury Hill, but the fact there was no kill did nothing to take from the perfection of the autumn day of misty sunshine. It seemed to be confirmation that what they had done was right.

When Mike had first talked to Gillian about acquiring the Humphreys' bungalow and land, he had suggested the accommodation might be useful for staff. But they had second thoughts. Most of the staff had roots in the village; all except the chef who had been given the rooms over the greengrocer's shop in return for his wife working four hours a day in the shop beneath. It was her first venture into what she termed "dirty work"; until they'd come to Ockbury she had served on the cosmetic counter at Boots the Chemist. With no hope of a house of their own they had clutched at the chance of moving into the rooms above the shop. Once they were settled, they were remarkably comfortable and she had enjoyed chatting to the local housewives as she weighed out their vegetables. The idea of moving up the hill and being surrounded by fields held no attraction.

Mike saw no need to move out of his accommodation, a conversion of the one-time hayloft, and as the national shortage of housing was expected to last for years, their decision had to be whether to take a tenant for the bungalow or sell it outright.

'It was your investment, Mike, so it's your decision,' Gillian said.

'My investment was in Hunters' Lodge, all legal and correct. So if we sell, then the money we make belongs to the business.'

'With a property in Ireland crying out for attention, I'd have thought you'd be glad to make use of it.'

'At the back of my mind I have plans,' he answered, giving her a thoughtful look but no explanation.

'Tell me,' she prompted him.

'One day I will. But we have things to think about here for the time being. So, the bungalow ... shall we go and see the estate agent in Brindley, or shall we advertise it ourselves?'

'When David first heard about Hunters' Lodge – only it wasn't called that, it was Hindley Farmhouse – he read it in the weekend newspaper. Let's advertise the bungalow ourselves – there may be some young family out there who will read the advert and know it's just what they are looking for, just like David knew the old farm buildings were right for him. Anyway, if someone writes in answer, we shall see the letter ourselves, it won't go through an agent.'

So in February of 1950 that was what they did. The notice appeared in the Saturday morning edition of a national newspaper and on the following Tuesday two letters arrived. One was perfectly typed and very businesslike, from someone in London who, subject to a surveyor's report, was prepared to make an offer only slightly below the asking price and pay cash. The other was handwritten, from a man who signed himself Derek Denvers, who told them he was keen to see the house as soon as it could be arranged and asked them to let him know when it would be convenient. His address was in Kent.

Gillian sent a reply by return post suggesting any day later that week and suggesting he telephone to say when he was coming. Her letter was in the evening collection on that same Tuesday. Wednesday evening his call came.

'I could come tomorrow,' he told her. 'I've enquired about trains and I should get to Brindley station at ten past one. How far is that from the bungalow? Are there buses? If not I'll find a taxi.'

'About four miles. There's only one bus a week between the village and Brindley. There is one taxi, but at that time of day he'll probably have gone home for dinner,' she said, and Derek Denvers could tell from her voice that she was smiling. 'We really are in the sticks here. Would you mind that? Perhaps you have a bike? Or do you think you'd find it too cut off?' She was surprised at herself. She ought to be trying to persuade the enquirer that the bungalow was right for him.

'Deep in the sticks sounds like what I'm looking for. If I can't get a taxi I'll walk, in which case I shan't be with you until about quarter past two. But don't give me up, I'll definitely get there.'

Gillian had no idea what sort of a man he might be. Clearly he was fancy free to make his home anywhere, so perhaps he was elderly and retired. Yet his voice conjured up an image of a young man.

'I'll come and meet you. How shall I know you? Not that many people get off the train at Brindley as a rule. Are you tall, short, fat, thin? What will you be wearing?'

There was a pause, a pause long enough that she thought perhaps he hadn't heard what she said.

'Hello? Are you still there?'

'Forgive me. I'm sorry. You offered to meet me. That's awfully kind of you. I'll be wearing a brown hat with a wide brim.' Another pause, then speaking quickly and, she felt, forcing his

135

voice, 'Oh, damn it, this is difficult. You'll know it's me because my face is a mess. Burns.'

'You were a pilot?'

'I was but that's not how I was burnt; I'm not a war hero. It was an accident.'

'Just as painful however it happened,' was Gillian's opinion. 'I'll have been exercising the horses before I come, so I'll be the one in riding things. And if by chance I can't make it and my partner is there instead, the same thing applies. We shall look forward to meeting you and, Mr Denvers, I really hope you like what you see.' And it was true.

The next day three people left the train at Bindley Station: one elderly woman with a shopping basket, one boy who looked as though he should have been at school and a third in a trench-coat type mackintosh with its collar turned up and a brown wide-brimmed hat. In that second, as she held out her hand to him, Gillian felt an instinctive shock at his appearance, even though she had been warned, and she understood his desire to live deep in the sticks. One side of his face must be a constant reminder to him of the way he used to be, while the other was scarcely human. It was as if the heat of the blaze had withered him, making the right side of his face contract, the purple skin withered. Into her mind came the thought of crêpe paper that had been screwed into a tight ball and then unfolded. But Gillian was adept at hiding her thoughts, so she met his eyes squarely and took his hand in hers.

'Right on time,' she said. 'I'm Gillian Sinclair. The car is parked just by the way out.'

'Thank you,' he mumbled.

These days she no longer drove her elderly Morris Oxford; instead she used David's Riley and as she got into the car and waited for Derek to slam the passenger door closed, she was thankful that she would be driving and could keep her gaze on the road ahead as they talked.

'The bungalow was built in the early thirties,' she said as they started forward. 'Two bedrooms, a kitchen leading off the sitting room and beyond that the bathroom.' She hesitated, uncertain how to find the right words for what she wanted to say. 'You can see already, now that we've left Brindley – which isn't much of a town – we really are in the middle of nowhere. Lovely walking country, or riding. Do you ride?'

'No. And lately ... lately I haven't even walked. But here it might be different.' Then, turning to look at her, he almost shouted, 'How can I walk? Would you go out, looking like this?'

Gillian slowed the car almost to a standstill on the straight, empty road, and then turned to look directly at him.

'Of course people are surprised when they see you for the first time, you wouldn't believe me if I said differently. But now that we've met and talked, well you are just *you*, the man who seemed keen to come and see the empty bungalow. But tell me – not that it's my business – what about work? Most people would find the position of it unsuitable.'

'I don't go to work.' Then, hearing what he'd said, he laughed (pulling his face into a hideous grimace). 'Oh, I'm not one of the idle rich. I said I don't *go to work*. I paint.'

'You can live on what you earn from painting? I've never met a professional artist before. Do you get commissions for your work? Or have exhibitions?'

'Neither at the moment – not since the accident. I paint, of course I do. It's my hold on sanity.'

By now the car was stationary and, surprising herself, she reached out her hand and touched his.

'Wait till you've lived out here for a while. It has a healing effect on your spirit. Believe me. The bungalow is right next to my hotel, Hunters' Lodge.' So she explained to him how it was that it was on the market. 'The few of us at the hotel will soon be familiar. Then you'll take the plunge and go into the village. Small communities do have a healing effect, truly. They draw you in and make you feel part of them.' He didn't answer and she suspected he was battling to hang on to his control, so she eased her foot off the clutch and the car started forward. 'I came from London and took over the hotel last year. It was seven years since my husband left me, seven years of being surrounded by people and yet feeling utterly alone. I'd not realized it, not thought about it, until now, but here in the country with no mass of unknown people, every one of us matters. Well, you'll find out for yourself if you take the bungalow. We're almost there.'

When she drew up outside the little wooden gate Mike was there waiting for her. Not for the first time, she thought, 'He never fails', as he opened the passenger door with a welcoming smile and his hand outstretched.

'You'd better trot on home, Gill. Debbie was hopping about with excitement, looking for you. She wouldn't tell me what it was all about. Mr Denvers and I will be OK to go over the house.' Then, giving his attention to the visitor, 'Did Gillian explain, she and I are business partners? Come on in and see what you make of it.' Not a hint of the shock he must have felt at the first sight of the disfigured face.

Gillian drove on to Hunters' Lodge, parked the car by those of the guests and hurried to the side entrance leading to her own rooms.

'Mum! Mum, got a surprise for you,' Debbie yelled before she had time to close the door behind her. 'Mum, you were wrong. You told me I'd never had a Daddy, but you were wrong. Why did you fib to me, Mum?'

'What do you mean?' Stay calm ... don't begin to imagine...

Helen was standing in the doorway of the sitting room. What had she been telling Debbie? Gillian's instinctive surge of hope vanished in a rush of anger. How dare Helen interfere! Then anger was overtaken by something else as she saw him.

Five

'Mum, he didn't know about me and I didn't know about him. Mum...'

'Hush, Debbie.' Empty words spoken while Gillian tried to recapture control and make sure her face gave no hint of her tangled emotions

'Debbie and I were just going to pick some snowdrops when Stephen arrived.' From Helen's manner, his appearance might have brought nothing but pleasure. 'There are masses in the copse at the bottom of the garden. Come on Debbie, let's go and see what we can find for the visitors' lounge. They're such a promise of spring.'

'But Auntie Helen...'

'Go with Helen.' *Yes, go, just go, both of you*, Gillian screamed silently even while she told herself that she was a fool. How could she let the sight of him make her feel like this, hope tingling in every nerve? And yet as the side door closed on them and through the window she saw Helen helping the little girl on with her anorak, she wished they were back, a barrier between her and the longing she had no power to control. If only he'd move towards her, make some sign that would tell her what she'd dreamed of hearing. Yes, that was the truth, a truth she'd refused to acknowledge; but now there was no running away from it. Why else should he still have the power to do this to her? *Pull yourself together*, she told herself, *don't be a fool. What has he come back for? Why couldn't he have left me as I was? I was winning, I was blotting out the memories ...* but he stood quite still, his expression inscrutable. She felt inadequate, helpless in a way that was alien to her nature.

'You're looking remarkably well,' he said in a voice that might have been addressed to an acquaintance he'd not seen for some time.

'I don't imagine you came here to tell me *that*.' She made certain that her voice was as expressionless as her face.

'And you imagine correctly. Did you know when we parted that you were carrying my child? Did you let me go, knowing you were depriving me of something I had a right to know?' Whatever she'd expected to hear, it certainly wasn't that. 'Gillian,' he said, for the first time calling her by name and sounding more like the Stephen she remembered, 'that evening when we admitted our marriage was over, why weren't you honest with me? Perhaps you didn't want me any more than I wanted you, but we had more than ourselves to consider. Debbie is as much mine as she is yours and, even though we were divorcing, that's the way the court would have seen it.'

Physically Gillian seemed to feel herself

141

standing taller and, in the incongruous way a mind can work, at that second she was glad she was wearing her riding habit, knowing that it suited her well.

'When you came to the flat telling me our marriage was over, I was *not* pregnant.'

His laugh mocked her. 'Don't try and make me believe she isn't mine. Take a look at her. She must be a constant reminder to you. She belongs to me as much as she does to you and she has a right to a proper family.'

'It's a bit late to think of that now ... and Debbie *belongs* as you call it to no one, no one except herself. We are all free agents, not possessions.'

'Damn it, Gillian, stop splitting hairs.' He crossed the room and took her by the shoulders. 'I told her who I am, that I'm her father. You were out – leaving her for someone else to look after while you enjoyed yourself – so you didn't see the way her face lit up. You know what she said? "But Mum said I never had a daddy." Easy for you, but what about her, just a baby and told the basic foundation of family life could never be hers?'

Gillian's voice was cold as she told him, 'I hardly think her mind works that way. Debbie and I are perfectly content. You have no place in her life, nor in mine.'

There! She'd said it, she'd said it as if it were the truth.

'I can accept that when you lost David and inherited this place you took the course you did,

142

even though when I wanted you to give up your job you refused.' He spoke more gently, somehow the way he spoke David's name making it harder for her to fight him. 'And as for Debbie, she must be better with the young woman I talked to, Helen, the girl who was to be David's wife, than with some stranger paid to look after her. But Gillian, you say yourself a child isn't a piece of property to be passed around, she is living proof of what was between you and me.'

'Fine words!'

'Fine words which we could back with fine actions.' He took her chin and raised her face. She wanted to close her eyes or to lower her gaze, but Gillian never ran away from the things she feared, so she looked directly at him. 'We could start again. Think what it would mean to Debbie. You carry on here, I know you are doing that for David. I didn't say – I didn't need to say – how sorry I am about what happened. Rotten for all of you – even for Debbie. I'm back in my old job, European correspondent for the *Daily Gazette*, but even if I'm not able to be here all the time she would know we were a proper family – a family just as we intended when we took those vows. Say yes, Gillian. There's no one else?'

'No, no one. Stephen you can't come walking in here and expect me to cut out more than seven years of my life and pretend they haven't happened. Anyway, we've nothing to build on, all that held us together was sex.' She semed to spit the words at him.

143

'We were inexperienced, we're older now. And wiser?'

'I thought you wanted a wife who would be there for you like a comfortable pair of slippers, one whose interest would be in the things *you* did and the places *you* went to.' She hated the unpleasant tone of her own voice and yet only in talking to him like it could she keep her resolve. He had cast her aside, even her memories of the glory of what she had believed was perfect had been stained by the way he had spoken on that last evening. Yet now he counted all that as nothing.

He laughed. 'I'd pretty well forgotten how stubborn you were about hanging on to that job of yours.' Not a bit uncomfortable with the situation, he seemed prepared to reminisce. 'Not like Edna Ferguson, yes, that was her name. She and you were poles apart, she would have let her life revolve around me.' He laughed softly as if at some private joke. 'Edna Ferguson ... I haven't thought about her for years. If it hadn't been for the Japs bombing Pearl Harbour I was about ready to land up with her. She just about fitted what you say I wanted, used to hang on to my every word. Her mother ran a guest house in Manchester where I used to stay when I went north. As different from you as it's possible to be. Dumpy little thing with a big smile. Did I honestly think she and I could have lasted? Jeez, but I haven't given her a thought since I shipped back home to fight for my country.'

'Not her nor me either,' Gillian said coldly. 'Or any of the others from your high school days onward and through the years since we broke up I have no doubt.'

Unabashed, he laughed aloud. 'Sure and I've had women aplenty, if I denied it you'd know I was lying. You know the way I am.' Then, the smile vanishing, he was suddenly serious, 'Yes, you know the way I am, none better. But who, seeing you, would know what smoulders beneath that icy facade? We were made for each other. I've never known a woman like you.'

'Don't, Stephen. There's no point in stirring up dead ashes.'

'Yes, yes Gillian. Tell me the truth, the honest to God truth: did what we had mean nothing to you? If so and the ashes are dead, then nothing can stir them. But they're not, they are red hot. We can bring back the flame.'

'It's years ago, Stephan. We're not even the same people.' She grasped the first thing she could think of to hide behind.

'No, we're not. We're older, we've had time to look back and see what fools we were to let it all go on a whim. My whim, I don't try and excuse myself. If you don't care about how I feel, about how often I've looked back on our glory days and ached just to touch you, to hold you, to feel the heat of passion that drives you, then the ultimate...'

'Stop it, damn you!' she rasped, then hated herself that she should have let him see what his words were doing to her. 'I told you, I'm not the same person. All we had was sex – your words – and I've lived well enough without it all these years.'

Just as he had before, he held her chin in his hand and raised her face, defying her to look away.

'You lie,' he said softly. 'You've craved love. You're more than attractive, there must have been men willing and eager to give you want you wanted – what you want now, this minute, just as I do – but you preferred memories. What we shared couldn't be found with someone else.'

'My life's been full. So it still is. I don't need you or any other man.'

'Then think of Debbie.'

'I've thought of Debbie all through those years. Go away Stephen and leave me to make a life, why can't you?'

'Why can't I? Because even if I made myself forget you, we are a family. You, me and Debbie belong together. Ask *her* if you won't listen to me. If you'd been here when I arrived instead of leaving her to be looked after by someone else, then you would have seen the look on her face when I told her who I was. I swear to God – something I don't often do – this is the most important thing that's happened to me.'

'And to me – Debbie, I mean.'

'So? Am I so repugnant to you? Is that what you're trying to make me believe, that you haven't wanted me just as I've wanted you?'

Loosening his hold on her shoulders, he moved

146

his hands down her arms, then gripped her hands, crushing her fingers. 'The truth, Gillian, tell me the truth. Is there someone else?'

'No,' she answered. 'There's more to life than marriage. My life is full, I told you. I have Debbie, I have David's trust for what I do here...'

'I know you as no one else ever has.' He spoke softly, earnestly. 'Do you imagine this cold facade of yours fools me? No, my darling Gillian. Only *I* know the woman with a passion to match my own. Darling, darling Gillian, take me back. I want to be with you, deep inside you, inside your heart and inside your warm, beautiful body.'

'Oh yes,' she seemed to spit the words at him, 'sex, we shared that, that and nothing else. It was you who said it.'

'It'll be different now. Now we share Debbie. Now we are older, we know what life is without each other. Say something, Gillian.'

'Don't know,' she muttered, feeling her resolve ebbing away and not having the courage to hold on to it. She closed her eyes as if that way she could distance herself from him. And when she spoke, they both knew the facade had dropped. This was the truth. 'Yes, I've wanted you, wanted you, loved you, hated you, mistrusted you, dreamt of your coming back and yet dreaded seeing you.'

'All that's gone. Now Gillian, we are honest with each other, we aren't hiding behind pretence. I beg you.' Again he tilted her face up to his, willing her to open her eyes and meet his

147

gaze, moving closer so that she could feel the warmth of his breath.

Her lips were parted as his mouth covered hers. Still holding her, he moved his right hand and forced it between them to unbutton her jacket, then she felt the warmth of it on her breast, his thumb outlining the telltale raised nipple. She knew she was lost and she rejoiced in it.

They were sliding out of control. A thousand times it had happened to them in the years they'd shared and willingly they had followed their instinct. But this was different, any minute Helen and Debbie would be back.

'See the state you've got me in,' he mumbled into her hair, his hands on her buttocks pulling her tight against him. 'Gillian, this is right for us. Say yes, say yes.'

'Yes, yes, yes,' she whispered. Then glancing out of the window to where Helen and Debbie were coming back across the lawn, carrying a trug white with snowdrops, 'Quick, Stephen, they're almost back. The bathroom's on the right along the corridor, go and ... and tidy up.'

For a moment their eyes met, a moment that held the sort of intimacy she had schooled herself to live without. She turned to the mirror and smoothed her hair back into place, then re-buttoned her jacket.

'We got lots of snowdrops, Mum. See! Auntie Helen and me are going to do them to make the hotel lounge pretty, but she says there will be enough for out here too. 'Cause, like she says, today is so special, me having a daddy after all.'

'Where is Helen? I saw you coming across the lawn together.'

'She's putting our coats away and finding the right vases, little ones, 'cause snowdrops are small. She's good at flowers. Well, silly me,' she giggled, 'you know that, don't you? That's why she does them for the dining room tables, 'cause she's good at them. Where is he Mum, where's *Daddy*?'

'In the loo. And look at the time! Here he comes, so now I'll go and have a quick bath and get dressed. Before I know it, it'll be time for guests to be wanting drinks.'

Stephen and Helen met in the corridor and exchanged a silent glance, hers a question and his the answer. Yes, all was well, he and Gillian were making a fresh beginning. But even as the wordless message was passed they heard what Gillian said.

'Oh no, Gillian.' Helen voice was shocked. 'Not this evening. Let someone else look after the bar and the restaurant, this evening you must have your meal out here, the three of you together. Debbie deserves to stay up that bit later. And tonight you'll want to see her off to bed together.' It was fifteen months since Gillian had inherited the running of the hotel, months in which time and again her lack of sensitivity had shocked Helen. But to expect *this* evening to be no different from any other truly hurt her romantic heart. 'Let me go and speak to Sarah before she finishes for the day,

149

she wouldn't mind staying when she knows ... when she knows ... oh but I'm so happy for you both, for all of you.'

'Great idea, whoever Sarah might be,' Stephen said with a broad grin. 'Set the tongues wagging, I bet. What had you told them, Gillian? That I was dead?'

'Told them?' Gillian was genuinely surprised. 'I've told them nothing. Why should I? I hardly think my affairs would be of much conern. And the idea of asking Sarah to stay is ridiculous. What Stephen and I do is our own affair.'

Biting her bottom lip, Debbie looked on anxiously. Why wouldn't Mum do as Auntie Helen suggested? The beastly people in the hotel always had to come first. When Uncle David was here, he always had time for playing with Helen and her. Now this evening would be just like any other. From anxiety, her expression changed to sulky rebellion.

'Beastly hotel,' she mumbled. 'It spoils all the fun.'

'Don't be silly, Debbie.' Gillian's rebuke was automatic. 'Anyway I must go. It's getting late.'

Helen's romantic imagination was again working overtime.

'I came back to collect Debbie to help me with the flowers,' she said. 'Come on Debbie, you and I have a job to do.' She ushered Debbie out of the room. How must Gillian feel, after all this time to have him come back? Well, it was obvious, Helen answered her own silent question, Gillian must be in seventh heaven. If she weren't, she would have sent him away. No one ever persuades her to do anything against her will. Just think, now this very minute he'll be with her as she pulls off her riding things ... he'll ... he'll... Imagination can only go so far. Helen had never been more conscious of the virginity that now mocked her. But even her naive imaginings went further than reality.

Walking ahead of Stephen, Gillian went into the bathroom, then closed and bolted the door.

'Gillian, don't do that. Gillian, undo the door.'

Memories crowded in on her and for a moment she was tempted to do as he said. But it was more than the knowledge that she had responsibilities waiting for her in the hotel that prevented her from pulling back the bolt and letting him in. Other memories fought for pride of place and, as it had so often through the years, his voice echoed in her mind, scorning her that they had nothing to keep them together except sex. Perhaps he'd been right but, if he had, then it had been all she'd needed and each time he had arrived at the apartment she had welcomed him with open arms. Well, she was wiser now.

'Go and watch the flower arrangers,' she called cheerily. 'I shan't be long. I mustn't be long.'

'Damn the bar or whatever it is you're rushing away to. Let it wait. Gillian–'

'I'm turning the water on, I shan't hear you.'

Even though she hadn't started to take off her

clothes, she turned the bath tap on as if to prove to him that he had lost his power over her. Then, listening from behind the closed door to his retreating steps, she opened her mind to honesty. Perhaps he'd been right and that welcome he must always have taken for granted had been no more than an expression of her yearning for his touch. She wouldn't be such a fool again. And yet ... and yet ... Stripping off her clothes, she stood in front of the long mirror, her hands cupping her naked breasts. How many times have we stood together under the warm water, his hands massaging every inch of my body, my hands on his until ... that train of thought was overtaken by another, as she recalled the time when their excitement had been beyond holding. He had turned her around and without a word, bending her forward, had thrust into her. Even at the time, excited though she had been by his loss of control, in those minutes (minutes? hardly more than seconds) as he had pounded frantically to a climax that left them both in an uncomfortable heap in the warm water, she had felt that she'd been *used*. Other times, lovemaking had more than simply satisfied a burning physical need – in the glory of it she had known herself to be cherished.

Willingly she let her thoughts carry her to those times of wonder as she smoothed the soap over her body. Tonight he would stay with her, tonight would belong just to the two of them. Until then she must let him see her in her new role, as owner of Hunters' Lodge, in control of

the establishment and of herelf too. As an aid
to getting her mind on track, she thoroughly
rinsed away the lather, then stepped out of the
bath and towelled herself vigorously, forcing
her thoughts on to other things. Mike ... would
Derek Denvers still be with him? As she imagined the two of them, she was sure that if
anyone could help the poor man to find confidence it would be Mike – oh, but how hard it
must be, always he would be aware that people
seeing him for the first time must momentarily
recoil – yet even in the time of their drive from
Brindley she had schooled herself not to be
repelled by his appearance.

Perhaps the two of them would come over to
the hotel; yet, even as the thought came to her,
she rejected it. The day must have been ordeal
enough for Derek, he certainly wouldn't face a
restaurant full of strangers. When he had seen
round the bungalow, and perhaps made a decision, Mike would drive him back to Brindley.
With the towel wrapped around her, she stood
still while her thoughts went on a journey of
their own. Mike was different from anyone she
had ever known. Through all the months she'd
been here he had been her friend, unchanging,
always ready to boost her when her confidence
flagged. Behind the closed door of the office
they were business partners; exercising the
horses on the downs they were often silent but
the companionship was always there. What
would her time at the hotel have been like without him? From the first time they'd ridden out

153

together, the day her bubble of pent-up emotion had burst, he had been there for her.

Wiping the steam from the mirror with the towel, she looked critically at her reflection. Mike was forgotten.

Every evening, Gillian was austerely elegant, but on that particular one she took even more trouble than usual. The figure-hugging, steely blue dress flattered her and the impression of elegance was enhanced by the silver necklace and earrings. Even standing as she did most evenings, frequently for as long as six hours, she was always comfortable in high heels. In truth, many a woman brought to Hunters' Lodge for an evening out felt either overdressed or dowdy when confronted by her cool assurance. By contrast, Helen never failed to be the prettiest person in the dining room. She, too, dressed simply, though she loved soft pastel shades. But clothes had very little to do with her natural loveliness; loveliness that was part of her gentle nature and never made either the overdressed or dowdy brigades feel inferior. Helen's beauty came from something within, as every one of the guests would agree. And yet Gillian was so often irritated by her, in her mind likening her to a pretty kitten, stroked and petted by everyone as it ensured itself the most comfortable place to settle.

On that particular evening, she assumed Debbie's bedtime routine would be the same as usual: she'd slip away into their own rooms for just long enough to say goodnight, then Helen would take over, coming to the dining room only when she was happy that Debbie was comfortably settled for the night.

'Mum,' Debbie greeted her when she came away from the bar where the pre-dinner drinkers were happily sipping. 'Mum, you know what? Daddy's going to see me have my bath and he's going to read me my story.'

Gillian's expression was inscrutable.

'A new experience, Stephen,' she said. And what was he supposed to read into her words? Pleasure? Jealousy? Annoyance?

'Unfortunately, yes. Debbie and I surely have a lot of ground to catch up on.'

'You'll be there too, Helen? He's a novice, remember.'

None of them understood exactly what there was in the atmosphere that made them uncomfortable. Even Debbie was aware of it. It had all been lovely until her mother had come in. The little girl scowled. What did "novice" mean? Was Mum being cross about him coming?

'I must get back to the bar,' Gillian said. 'The place is bursting at the seams this evening.'

'Why can't someone else take over? If you own the place, why in the world do you turn yourself into a barmaid?' Even her newly-discovered father sounded different from how he had a few minutes ago. Debbie wriggled uncomfortably on her chair. They'd been playing a lovely game of Snap; now it was all spoilt.

'Hop down and kiss Mummy goodnight,' Helen whispered. Well, at least she sounded the

155

same as always. Willingly, Debbie did as she was told, Helen's normal voice restoring hope that they'd be back with the game in no time.

'Night, night Debbie pet. Go to bed nicely, won't you. I'll see you in the morning.'

They had their nightly hug and Debbie forgave her for her unsmiling expression. Mum was always like that. It was a bit sad, that was the seven-year-old's opinion. Everything was so much more fun if you made your face all smiley.

'Just a second,' Helen whispered urgently to the other two as Gillian closed the door behind herself. She followed the retreating figure along the passage. 'Gillian,' she hissed. 'I don't know how to say this but ... tonight, would you like me to have Debbie in my room with me? She's so excited that Stephen's here ... perhaps she'll wake ... I mean...'

Gillian looked puzzled and Helen wished she'd not made the suggestion. But in the books she read, if lovers came back together after a separation ... even in her mind she didn't know how to finish the sentence. She felt uncomfortably aware that in her imagination she was trespassing into Gillian's private world.

'I wouldn't make a big thing of it,' she blundered on. 'I'd say it would round off this special day as a treat. But I don't want to push in, I mean Stephen is so over the moon with her. It's just ... I thought...'

All Gillian's irritation melted as she saw Helen's embarrassment.

'I do appreciate your offering, honestly I do Helen.' She too spoke quietly, somehow Helen's discomfort seemed to demand it. 'If you want to have her another night, that would give her a treat. But she's been pushed around too much already and tonight it's important she stays in her own room. She almost never wakes.' And then with something resembling a laugh, 'And if she does, then he can have some practice in parenting.'

'He's so thrilled about her. I didn't know he hadn't even realized you were pregnant. What a sad muddle it all was.'

'See you presently, when Debbie's in bed. And thanks Helen. If you're there I know they'll be OK.' And she meant it sincerely. Being Gillian, she would hardly have made such a remark had it been anything less than sincere.

The game of Snap picked up where they had left it, but the hands of the clock were getting towards the hour of seven, time for Debbie's bath. So it was that *her* pile of cards started to grow bigger and both Helen and Stephen's dwindled away as they were slow in shouting, 'Snap'.

In the bathroom, Debbie undressed independently, a nightly feat in which she had taken great pride ever since they'd been at the hotel. Helen encouraged her and, even in the beginning, had never hinted that it would have been much quicker if she'd had help.

157

'There!' Debbie exclaimed with pride as she peeled her vest off over her head. 'Now I'm ready...'

'Well done,' praised ever faithful Helen, but Stephen said nothing. Suddenly he was afraid to trust his voice as he gazed on the small naked form in front of him. As he'd said to Gillian, there was no doubting that Debbie was his child – young as she was, the resemblance was clear. He wanted to touch her, to move his hands on her small body, flesh of his flesh. Her dark eyes were fixed on him; was it his imagination or did she know the moment was special? He was quite sure that Helen did, he knew it from the way she turned her back on them and scooped up Debbie's discarded clothes.

'I'll lift you in,' he told his daughter. 'Squeak if the water's too warm.' Picking her up, just for a moment he held her close, an action not lost on her. Her arms were around his neck as she threw back her head and laughed. This was the most special day she'd ever had.

Later, he read the promised story while Helen was tidying up the bathroom and making sure the sitting room looked what she imagined would be in keeping for the re-united lovers to spend the last minutes of their day. She was glad she'd picked enough snowdrops for that shallow black vase on the table there as well as in the residents' lounge – flowers were important. At least, she imagined they were. Supposing it had been David suddenly come back, supposing ... but that could never happen.

Standing in the centre of the sitting room where the two of them had so often been together, she felt utterly alone. She ought to go away from Hunters' Lodge, she knew she ought. It belonged to Gillian now, everything there was different. If it weren't for Debbie she would find the courage to look for a job somewhere, perhaps somewhere miles away where every way she turned ghosts of yesterday wouldn't be waiting for her. No one knew how desolate she was, how could they know? But David knew, of that she was certain. Wherever she went he would always be close to her. And telling herself *that*, she stood a little straighter and went along the corridor to Debbie's bedroom, just as she recognized the last sentence of one of the favourite stories.

'Prayers time?' Debbie wriggled out, pleased to show off to her newly discovered father how well she knew the routine. And this time she needed no prompting as she dug in her mind for the things she had to say "thank you" for. 'I know I've never actually *asked*, but I have thought it, about wishing I had a daddy. Now he's come and that's the most important thing I've ever had to thank you about. Please make him stay – not like Billy Hatcher's father at school, he's gone away and left Billy and his lot. Please don't let that happen to me now that you've let him come back and find Mum and me – and Auntie Helen,' she remembered to add, fearing Helen might feel left out and sad. 'Amen. Oh no, something else. On Sunday

159

when Mike puts the jumps up for me, please make Lyndy and me do well and my Dad watch. Amen.'

It was a very satisfied little girl who climbed back into bed, pursing her lips not once but twice tonight as first Helen and then Stephen bent to kiss her goodnight. Excited as she was, she wanted to stay awake and remember every single second of the last few hours, but her eyes wouldn't stay open.

As Gillian had said, the restaurant was full and on that Friday night no one seemed in a hurry to go home. Once or twice during the busy evening Helen crept along to make sure Debbie hadn't woken, but most of the time, once dinner was over, she and Stephen had been back in the bar sitting over their coffee at the far end of the room. Watching them – when she had the chance, which wasn't often, kept as busy as she was – an expression of her grandmother's she remembered from childhood came to Gillian: "He could charm the birds off the trees." Words that might have been written to describe Stephen. Her emotions were confused: resentment that his attention was fixed so firmly on someone else, anger that he'd come back expecting her to fall into his arms and that anger mixed with shame and humiliation that, despite herself, she had been putty in his hands.

All these years when she'd been telling herself he was out of her life and out of her mind, deep in her heart she had known it wasn't true.

He'd been her first love, and that at an age when many women are married and with children; he'd been her only love. But what had become of her pride that when he'd begged for the years of separation to be put behind them, her resolve had melted like snow in sunshine? He had sounded so sincere; she tried to find excuses for her willingness. Then there was another strand to her emotions, one that was weaving itself into the pattern: if ever a girl was a true romantic it must be Helen, poor heartbroken, lonely Helen. Watching the two of them, Gillian's habitual irritation vanished. For herself, she was tough, she could fight her own battles, but Helen was vulnerable.

Though the two in the far corner of the room had sat long over their empty coffee cups, their evening was passing much more quickly than Gillian's. Helen was a good listener and Stephen loved talking, talking of his past, talking of his regret about the break-up of his marriage, talking about his life as a roving reporter, talking about what it meant to him to have found Debbie.

'You have a rare and wonderful gift, Helen,' he told her, not missing the fact that at his words her face grew pink as might have a girl's half her age with her first crush on a handsome man. Stephen was enjoying himself. This fragile and utterly gorgeous Helen was one of a dying breed. 'I mean it sincerely. You are a listener. And these days most people clamour to be heard. No one cares enough to be still and listen. You should have shut me up, I must have been boring you rigid.'

'Oh, but you weren't,' she hastened to assure him. 'I didn't know much about you, you see. David never talked about what went wrong between you and Gillian...'

'Not very likely that he would. He couldn't have known. There are things in marriage no outsider can know. It was my fault we parted. I'd had woman friends since I first considered myself a man. It goes against the grain when because you're married you become "husband" – or "wife" in the woman's case – and not the person you have always been. I married Gillian feeling so sure I could be faithful. But – oh damn it, Helen, how can I put it so that you will see what I'm driving at? If you have a box of chocolates the centres are all different. Your favourite might be the caramel, so why don't you elect to have a bag of chocolate caramels instead of that variety?'

Helen was out of her depth, she shook her head helplessly and waited for him to go on talking. 'I'll tell you why, Helen my friend. Because there is no excitement in a bag of just one flavour. In a box, some may be sweet and delectable, some may not appeal at all, but you have to try them. Gillian and I had been lovers for about three years and for me there was no one like her – there still isn't nor has been during the time we've been apart. So we married and I felt the door of the cage click shut. She wouldn't give up her job, she took no

162

interest in my career, a career that took me into Europe until the war started and after that all around the United Kingdom. We were together only when I was in London. But there were things in my relationship with Gillian that made everything else worthwhile – for a time. You see, she never had time to be a listener, Helen, she always had to be driving herself, over-coming some challenge or another. She be-lieved *her* work was every bit as important as mine. But I'm an old-fashioned kind of guy when it comes to marriage. I believe the man ought to be the main breadwinner.'

'But what about now? She works so hard here and, to be fair, it's a seven day a week job. I'm thankful I'm here for Debbie.'

'And so am I,' he endorsed her remark, touching her hand lightly with his. 'But it's not what you expected, you were dealt a rough hand.'

Helen nodded. 'Sometimes I wonder how it would have been if David hadn't been killed, if instead he had been left paralysed. For me, it would have made no difference, he was – he was my whole world. But he and Gillian are alike. He probably would have refused to go ahead with the wedding.' She bit her trembling lip. 'Hate horses,' she mumbled.

'I bet you do.' He took her hand firmly this time. 'Who wouldn't, in your position? But things have a habit of working out, Helen my friend. Gillian is efficient to her fingertips, but if you weren't here the spirit of Hunters' Lodge

163

would be changed. I could feel that from the moment I arrived.'

'I *do* try,' she said, her lovely blue eyes seeming to him to plead for his understanding. 'With children I know I do well. Teaching little people was sheer joy.'

'I thought there was a scarcity of teachers.'

Was he implying that she ought to be earning a living? Did he see her as an encumbrance there in the place that Gillian had inherited? She explained to him about the letter David had written and left for Gillian, not expecting that it would ever be needed.

'Our future was so certain,' she finished. 'Now he's gone and – and there's just *nothing*. He would want me to be here, I am sure of that. And Debbie is my salvation. Gillian is so busy, busier than when she had a full time job in London, because there at least Debbie had her for the evenings. But now she never seems to have time for anything. And on Saturday, the day with no school, there's hunting.'

'I'll get us a drink,' he said, guiding the conversation away from where it was heading.

'And I'll just have a peep to make sure Debbie's still sound asleep.'

So the evening finally came to an end, the last of the residents gone on their way, and Gillian put the remaining glasses in the dishwasher. Thus it was every evening, Fridays and Saturdays always later than the rest of the week, while the weekenders made the most of their break. The kitchen staff cleared up and went home and Gillian was left, the last to finish. It was only as she finally pulled down the grille in front of the bar that she remembered Derek Denvers and was surprised that Mike hadn't walked across to tell her the result of the viewing.

Long though the evening had been, at last it was over, and Helen had gone up to Room 14, the room which had always been reserved for her. Gillian and Stephen went through the door marked "Private". This was her hour, he'd come back to her, she'd haunted his dreams just as he'd haunted hers. That was the way her mind was turning, but uninvited came the memory of his leaving her. Pride was pushing to the fore: she would be calm, she wouldn't let her craving body make her no more than a puppet waiting for him to pull the strings. But her intentions were thrown off course as they crept along the corridor and, reaching Debbie's tiny bedroom, he took her hand to hold her back. Then soundlessly turning the handle, he pushed the door open so that, in the light shining from the corridor, they could see the sleeping child.

'Like a miracle.' His whisper was so quiet she could almost believe she'd imagined it. Then, just as gently, he stepped back to the passage and pulled the door closed behind them.

Now it's us, just *us*. Her brave intentions were vanishing, she had no power to hold on to them. And why should she even try, she asked herself. She loved him, nothing could ever destroy the hold he had over her. At first it might have been because he was handsome and charming that so willingly she had rushed headlong into love with him. He'd brought her joy beyond anything she'd imagined, physical joy beyond anything she had known before or since.

Upstairs in her lonely bedroom, Helen imagined what must be happening. She had left a soft light on in Gillian's lounge and the gas fire was still burning. They would be sitting on the settee, and Stephen's arm would be around Gillian. That's how it used to be for David and *her*. Gillian was so determined, so busy always, it was hard to imagine her relaxing and leaning against Stephen, holding her face so that his mouth could find hers. All the romance in Helen's lonely soul was with the two downstairs. It must have been an hour later when she got out of bed and looked down from her window, surprised to see a glow of light coming from the lounge. Ought she to go down and make sure they'd remembered to turn off the fire? No, they might hear her creeping past the bedroom door.

Had she gone down, what she would have seen might have shocked her. To Helen, romance belonged to the scent of flowers on a summer night, to moonlight, to soft music. She would have been disillusioned and puzzled by the sight of the two on the sheepskin rug by the fire.

The next day was Saturday, always an early start for Mike who got the horses ready and then in their trailers so that there was nothing to delay the participating guests setting out for the meet. For Gillian too it was an early start, for she aimed to be in the stables in time to help him and walk Bella and Brutus into the horsebox so that they could lead the way to the meet.

With Stephen still sleeping, she wriggled to the edge and then, gingerly, got out of bed. It seemed he'd been nearer waking than she'd imagined.

'Hey, lady, come back here. What time do you call this?'

'After half past six. I'm always early on Saturday. Remember, I told you, I go with the guests to the hunt.' Even though he seemed more wide awake by the second, she whispered. 'I tried not to wake you. You needn't get up yet. I always give a hand with the horses before we set off.'

'Come back.' He tempted. 'Just five minutes. Our first morning.' He reached to take her hand and guided it under the bed covers. 'Don't go, Gilly. Just five minutes – two minutes more likely.'

She had no resistance. This was their first morning, and it was to start as so many had in the past.

'Remember last night,' he said softly, as he drew her to lie on top of him.

'Every second of it,' she murmured, her mouth close to his. Where was her willpower? It had melted just as it always did at his touch. Yes, she remembered last night. They had followed every erotic avenue, their passion heightened by each turn of the way. Morning was different. Only half awake when he had pulled her back into bed, his returning consciousness had only one aim. For her there was no joyous climax, she didn't even want there to be. As she moved on him she gloried in looking down at him as he lay with his eyes closed, his mouth slightly open, and knowing that his control was lost while it was she who was doing this to him, she who had the power to strip his mind of everything beyond the driving need that only she could satisfy.

'Are you OK?' Mike greeted her when, some forty-five minutes later, showered, her face made up with the same care as every other morning and immaculate in her hunting habit, she joined him as he led Bella into the stable yard.

'I'm late, aren't I? Sorry, Mike. If you'd come to the hotel yesterday evening you would have known ... Mike, Stephen's back.'

'Your husband?' Just for a second her announcement stripped him of the natural friendly manner she had come to take for granted.

'My ex-husband. Debbie's father.'

'You say he's "back"? You mean you're together again?'

She nodded. 'Tell me I'm crazy. Perhaps I am. All these years I've told myself I didn't care about him. Then, out of the blue he was there, Debbie's father. She's over the moon. I never realized – never gave it a thought – just how much it meant to her that she had no father.'

'You can't shape your future on her need for a father. Gillian, suppose you fell for some other guy, are you saying you're willing to tie yourself to a failed marriage so that Debbie has a father?'

'I didn't say that. Mike, please be happy for me. If David were still here it would have been vitally important to me that he understood. And since he's been gone, you have – no, I can't say you've taken his place, no one could possibly do that – but you have been my very dear friend. It's important to me that you understand and are happy for me.'

Still leading Bella, he came to her side and took her hand in his.

'Yes, our friendship is important, more important than I can say. And yes, Gillian, I guess happiness is what I want more than anything for you. You never told me what broke your marriage, and I don't want to know. If you love him, then he's the man you want to be with. But don't push yourself into it for Debbie's sake. A bad marriage is no setting for a child to grow up in.'

'If I didn't love him I would have sent him packing, believe me.' Her voice was firm. She didn't want advice from Mike or anyone else. She intended to make her own decision just as she always had. She was disappointed – disappointed and deep down she was angry too – at Mike's doubtful acceptance of what she

169

had done.

'Here come the guests. Brutus is aboard. I'll just get Bella into the lorry, then we'll be on our way.' And as he called a smiling greeting to the four who were making up their party, he drew a line under the intimacy of the last few minutes.

As he drove the five miles or so to the venue for the meet, Gillian steered the conversation on to a different track.

'I thought you would have come over to the hotel to tell me how you got on with Derek Denvers. Didn't he like the bungalow?"

'Sure, he liked it. Nice young man. We got along fine. In fact, he stayed the night on the sofa in my living room. He had a train timetable with him and we aimed for the seven-twenty, which would have got the connection in Reading in time for the last bus when he got the other end. When we got to the station we were told the seven-twenty had been cancelled, the next was just after eight and too late for him to get the connection. So we picked up a few beers from the off-licence and some fish and chips and came back to my quarters.'

'That was nice of you, Mike. But we had vacant rooms at the hotel, he could have stayed there instead of on the sofa...'

'You've met him, Gillian, you've talked to him. Can you see him checking in at a hotel, eating in a full dining room? Poor young devil. I don't know when I've felt so sorry for anyone. But I knew better than to let him suspect what I was feeling.'

'You say he liked the bungalow? Is he interested in buying?'

'Sure he is. And he didn't come in with an offer less than the asking price, either. I had the feeling money wasn't his chief concern. What he's looking for is seclusion. Did he tell you how he got so burned?'

'Only that he'd been in an accident. I suppose that's why he isn't driving, he must have lost his nerve.'

While they'd talked Mike had kept an eye on the driver's mirror, making sure that the two cars and horse trailers were still behind them.

'Lost his nerve to live, poor devil. But it wasn't a motoring accident. After we'd sat drinking our beer and eating the fish and chip supper, he opened up quite a lot. He was living with his parents down in Sussex. It seems they'd just had their boiler adapted to use gas instead of oil. God knows whose fault it was but there was a goddamned explosion, right there in the kitchen where all three of them were. Even talking about it turned him into a shaking wreck. They were thrown by the blast. The place looked as if a bomb had fallen on it, except that a bomb does its damage and it's over. My guess would be that the blast extinguished the flame in the boiler, but the gas was full on. The light was on, gaslight with a naked flame. By the time he had picked himself up from the blast and tried to shift some of the debris off his parents, suddenly the room was a blazing inferno.'

171

'Surely he could have got out of the room and dragged his parents?'

'His parents were buried under the rubble, both unconscious; the doorway was blocked. Maybe he panicked, God knows he had reason enough. There was no way he could turn off the gas, the tap was in the garage, he was trapped in the little kitchen, trapped just as surely as his unconscious parents. There were no very near neighbours, but a motorist passing by in the lane saw the cottage with its windows blown out and a pillar of smoke. He called for help or Derek might have ended like his parents – both were killed. Yet their bodies weren't burnt like his, apparently. His clothes caught fire, he remembers trying to roll on the ground – then nothing else until he woke up in hospital. It's not just his face, you know; his body is a mess too.'

'Awful, just awful. And now to have to build a new life ... poor lad.'

'He's not as young as I first thought. He was a flyer for the last year of the war, then he went to art school. He'd just had his first exhibition and his work was selling. But this seems to have knocked the chocks from under him.' By now they'd come to the point where riders were already assembling. Gillian realized that for the whole of the drive she hadn't given a thought to Stephen or, for that matter, to the excitement of the day ahead. 'Out we get. There's more to tell you, but it must wait now until we're on the way home.'

'We're so lucky, Mike,' she said, as she jumped to the ground from the cab of the lorry.

'Yep. Come on, my friend Gillian, what we both need is a good hard ride.'

'Blow away the cobwebs,' she said, recalling that first ride she'd had with him.

Just for a second her gaze met his, but almost immediately she looked away. Surely she must have imagined what she'd read in his eyes.

On the drive home, he told her the rest of the story. There was nothing to hold Derek in Sussex, and it had been Mike's suggestion that rather than waiting for the legal ends of the purchase to be tied up, he could move into the bungalow as soon as he liked.

'Poor young devil, I reckon what he's craving is solitude to lick his wounds.'

'I thought that too,' Gillian agreed. 'But if you can make yourself look directly at him without letting him see what the sight does to you, I found that even in the time I was with him I started to get used to his appearance. Don't you think that's the way it is with everyone? Even someone like Helen, who must be the prettiest person I've ever seen, once you know a person you almost don't see what they look like.'

'Yep, I guess so. But it's that initial hurdle he has to cross. He's not long been out of hospital, I don't think he's got used to his face himself yet. And it's not just his face. He must have been in a hell of a state – imagine the pain, Gillian.'

'So how soon does he expect to move in?'

'I guess he's probably there by now,' Mike said with a laugh. 'I told him he can carry the bedding he used on the sofa last night, and until his things come he can eat with me.'

'He can't live like that – sleeping on the floor, no furniture.'

'This morning he's going to walk to the call box down the hill and phone to have his things sent. He's going to speak to an old buddy who lives in the same village, they've been friends since they were kids at school. That's where he's been staying since he came out of hospital. One side of the house was virtually undamaged except for smoke. His mate will get it organized for stuff to be collected. Apparently the two of them had been into the house together and collected his own personal stuff – any clothes that were still OK. Now he'll get some furniture sent as soon as it can be handled, so he won't have to bed down on the floor for long. And I thought I'd run him into the village to pick up bits and pieces he'll need for cooking. Going with someone the tradespeople already know won't be as hard as walking into strange shops on his own.'

'Are you always this kind?' Even though it wasn't a serious question, she was surprised that he should be going so far out of his way to help a stranger.

'There was something about him – sort of touched me somehow. I hope he finds his way to making a collection of paintings for another

174

exhibition. There's nothing like the country and solitude to mend a broken spirit.' Then, changing the subject, 'We'll be home early today. The fox must have known you have a husband impatient for your company.'

But he was wrong. When they got back to Hunters' Lodge the first thing she noticed was that Stephen's car was gone. And the second that Kathleen's was in the car park.

'I'd better go in and say hello. But I'll come out again and give you a hand.'

'See how things go. Fine if you do – but if not, I'll get our young friend out and introduce him to stable life.'

She found Kathleen in the visitors' lounge having tea. It seemed that Ella had been determined to come over, even though she knew neither Gillian nor Mike would be there.

'She trundled off on her own in the direction of the stables. I noticed she had her sketching things with her, but what she's up to I've no idea. What's all this I hear about Stephen being here?'

'Helen's told you?'

'The reception girl – Sarah do you call her? Full of excitement about it. Like all the youngsters, a head full of romantic notions.' She paused, waiting to hear the whole story.

So Gillian told her, or at any rate gave a clear outline of how Stephen's chance meeting with his cousin Stanley had led him to Hunters' Lodge.

'Have you met him, Kathleen? Was he here

175

when you arrived?' Suspecting Kathleen was less than enthusiastic, Gillian was sure that once Stephen had charmed her she would be captivated.

'No. The girl told me he had taken Helen and Debbie out in his car. Gillian, Gillian my dear, are you *sure* you want to slip back into a marriage that failed once?' Not many people on hearing the news would have been so outspoken, but it was that very outspokenness that made these two understand each other so well.

'In my mind, I've fought it all these years. But, Kathleen, when I saw him I knew it was useless to fight. And Debbie, honestly you'd think heaven had fallen at her feet. I never realized how much she wanted a father.'

'Sometimes the right stepfather can be better than the wrong father,' Kathleen said, then listened to the sound of silence as her words sank in.

'You may well be right in some cases. Anyway, there wasn't going to be a stepfather, right or wrong. Stephen is the right father for Debbie and when you see them together, you will agree.'

'And are you the right wife? You weren't last time.' She was certainly taking liberties with their friendship.

'If I weren't, would he have come here begging me to let us have a fresh start? Just one thing, though, Kathleen. I see no reason for us to re-marry. I already have his name, he is the father on Debbie's birth certificate. So as far as the ouside world is concerned we are husband and wife, just as we still see ourselves. And that's the way I intend to leave it.'

Kathleen looked at her thoughtfully, but made no comment. Instead, she reached to cover Gillian's hand with her own. 'Then my dear, I wish you every happiness from the bottom of my heart. But, one piece of advice which I hope you will never need: if this time round things go wrong, don't hang on to a dead relationship for the sake of a child. A bad marriage is no setting for a child's upbringing.'

'Almost word for word, that was what Mike said.'

Kathleen weighed up the remark, but again made no comment. When she spoke, it was to change the subject.

'It'll be getting dark before we know it. I must go and collect Ella. I wonder you didn't see her when you parked, it was the stables she was making for.'

But she wasn't there and neither had Mike seen her.

'Silly to worry about the child,' Kathleen said, 'she's perfectly capable of getting around in her chair. It's getting cold, though, and sitting still she'll be frozen.'

'No, she won't. If she were cold she would have gone to the stables and watched Mike with the horses.' In fact, that was where they had both expected to find her. Instead they went through the back gate, glancing up and down the empty lane. There were two horses grazing

177

in the field which used to belong to the bunglow next door, so they turned that way, expecting that's where they'd find Ella and her sketching pad. But they didn't reach the front gate of the bungalow, for as they came to the opening of a narrow track that ran alongside the fields they saw her.

'Wait!' Gillian said, instinctively drawing Kathleen back.

'But who is she with?' Kathleen's protective instinct was aroused. For Ella wasn't alone. Sitting on the step of the stile leading into the field was Derek, with Ella's chair drawn close to him while both of them were engrossed in the drawing she had been working on.

Six

Making the excuse that the cold air had made her sleepy, Ella wanted to be helped to bed soon after nine o'clock. During the evening she had said nothing to her mother about her meeting with Derek, and Kathleen was wise enough to ask no questions, even though what she'd learned from Gillian was at the front of her mind.

'He shuns strangers. I've already met him; I drove him from the station,' Gillian had said. 'So you go on to the car and I'll fetch Ella. She

178

must let him know she's told you about him before you meet him face to face. You can almost feel his dread of the shock and embarrassment of anyone who meets him.'

'Poor lad. We've seen so many scarred by burns over these last years – but at least those in the war were able to support each other. Yes, my dear, I'll wait for her in the car,' Kathleen had agreed.

On Gillian's way past the stables, Mike called out to her.

'I told you not to bother to come back. I can manage. You go and get warm.'

So there was a brief delay while she told him about Ella and Derek being together.

'That's great,' he said. 'What if I go and find them and wheel her around to the car? He's getting used to being with me. Then I'll suggest he give me a hand here. Say, but that's good, Gillian, the two of them out making friends by themselves.' Then, his eyebrows raised and a smile on his face, 'Isn't that just proof of the country magic? Off you go, before that husband of yours comes looking for you.'

'Not very likely,' she'd laughed. 'He's taken Debbie out in the car – and Helen, of course.'

Mike's frown didn't pass unnoticed.

Gillian had gone back to her room at the hotel, Ella had been collected and Derek had been persuaded to have his first lesson in horse care, something he had agreed to out of politeness as Mike had been so generous in his hospitality. For him it had been a new experience, as

179

new as the feeling of undemanding comrade-ship.

Driving back to Streatham Manor, Kathleen had asked how Ella's afternoon had gone, sure she'd be taken into the girl's confidence.

'The afternoon flew. I went to watch the horses in the field, and it seemed no time before Mike was home and came to say you were waiting.'

That had warned Kathleen off asking more questions and late in the evening, with Ella in bed and the Aga banked up to keep the kitchen warm for morning, she thought about the girl's unusual reticence. On the rare occasions when anything out of the ordinary happened, what-ever they were talking about, Ella would steer the conversation back to the thing, or the per-son, at the forefront of her mind. Kathleen was surprised at today's silence; she even wondered uncomfortably whether Derek had been of no interest because of his appearance.

Wide awake and revelling in the thought of the hours of solitude ahead of her, Ella relived her afternoon. Would he be remembering it too? She wondered why it was she had been so secretive with her mother. Did she feel that by not talking about her new friend she was allowing him the privacy she instinctively knew he craved? Yet he hadn't run away from *her*. Wriggling to sit up in bed, she switched on the bedside light and reached for the sketch pad she always kept close to hand. Then she started to draw. She could remember exactly what he looked like, but that wasn't what she sketched. There was no disfigurement in the face she drew. Even on his unscarred side, it probably wasn't terribly like him, but it was the nearest she could manage to the image in her memory.

Smiling, she tucked her pad under her pillow, turned off the bedside light and lay down. Derek Denvers ... that was a lovely name. Fancy being a proper artist. And he hadn't been a bit condescending when he'd talked to her about her sketches. He would teach her. Her mind was flying high, carrying her where it would ... when he had another exhibition, she imagined some of her work hanging next to his. Then she relived the moment he'd walked out of the back door of the bungalow and seen her by the stile in her wheelchair. Would he have come over and spoken to her if she'd been ordinary, like everyone else? She knew he wouldn't have. Was she falling in love? She asked herself the question, entirely forgetting how many times in the past she had been sure the answer had been "Yes". On that night, none of those other times had any place.

Never in my life, she said silently, *never once – that's true, yes, that's the honest truth – when I've met someone, have I felt like I did today. Always I've been the one who had to be taken care of, I've sort of lapped up their attentiveness. Oh well, I can't walk, we all know that; but I don't feel like I just know he does, numb with terror at being looked at. When he walked over to speak to me it was a sort of magic*

181

moment, I felt he was frightened to see my expression. But he needn't have been, because I – I – I wasn't a bit shocked, it was as if I felt his pain for him. I know why he came to talk to me: he came because he saw me as a cripple. But I'm not; I'm just me who can't walk. And Derek, Derek Denvers – one day, when he's famous, everyone will know his name – he's the same person he always was, except that he's shy of being looked at. But that won't last. He didn't seem to mind Mike. But then Mike's special, he sort of understands how people feel. Am I in love with Mike? I truly thought I was. But of course he's really too old for me. I wonder how old Derek is?

She, who had thought she had hours of night ahead of her to indulge in daydreams, was being lulled into sleep.

Next morning Debbie rushed to the stables as soon as breakfast was over.

'Mike! Mike! Mum must have told you! I was wrong when I said I hadn't got a daddy, I *have*. Mum must have told you. And he's going to live with us so we are a proper family the same as everyone else.'

'Sure, honey. Your mum told me. I bet you can't wait to get to school in the morning and tell your mates, eh?'

'Well.' Debbie pondered the question, frowning, 'The thing is I just never talked about fathers. No one does really, it's always mums who meet them from school – except for me,

182

and Auntie Helen comes for me. But I tell you what, Mike, I bet sometimes now Daddy will come and get me. Only he says he won't always be here because he is a writer for a newspaper and he goes everywhere, even across the sea.'

'He'll be here as often as he can, Debbie, you may be certain of that.'

'Yep,' she mimicked the way she'd often heard him say it, the single word full of confidence. 'Anyway Mike, why I came quick as I could as soon as Mum said I could leave the breakfast table was to ask you if you would put the jumps out for me. 'Cause you see, I want him to see how well I can do.'

'Sure I will, honey. You go and get your kit on while I see to it.'

'OK. Thanks Mike. I'll be quick as anything. And when I come back I expect I'll bring my dad with me. But isn't it ... isn't it ... spiffing!' And as if the word fell short of just how wonderful it was, it was emphasized by the way she gripped her hands together and jumped.

Ten minutes later she was back and, with her was a tall man dressed with casual elegance. So this was the one who must have held Gillian's heart all these years.

'You'll surely be Mike,' an American voice greeted him as he led Lyndy out of the stable. 'Stephen Sinclair.' Stephen held out his well-groomed hand. By comparison, Mike felt his own to be work-roughened.

Debbie looked on, saying nothing, her own small hands gripped under her chin and her

183

eyes shining with excitement at the wonder of it all.

'You'll be proud of how well Debbie here is riding. By summer she'll be in the gymkhana,' Mike said, with an affectionate glance in her direction. 'The jumps are out, Debs, you know what's expected of you. I've not started you off too high, so when you're ready, ask your father to raise it another notch. OK?'

'Aren't you going to watch me?' A small cloud appeared on her horizon.

'Hey there, but how big an audience do you need? This performance is for your father. Lyndy is all set, so get on the mounting block and he will give you a hoist up.'

She nodded, partially restored, looking to Stephen for corroboration.

'Oh no, no.' Stephen laughed. 'I guess horses and I aren't on familiar terms like you folk here. I'll watch from this side of the gate; you won't catch me going within kicking distance of the beast.'

'Lyndy wouldn't hurt anyone.' Debbie was quick to the defence of her adored pony. She wasn't going to listen to anyone, not even her newfound wonderman, calling Lyndy a "beast" in that unfriendly tone. 'You come, Mike. Please.' And Mike could sense that her excited happiness was too new yet to withstand disappointment. Just for a second his face reflected his feelings, but he soon had it under control again even though he was silently asking himself how Gillian, Gillian of all people, could

184

have fallen in love with a man so alien.

'Sure I'll come, honey. Up you get then.'

With Debbie mounted, they made their way to the paddock where Stephen, true to his word, closed the gate behind them as they went through and leant against it, waiting for his daughter's performance.

'Ride right round first,' Mike told her, 'then take the jump the second time. I'll be here watching.'

Of the two men, it was Stephen whose emotions were clear, his gaze never leaving Debbie. Mike wasn't prepared to acknowledge his anger and frustration, and even if he had, anger and frustration were more straightforward than something he tried to stamp on before it had time to form. For Debbie's sake, he knew he ought to be thankful that her father had reappeared, but there was a wide gap between how he *ought* to feel and his true sentiment. Then he glanced at Stephen and saw the pride, more than pride, in his eyes. Mike knew that it was *he*, himself, who was the outsider.

'Look Dad! Watch me! Jumping next time round!'

Mike looked around: the hotel, the paddock, the grazing land beyond, all this had woven itself so surely into his life. The years that had gone before had been overshadowed as if they were no more than the precursor to his time at Hunters' Lodge, the bond that had grown between Gillian and him, the pride he had in Debbie. From now on, even though often Stephen

185

would be away, nothing could ever be as it had been.

Through the months since October the new order of things in the hotel had got off to a satisfactory start, so what was he doing staying here as nothing more than a stable hand? Until that moment he had never thought of himself as being "used". When he'd become a partner in the hotel the idea hadn't occurred to him to alter his role there. He and Gillian each played their part, riding together, hunting together, often going over the books together; but beyond all that he was the stable hand. Could he stay here now, watching her with Stephen, seeing the change marriage must make to her life? He had work waiting for him at Dalgooney.

But suppose her sod of a husband walked out on her again? Memories flooded back of that first time they had ridden together, the day she'd lost her hard-fought battle for control. Imagine if she'd been alone.

'Can I try a bit higher Mike? I flew right over that one.' Debbie young voice broke into his reverie.

'I reckon you can. Trot round the paddock while I raise it. You're doing fine.' Then to Stephen, 'She's a natural. Like her mother – and David.' He had to say it, taking some sort of satisfaction in feeling himself close to the whole family.

'She's a smashing kid,' came Stephen's proud reply.

Mike raised the jump, then stood close by

while he watched her approach.

'Well done,' Stephen called to her. 'That's enough for today. Get Mike to help you down and we'll drive into Brindley. I want to get a newspaper.'

'The papers are in the visitors' lounge,' Mike called back to him, again deriving satisfaction in his own familiarity with Hunters' Lodge.

'Not the one I read.'

Debbie rode over to him. 'I did do well, didn't I?' She needed to hear his praise.

'Yes, sure you did. I told you so. Get – Mike do you call him? – to help you off, then leave him to put the pony away.'

Debbie chuckled, looking at Mike.

'Daddy doesn't know about horses, does he, Mike? He thinks they're like cars, you just go indoors and forget them.' Then, to Stephen, 'I have to put my tack away and give Lyndy a carrot. That's all part of having a pony.'

'Mike can see to it for you today. I'll go and collect Gillian.'

'Mummy won't come. She'll have things to do. She's always busy on Sunday morning. Me and Helen usually keep out of the way.'

Stephen laughed. 'Want to bet? Of course she'll come. Get off now, Debs, and leave the clearing up to Mike like I said.' And with that he turned back to the hotel.

Mike steadied her as she climbed to the ground.

'I'll see to Lyndy this time,' he told her. 'Your father's first morning home, he deserves to

187

have you with him.'

Still she hesitated. She always enjoyed it after her ride when she and Mike worked together. 'Mum says Lyndy is my responsibility.'

'And so she is. But as today is special, I guess your Mum will think it's OK. Lyndy and I are pretty good mates.'

'Thanks, Mike. I'd better hurry or he might go without me.' Then, standing as tall as she could and planting a loud kiss somewhere below Lyndy's ear, she turned and followed the way Stephen had gone, running as fast as she could.

Debbie was proved right. The sound of their voices met her as she ran along the passage from their private quarters to the restaurant, where Stephen had tracked down Gillian.

'Hey, but that's nonsense. What sort of staff do you employ in this joint? You've got a family to consider – and a husband.' He wasn't used to not getting his own way.

And from the tone of Gillian's reply she clearly wasn't prepared to accept criticism, whether of her organization, herself or the staff.

'This joint as you call it has an excellent staff. Suddenly discovering I have a husband doesn't alter the way I run things here any more than you would let having a wife get in the way of your work. If you want to take Debbie out, that's fine. Will you be back to lunch?'

'To watch you faffing about with your horsey friends? You bet I won't. Debs and I will take a trip somewhere.'

Gillian's main reaction was relief, but there was no way she could keep the smile from her eyes as she looked up at him.

'Have a good time,' she said softly, automatically moving close to him and resting her hands on his shoulders as she held her face to his.

'You're a witch, you know that?' He too whispered, even though neither of them were aware of Debbie standing in the doorway. 'You cast a spell over me.'

Debbie watched them. What a funny way he was kissing, as if he was hungry and wanted to eat Mum's mouth. And Mum looked different from usual, as if she wasn't strong and certain. 'Perhaps I won't go out,' he was saying, moving his mouth from side to side on her mother's as he spoke, 'perhaps I'll carry you off and give you just what you're asking for.' Debbie frowned. Asking for?

Gillian's moment of weakness was short-lived. Firmly, she pushed him away.

'Go and have a good time. Why don't you take Helen along?'

'Doesn't she have a mass of Sunday morning responsibilities? And, if she doesn't, why can't you let her do whatever it is you look on as so important?'

'Don't interfere with the way I do things here, Stephen.'

Debbie moved back into the passage. Why couldn't Mum just be happy and do as he said? Why couldn't she let them go out together and be excited that he'd come to live with them and be a proper daddy?

'You're theirs in the day and mine at night, is that the way you want it?'

'It's the way with most marriages when two people work. I can't just down tools and go out, Sunday lunch is important.'

'I thought you told me you had a partner in the business. Why can't he get some decent gear on and come in to serve their drinks or whatever it is you consider so important?'

At the thought, Gillian laughed. 'Mike? Don't be daft. What Mike does is every bit as important as anything I do. Now off you go, Stephen. Collect Debbie, and if you want someone with you then you'll find Helen in the visitors' lounge. She'll jump at the chance of lunch out.'

With a shrug of his shoulders, he left her, and Debbie came out of hiding in the shadowy passage. Less than five minutes later, Gillian heard the excited chatter and laughter as the three of them passed the window on their way to his car. Did she regret her obstinate decision – not that she thought of it as obstinate – or was she simply relieved when she heard the car drive away? Uninvited, the question sprang into her mind, only to be pushed away. And what had he said about her belonging to the hotel by day and to him by night?

Memories of the night crowded in on her, a night driven by years of frustrated longing. Immediately, her thoughts were pulled up short; she was faced with that other image, times

190

when in the isolation of her lonely room she had found fleeting joy only to fall immediately to self abasement and empty hopelessness. Now all that was over. Through the years when she'd thought he'd forgotten her, he had remembered; he had wanted her just as she had wanted him. Then came that other ghost: the echo of his voice telling her all they shared was sex, and that that couldn't be enough in a marriage. Last night it had been enough, for him and for her too. Anyway, she told herself, everything was different now; no longer were there just the two of them, now they were part of a family. Thinking of Debbie and the little girl's excitement that she had a father, Gillian smiled.

Then she made herself give her full attention to the tasks of Sunday morning. When parties of riders weekended at Hunters' Lodge, they arrived as strangers. Two or three days either riding on the downs or going out with the Downland Hunt soon destroyed the barriers. Their short stay ended after lunch on Sunday, a meal with a party atmosphere. When they arrived they had tables for two – occasionally for one – but for their last meal the dining room furniture was rearranged to give them a long table, and the easy chatter and laughter was evidence of the success of their stay. By the time they said goodbye to Gillian and Mike, some had already booked to come again.

'That's the last of them gone,' Mike said unnecessarily as they waved their departing guests on their way. 'Don't worry about Brutus, I'll give him a gallop for you.'

'Not likely, you won't. Give me five minutes to change and I'll be with you.' Then, seeing his uncertain expression, 'The others are out. Don't look like that, Mike. The best time of the day is when we exercise the horses.'

'Sure it is. But I guess at weekends you ought to leave it to me. A shame your husband isn't a horseman.'

She laughed. 'I can't imagine it. Let's see ... the Browns didn't bring their own mounts did they, nor the Shelleys', so none of the other horses are desperate for an outing.'

'Nor Brutus or Bella, come to that. They've had as much exercise as any of them.'

'Don't be mean,' she laughed. 'They'd love a hard gallop. So would I. Five minutes and I'll be back.' And she was gone.

The best time of each day was when she and Mike rode together. Sometimes they talked but more often they didn't. Their companionship came from shared enjoyment in what they did.

That weekend saw a turning point in all their lives. Stephen's assignments took him all over the country and sometimes to the Continent, sending home reports of Europe's slow road to recovery. But even though he was seldom at Hunters' Lodge, the very fact of his return influenced everyone. Debbie had told Mike that fathers weren't discussed at school – but after that weekend *hers* most certainly was. Young as she was, instinct guided her into how much or how little to tell her friends, so the story soon spread that because he worked for an American newspaper, that's where he had had to be since he stopped being a soldier when the war ended, but now he had managed to be sent to England so that they could be a proper family again. Once his presence was accepted, how could she help boasting about his exploits? 'My Dad has been to an air show ... a flower show ... across the sea to France so that he can tell the people in America what it's like...' Her audience was duly impressed; Stephen's exploits were grand indeed compared with their own fathers' in Ockbury or, at furthest, in Brindley some four or five miles' cycle ride away.

Gillian's life took on a new meaning. Had Stephen worked locally and come home at the end of each day, the heights might never have been so high, his resentment at the hours she spent in the hotel might have been more evident and for her the newfound romance might have been overtaken by monotony. As it was, he was usually away for four or five days at a time, home for perhaps two, or at most three, days – long enough to be at the school gate to surprise Debbie, long enough to appreciate the one thing that he and Gillian had shared, but not long enough to grow resentful at having to bide his time until the hotel had finished its daily claim on her.

Helen with her gentle manner was always there for him. Indeed, so she was for any guest, that was the role she had created for herself, but Stephen neither knew nor cared about the time she spent listening to lonely travellers or playing Scrabble with the elderly spinster sisters. Sometimes they went together to meet Debbie from school; before Debbie's bedtime and while Gillian was already in the bar, he made a third in the routine game of Ludo or Snap, then after dinner he and Helen would sit together in the bar. As often as she could, when Gillian brought them their drinks she would include one for herself and join them. Those were the times when she wished Helen would follow her former routine and take her book to the visitors' lounge. But mostly she was glad to see they got along so well; she knew her own work would have been made much more difficult if he'd been alone. Helen's greatest talent was as a listener and Stephen's was words, whether spoken or written. She would hear again of the things he'd seen on his most recent mission, her eyes bright with interest in all he told her. And so it was that his return played its part in changing the lives of each of them, Gillian, Debbie and Helen, too.

More that that; nothing could ever be the same for Mike. For more than a year, almost without his realizing what was happening, Gillian had become the centre of his existence. Without his realizing it? In the beginning that had been true, but over the months as they had worked closely together, then seen the fruition of their plans, the intensity of his feelings for her had grown into something he had never before experienced. Some inner voice had warned him to bide his time, even though he knew she was fond of him. They were friends, they trusted each other completely; but if she knew the way his mind was working, if she knew that she filled his every waking thought and his dreams too, would it put a barrier between them and destroy what they had? And then Stephen had come into the picture and Mike had seen in Gillian a new radiance. She still came to the stables just as she always had; they still rode together. Sometimes he tried to make himself believe that he imagined the change in her, that she was as close to him as she had become over the months. But he wasn't a man to hide from reality.

'Things are going well,' he said to her one June morning. 'So well that the time has come for me to get started on sorting out what has to be done at Dalgooney.'

'You ... go?' The idea of it came as a shock to her even though she told herself she ought to have realized his interest must be in the future of the estate in Ireland.

'I don't mean to leave Hunters' Lodge in the lurch, Gillian. But this is a good time of year to take on a new stable hand and let him get used to what's expected of him while the weather is kind and before the hunting season begins. This time of year the visitors are more evenly spread than in the winter.'

'We shall have to alter our advertisement if

195

you aren't here. You have been the one to train the novices on holiday.'

'You or me, where is the difference? We don't get that many and their lessons are never for more than an hour at a time.'

She frowned. 'That, and taking them out for rides. I have a job of my own to do, I can't spend hours of the day in the stables.' She was being unreasonable, she knew she was. But how could he announce so calmly that his time at Hunters' Lodge was over, that he could turn his back on all they shared without a backward glance? She needed to hurt him, to burst his bubble of anticipation for the excitement of his own future – a future in which she would have no part.

He reined in his horse and instinctively she did the same. Side by side, sitting astride, they looked helplessly at each other.

'It'll be different for you,' he said. 'Do you imagine I don't know that? But things – all things – are different now. You have a husband.'

Again she frowned. 'He's no help when it comes to running Hunters' Lodge; put him in the paddock with the horses and he'd be over the hedge before you could say "knife".' Suddenly her frown was gone, driven away by the image of Stephen scrambling over the stile to get away as a horse trotted amiably towards him. Looking at each other, she and Mike both laughed. 'Mike, we've had such a good time together. Without you I don't think I could ever have faced doing all David would have wanted.'

'Sure you would have done it all, Gilly my dear – my dearer than you know – friend.'

Their smiles had faded, but they still held each other's gaze, seeing nothing of their surroundings, seemingly cut off from everything but each other.

'I can't stay, Gillian. Don't ask it of me. God help me, I have to find a life away from here – away from all that has come to mean so much to me.' Then, forcing a smile and just for a moment reaching to touch her shoulder, 'I ought to rejoice for you. I ought to be thankful that you have found the happiness you believed was gone for ever.'

What was he telling her? She felt the image of him was imprinted on her memory, there to be recalled for as long as she lived. Perhaps, taking him for granted, she had never looked at him so deeply. Such a manly man, strong, lithe – even his coarse curly hair denoted strength, and his surprisingly well-cared-for hands too. Mike, her never-changing friend, her rock. Her eyes filled with tears, not tears of sadness but of some nameless and confused emotion rooted in her own newfound happiness and mingled with the unimaginable void that would be left when Mike went away.

'When will you go, Mike?' she heard herself ask, attempting to speak as his friend and business partner. Anyway, she told herself, he is being sensible. Yes, I am gloriously happy, and if he imagines he is getting too fond of me, then it's right that he strikes out for himself.

'In an area like this there might well be someone qualified to step straight in,' Mike answered, 'someone trained in one of the racing stables. I'll ask around locally first. The accommodation will be a big draw. If I can't get anyone suitable pretty quickly, we'll advertise further afield. Don't let's have a long drawn out period of waiting. I've known for weeks that it's what I had to do.'

'But Hunters' Lodge? It's partly yours. Are you saying you want me to raise the capital to buy you out?'

'We're partners, you know that. But my accountant can see to my side of things.'

His mind was made up. Starting forward, they rode home in sombre silence.

Ockbury had become used to the sight of Derek. He had needed all his courage to make his first visits to the village, but with each one he became more relaxed. There were seldom any strangers there and, as Gillian had said on the day of his arrival, once you knew what to expect you didn't give it a thought. Certainly many a local was sorry for the young man, but something in his manner warned them that he wasn't open for sympathy.

The second time he walked there, he called at the local garage and asked Bob Crighton, the owner, if he knew of a car he might be able to buy. Like everything else, second-hand cars were hard to come by and waiting lists long for new ones. But Bob happened to know that George Mildew, the undertaker in Eldon Lane, was about to take delivery of a new hearse. For nearly twenty years (even during the war when most people had to lay their vehicles up for want of petrol) Bob had serviced the old hearse and he would stake his reputation on it being a "fair grand engine with many a good mile left in it". Of course the inside would need a bit of alteration once it wouldn't be carrying the deceased to their last resting place, but it was work right up his street.

'Nice and roomy at the back, that's what I was thinking,' the garage owner told Derek, keen to clinch the deal and aware that a hearse wouldn't be the chosen mode of transport for the average villager. 'I've heard that you are an artist; that being the case, like, they'd be plenty of room for your easel and whatever it is artists carry around.'

Derek had agreed with alacrity. It hadn't been an artist's easel he'd had in mind.

So over those weeks of spring a change had come in Ella's life as well as his own.

Bob Crighton had to be taken into his confidence and between the two of them they designed fittings for a ramp so that the wheelchair could be pushed into the spacious back area, then secured so that it was stable.

By that June day when Mike and Gillian faced a future apart, Derek and Ella were enjoying the early summer sunshine at a high point on the downs. Both of them were sketching, she consciously making sure her expression was one of concentration even while she was filled with excitement that had little to do with the early summer sunshine. Derek was in a happier position; his whole attention was given to watching her every movement as he made his preliminary sketches of the girl who had given new meaning to his life. Six months ago when he lay in a hospital bed, his parents dead, his home partially destroyed, his career seeming to be as lost to him as his familiar appearance, how could he have imagined the time would come when he would feel as he did now?

With his pencil poised, the sketch forgotten, he gazed at her. And in that same second she turned her head just a fraction, just enough to let her peep at him without it being obvious – or so she thought.

'You're so lovely.' He voiced his thoughts, speaking in little more than a whisper, even though they were alone "on top of the world" as they called this, their favourite place.

Ella felt her cheeks grow warm; no one had ever said such a thing to her before.

'Silly!' Embarrassed, not knowing how to accept the compliment, she gripped her bottom lip between her teeth. 'Anyway, how could I be?' She sounded aggressive.

He shook his head. 'Yes, you are lovely. But it's not just looks. Ella – oh hell, what's the matter with me? I shouldn't talk to you like this. But when I'm with you I forgot – forget what's happened.' He covered the disfigured side of his face with his hand.

Throwing her sketch pad and pencil to the ground, she propelled her chair to bring her close enough to reach out to him.

'Doesn't matter about me,' she said, 'about what you said, I mean. I'm not upset, honestly. I didn't take it seriously. But Derek...' and suddenly her rush of words came to a halt. How could she tell him that to her he was perfect, perfect in body and soul? If she were normal, then she would say what was in her heart, but she wasn't normal, she was a cripple. Night after night in the solitude of her room she let her imagination carry her on a journey of wonder as she imagined herself walking by his side, running on the sandy beach with him, gliding around a ballroom in his arms, in wreath and veil walking down the aisle with him. It took but a second for those images to crowd into her mind, as from her wheelchair she reached her hand towards him and felt it gripped in his.

'Look at me, *look*,' he said harshly, bringing his face within inches of hers. 'Hideous.' Then as he saw her eyes brim with scalding tears, 'God forgive me. Ella, don't cry. Forgive me, Ella. I loathe self-pity. When I'm with you I forget I've changed, I feel normal.'

'And so you are normal. It's only your face that got scarred, not your spirit, not your soul.'

He turned his head away from her, but not before she'd seen the effort he was making to hang on to his own control. A moment ago she

201

had been embarrassed and ill at ease at his compliments, but that was forgotten. All that mattered to her was taking away his pain.

'You are my very dearest and best friend, Derek. I hate your face being scarred – not because you are less dear to me because of it, I don't even see it now that we know each other. I hate it because it makes you miserable. Of course you want to look like you used to. Just like of course I want to be able to run and skip and dance. Then I think how much worse it could all have been for both of us. You're an artist, so suppose you had lost your eyesight in the explosion; and me – well, I'm nothing special but I can see and I can hear, I love to draw and to play the piano or to read – all things I can do. And if I spent my life dashing around perhaps I wouldn't know what joy there was to be found in the things I do now.'

Still his head was turned away from her. Perhaps her words had been lost on him. Forgetting everything but that she couldn't bear to know he was upset, she reached to cradle his chin in her hand and willed him to turn his face towards her. He had hidden his feelings from everyone, even from Mike, who had accepted him on equal terms from the start, but now he had nowhere to hide. His face was wet with tears, his mouth, which even in repose was pulled down to one side by the shrivelled and shrunken flesh, was further distorted as he battled to hold back the misery that engulfed him.

He'd never felt for anyone what he did for Ella. He was a normal, healthy young man and for the first time in his life he had fallen in love. Occasionally, half waking in the night, he would think of her and know a moment of joy; but it would be gone in a flash with returning consciousness. He could have no future with Ella, not with her or any other woman. Like an evil spirit, the image of his disfigured face would be before him in the darkness. There would be no return to sleep.

For a second, he let his gaze meet hers, and a second was all it took for her to draw him towards her. All her life Ella had been the one to be taken care of and protected, but as she held him to her she had one thing in mind: to let him find comfort in her love. It couldn't have been a comfortable embrace for either of them, with the arm of her wheelchair between them, but as she cradled his head to her breast and felt the warmth of his tears through her thin blouse, discomfort meant nothing. When the sound of his stifled sobbing was over, still she held him.

'Forgive me,' he mumbled, his face pressed against her. 'Don't know what happened. My dear friend Ella.' There! He'd made himself say it, just as she had. A dear friend. That would help them back on to a smooth path again. 'And you're right. It could have been a lot worse. If I hadn't been able to see, I wouldn't have embarrassed you telling you how pretty you are, and none of this would have happened.'

She played her part in moving them along that
203

smooth path, telling him, 'I don't want to stop you saying nice things to me. Every girl must like to have compliments. It's just that I'm not used to them.'

He sat up, took his handkerchief out of his pocket and wiped his face, then from an inside pocked produced a comb and ran it through his hair.

'Dear, sweet, beautiful Ella, you've given me back my life, do you know that?'

'Don't know what you mean,' she said uncertainly, frightened to let herself hope just what his words might be telling her.

'I mean that being with you makes me forget – makes me feel normal and glad to be alive.'

She forced that stubborn hope to the back of her mind as she smiled at him. He was her dearest friend and so she was his.

'Of course we're glad to be alive,' she agreed. 'Both of us. How could we not be glad? Just look around us. Life is such a precious gift. To be sorry for ourselves would be ... would be ... a wicked sin. And what you said just now – it's the same for me too. That's how I feel, being with you. As if I could get up and run just like everyone else.'

He nodded. 'That's because I see you that way.'

'And Derek – I'm not a bit good at saying things, but I know you hate the burns on your face. But Derek, I don't seem to see them. I mean – I *do* see them, and yet I *don't*.' Timidly she reached to rest her hand against his shrivelled and twisted face. It was a special moment, they were both aware of it.

Then, almost as if the emotion were beyond them, he smiled that one-sided smile which was all his face could manage and winked with his good eye as he said, 'Like Nelson holding his telescope to his blind eye, eh?' Then, taking hold of the hand that still lightly touched his face, he held it to his lips. There was no passion in the kiss, rather it hinted at courtliness as he got to his feet and, without letting go of her hand, bowed his head before her. 'Madam, will you honour me with the next dance?'

Ella was confused. Such behaviour was beyond her experience and her ability too.

'Silly!' She tried to make light of it. 'Just because I said being with you makes me feel I could dance...'

'On your feet. *You* may have a beautiful face but I have two good feet; between us, there's no stopping us.' He helped her to stand, ready to take her weight and steady her. 'Put your arms round my neck,' he whispered, not knowing how often she had dreamed of doing just that. Then he lifted her a few inches so that she was off the ground and lying against him. 'A waltz, I think.'

In a pleasant baritone he softly sang the melody of the *Blue Danube*, moving away from the wheelchair and discarded sketch pads as he twisted and turned, waltzing her across the mossy grass. Although she was slightly built, she wrapped her dangling legs around his hips

205

in an effort to ease the weight; she wanted the dance never to end. In an afternoon when emotion was so near the surface and happiness gripped them both, it was impossible not to smile. From his voice it was clear he was becoming breathless and as he gasped to take in more air, both of them started to laugh. There was nothing funny and yet laughter was the only way of expressing their joy in living. He crouched down to lower her gently to the ground, then collapsed in a breathless heap beside her. If behind the laughter, pushed right to the back of Ella's consciousness, was the knowledge that being his dearest friend was a far cry from her dreams, this wasn't the moment to acknowledge it.

She lay back on the grass, listening to the summer sound of insects, gazing at the miraculously clear blue sky. She wanted to capture the moment, to imprint it on her mind to be remembered and re-lived a thousand times, and as if to lock it into her memory she closed her eyes. He had moved, she sensed it. Then she felt the warmth of his breath on her face. Then ... in her near-sleep dreams this had happened, but this wasn't a dream. His mouth covered hers. She drew him closer, her arms tight around him as if she could never let him go. Inexperienced, innocent, she was guided by instinct alone as she drew his hand to her and held it covering her breast. In the early summer heatwave she could feel the warmth of it through her cotton blouse and bra.

'Ella, Ella,' he whispered. 'My dearest, darling Ella.'

Her eyes shot open. What was he saying? What was he telling her?

'Am I?' Then, frightened that in pressing him she would frighten him off, she rushed on, 'No don't tell me. Just keep holding me, touching me.' Innocent she may have been, but Ella was as aware as any girl of the ways of the world, more aware than a good many, and as she moved her hand down his body she knew he was aroused with the same longing that filled her.

'Yes, yes, yes,' she whispered, hardly aware that she spoke or what would be the outcome of where instinct was leading her.

She felt him draw away. But of course he did, she told herself. She was nothing but a cripple – his friend, his dear friend – but not a proper woman. How could he know the aching need in her for a love that was full and complete? It was only her legs that had no power, the rest of her body was alive, yearning, burning with a half-understood desire that in those seconds she knew would never be fulfilled. Her heart was beating hard, her mouth was dry and she shivered despite the warmth of the sun.

'Yes, yes, yes,' Derek was saying, speaking in a voice she hardly recognized. 'Forgive me, Ella. What sort of a friend am I, for God's sake? This moment I want to possess every inch of your beautiful body.' He was sitting, his arms round his drawn-up knees, his head resting on them. 'Look at me!' All his earlier anguish was back as he sat up straight and turned to her. She wriggled to a sitting position, as close to him as only a moment before they had been as they lay on the ground.

'I'm looking,' she said, holding his gaze, 'I'm seeing *you*. You're not just a face and a body, and I'm not just a pair of useless legs. We're whole people. It's gone now, that terrifying, wonderful, overwhelming feeling I had. But just now there was nothing else except that I wanted you to ... to ... be so close nothing could keep us apart.' But she mustn't be so honest, she must let him feel free. So she forced a laugh that bore no relationship to the passionate way she had been speaking. 'I expect I was excited with the dancing – or the warm sunshine. I'm sorry Derek. But what I'm trying to say is, that if I can feel like that, so will some other girl when you fall in love.' There! That should make him see that she was just his caring friend. She felt she was back in control of herself. For weeks he had filled her every waking thought and most of her dreams, and this afternoon she had risked spoiling all they had because she'd not kept her racing imagination in check. Somehow she had to move them forward so that they were back on the familiar track.

'There's no other girl,' and again he turned away from her. 'There never could be any other except you.'

'But...' It was useless for her to try to hold back the joy that flooded through her. 'You

208

pushed me off...'

'Not true. I could never push you off. I was frightened of where we were heading. I love you, Ella. I want you with me always. But it's not fair on you. You've met no one. Suppose you imagined yourself in love with me and we married, then you met someone else – some chap who looked normal. And there you'd be, stuck with me. And I shan't get any prettier as I get older.'

'To me you'll always be ... be ... sort of perfect. Anyway, what about me? You might fall in love with a woman who doesn't have to be carried around the dance floor.'

'Darling Ella, I just pray that I'll always be the one to carry you.'

'I pray it too,' she whispered. 'I've prayed it with all my heart for weeks.'

He got to his feet, then bent to lift her as he might a child. Only this time he stood her on her feet in front of him, still taking most of her weight and yet somehow making her feel she was his equal. As his mouth covered hers, he drew her close. In his hold, she felt safe, she felt strong, she felt normal.

'In you sit.' He helped her to her waiting chair. 'We'll get home and talk to your mother.' He sounded more confident than he felt, for why should Kathleen welcome him as a son-in-law? An artist whose future was less than certain, his only asset the amount his father had managed to save through a lifetime of working as a bank clerk, the only home he could give her a far cry from Streatham Manor. How could he expect Kathleen Harriday to welcome him with open arms as a husband for her lovely daughter?

That evening the restaurant was busy, the bar smoke-filled and noisy with a party celebrating the twenty-first birthday of the youngest daughter of Brindley's foremost baker. No one watching Gillian would suspect the evening to be any different from those that had gone before or, indeed, those in the future. Only *she* knew that nothing could be the same after what Mike had told her that afternoon. He may not leave for weeks; he had promised to stay until he was satisfied that a replacement groom could be found and given time to settle in. But the die was cast; the easy, relaxed friendship she had come to depend on could never be the same.

When the door from the dining room to the bar opened and Stephen walked in, her heart gave its customary flutter. How was it that he could still have this effect on her? He had been in South Wales for two days writing up an account of a mining community, something to have in hand for when this adopted country of his seemed determined to deprive a newshound such as he of sensation.

'Hi, honey,' he called to Gillian. 'All OK?

'Fine,' she called back, equally brightly. 'Have you eaten or are you going to join Helen?'

'The latter. I've ordered. Just checking in on you. See you later.' And he was gone. The dull grey cloud that had lain over her had thinned, if not lifted. The hours of the long evening moved slowly on and seeing him sitting as he always did with Helen, Gillian found herself resenting the duties that kept her behind the bar, having to make friendly overtures to the baker. Why shouldn't she be the one to be with Stephen? When he talked he charmed his listener, that had always been his way and, watching him with Helen, she knew nothing had changed.

It was after eleven o'clock when she answered the telephone and was surprised to hear Kathleen's voice.

'You're a late caller. Is everything all right?'

'I've watched the clock for ages, waiting. I didn't want to ring you while you were up to your eyes. I have news for you – or perhaps you've seen it coming just as I have. Ella and Derek are to be married. Gillian, I can't tell you how happy I am. My darling little Ella – I've been so frightened life would hurt her. Had a sort of premonition.'

'Wonderful news. But I hadn't a clue.'

'Oh my dear, it was written all over them. And yet I was frightened. Can't say why but I couldn't get over this dreadful almost sick feeling I had about their future. Of course I don't believe in such nonsense. That's what it is – nonsense.'

Into Gillian's mind came the echo Helen's

211

voice after David's accident. 'I was so frightened. I *knew* something would happen to him. You feel things, don't you?'

Involuntarily, Gillian shivered.

Seven

On the day of the wedding, Hunters' Lodge was closed to outsiders at lunch time, although there were few guests at the reception, even including the Crosbie sisters who were looked on as "part of the establishment" and had become acquainted with Ella and Derek over the past months. The same couldn't be said for the numbers in the congregation crowding into the small village church, where after the first reading of the Banns, word had spread. Locals had filled the pews as nothing had since the thanksgiving service at the end of the war, as folk flocked in eager for a glimpse of "that poor pretty girl in her wheelchair" and the "young man with the face". There was more than plain curiosity in their wanting to be there, for each and every one was silently wishing the couple well in what they saw as the brave step they were taking.

Reverend Cyril Cuthbert was delighted to see his church so full, he even fondly imagined his sermons might at last have touched a nerve,

212

although reason told him just what held the local interest. The bridal couple had told him they wanted a quiet wedding, but he was more than glad to see the support given by the villagers; once it was all over, the new Mr and Mrs Denvers would look back with pleasure. Then, he put all thought from his mind and concentrated on the words of the service, his heart pleading silently that the young couple who had to face such obvious adversity would be blessed by a union of unending love and understanding.

Back at Hunters' Lodge, Kathleen tried to believe her heart was filled with thankfulness. She told herself that even though Derek's future career was uncertain, there was no doubting his very real love for Ella. And repeatedly she reminded herself that she asked for nothing more. There was no logic in the shapeless foreboding that would descend on her at unexpected moments. Ella was a normal, fit girl in every respect except for a congenital defect in her spine that prevented her walking. Suppose she had a child, would that defect make the birth difficult? Suppose ... suppose ... no, don't let yourself think it. Then her imagination would carry her in a different direction as she imagined the many times during each day that Ella needed help. When she had been a child, Kathleen had cared for her herself, then all through her adolescent life there had been someone coming to the house to help her bathe, to reach her clothes from the wardrobe and help her dress, to do a hundred and one things that were just out of her reach. But Ella was adamant: she and Derek didn't need anyone and any offer of financial help had been firmly refused. They were a team; they would do things together.

'I can understand they didn't want to travel anywhere for a honeymoon,' Kathleen said to Gillian at the reception, as the two of them stood apart from the others gazing out into the garden, 'but I do wish they'd accepted my suggestion that they should stay at the Manor for their first days. This evening I'm going back to Devon with Paul for a while. The Manor has always been her home; everything is familiar to her there. Going straight to that bungalow is a poor start to married life. Even tonight he'll have to help her to bed, then there's her bath and a hundred and one things she needs help with. I shall be driving away with Paul and worrying myself to death about her.'

'Of course you will. But you mustn't, you know. In a way I think they are right to want to do it their way. It won't always be easy for them but at least at the start there will be the thrill, the excitement of the unfamiliar intimacy. They both have what it takes to make a success of it.'

'I pray you're right,' Kathleen answered, something in her expression making Gillian rest a hand on her arm. 'It's just not fair. Perhaps it's my own guilt that gives me this frightening feeling that something – no, no, no, I mustn't say it.'

'Guilt. What guilt?'

'I've told you before: we were too old to be parents again. We had Paul and because I'd had a bad time, after that Gerald was always careful. This sex business is a rum thing. Just *once* we were careless and beyond caring, and that when I thought I was past conceiving. And, you know, after nine ghastly months carrying Paul and a confinement that nearly finished me, I went through Ella's pregnancy without a twinge then, a month before time, dropped her as easily as any sheep in the field. So tiny, so beautiful, so perfect, that's what we thought.'

'So she still is, Kathleen. Have you ever seen a happier bride?'

'I mustn't interfere with them. There's nothing worse than an interfering mother-in-law. But, Gillian, you'll keep an eye open, won't you?'

'Of course. You may bet they'll be at the stables a good deal. Derek has been helping Mike.'

Kathleen was watching her, something disconcerting in her gaze.

'When is Mike leaving?' she asked. 'You're going to miss him, Gillian.'

'Dreadfully. He's more than a partner; he's my dearest friend. I can't imagine it here without him. It sounds crazy, but I almost feel that he has been here for me because of David being gone.' She glanced around the room where some twenty people were gathered. 'Remember the last time we closed the restaurant, after David's service? It's like looking back at a

215

different life. Don't know what I'll do without Mike...' Then, as if she suddenly realized what she had said, 'But of course I'm pleased for him. He must be dying to get to grips with all he means to do at Dalgooney.'

'And do you think he won't miss you? Of course he will.'

'Oh yes, of course he will. We are great friends. But in a different place, with masses to do to fill his mind, he will be fine.'

'And so, my dear, will you. You have had changes in your own life lately; you have a husband.' Kathleen's spoke in a determined voice even though she knew what she said wasn't strictly true.

Gillian nodded, her pensive mood gone and her eyes a mirror to her happiness as she thought of Stephen. He had been away for more than a week, travelling in Germany. Before the day was over he would be home.

'He should be back in England by now. Perhaps he might even be here before the reception breaks up.'

Hardly had she said the words when the door opened and there he was. How he stood out from the rest of the group. What was it about him that set him apart? Any stranger watching him move across the room towards Gillian would have known immediately that he was different. If the English were still living in the long shadow of the war, the men's clothes hardly changed since the last years of the 1930s, it could hardly be wondered at, for most suits had been tailored in the pre-war days and because shirts, socks, underwear, raincoats, all the essentials still had to be given priority in the allocation of the meagre ration of clothing coupons, anything decent had been kept hanging in the wardrobe with a mothball or two in the pockets.

Not so for Stephen. America had experienced none of the shortages and in his few years in his own country after demobilization he had built up a wardrobe that must have been the envy of many a young Englishman.

Before he reached Gillian, Debbie saw him and rushed across the dining room to hurl herself into his open arms.

'And how's my princess been while I've been away?'

'Silly,' she giggled. 'Not a princess. I'm just me. Mum said you'd be home today. I've been watching ever since I got up. I was afraid you'd come when we were all at Ella's wedding. Look Dad, they're cutting the cake. Isn't it all...' words failed her, but not for long. 'Magnificent?'

'Sure, honey. All very pretty.' Then, with an intimate wink he stooped to whisper to her, 'Especially *you*. You're the prettiest of them all.'

Her reply was a satisfied giggle. Now that he had arrived, her happiness was complete. From the first there had been a bond between them, one which had grown closer as the months had gone on. Now, leaving his side to wriggle her way through the cluster of guests so that she had a good view of the cake cutting ceremony, she thought of that word, "magnificent". Yes, that's what it all was. Not just the wedding party but having a dad and a mum – and an Auntie Helen, too, she added silently. Anyway, how could he have said *she* was the prettiest here when Auntie Helen looked just like a fairy princess in that gorgeous peachy coloured dress she had bought for the occasion? Miss Jane had given her the coupons; Debbie had seen her pass her clothing book and seen the hug Auntie Helen had given her.

Glancing through a gap in the group around the table, Debbie could see her parents and swelled with pride as she noted the way her father gave a sort of dignified nod of his head as he shook hands with Mrs Harriday. That was jolly polite of him, for she knew without ever having been told that the two of them didn't really like each other. And didn't that just show what a silly person Mrs Harriday was? Someone was putting a plate bearing a tiny square of cake into Debbie's hand and her parents were forgotten. She didn't really care for fruitcake but she had heard talk about how lots of people had shared their ration so that it could be made.

Was it just Gillian's fond imagination or had Stephen's arrival breathed new life into the assembly? Surely the hostess was Kathleen, mother of the bride, yet with easy grace Stephen moved amongst the guests, exuding a spirit of welcome.

Then came the farewells as Derek pushed Ella's chair to the waiting converted hearse and lifted her to carry her to the passenger seat before loading and anchoring the chair safely.

'Where are they going?' Stephen asked Helen. 'It's a secret. I think Gillian probably knows. If Mrs Harriday does, then I'm sure she would have told Gillian. But when I asked her she slapped me down, said it wasn't anyone's affair.' He read her hurt in her startlingly blue eyes. 'I only meant to try and take an interest. But perhaps Derek didn't tell anyone and Gillian was cross because she didn't know. David had arranged where we were to go – he didn't even tell *me*. I wish he had. I could have thought about it – afterwards, I mean.'

Stephen led her away from the group of guests who were waving the honeymooners on their way. Of them all, only Gillian and Kathleen knew about the picnic hamper in the back and the plan that they would drive to somewhere they called their "special place"on the downs for a couple of hours until the visitors had all gone, before coming back to the bungalow.

Before they had turned out of the drive, Stephen's mind had moved on. 'While the school holidays are still on, how about if you and Debbie keep me company? Let's see.' He took his diary from his inside pocket. 'Nothing very world shaking next week, but enough to send a word picture of the pace of life here in England: a flower show in Surrey on Tuesday, a

219

gymkhana in Sussex on Wednesday – that should appeal to Debs – and a fair in Suffolk on Thursday. It's all low-key stuff, but then that's the way of folk in this country of yours. We might manage Surrey in a day, but there would be no sense in coming back here just to turn around and go off in the same direction to the gymkhana next day. And from there we'd go straight on to East Anglia. What about it, Helen? Would the idea appeal to you? I know it's no use suggesting Gillian might come, but if you're there to see everything's OK I wouldn't mind betting she'd find it a relief not to have Debs underfoot for a day or two of holiday time. Anyway, it's not fair to the kid, keeping her stuck here. I bet her friends have all had a break away somewhere.'

'Gillian has been so loyal to the hotel,' Helen defended her. 'I understand you must feel put out by it sometimes, Stephen, and I know poor little Debbie does, although I do try to make it up to her. But if Gillian were different, the place wouldn't be as well run as it is.'

'She has a good friend in you, Helen. She would never be able to do all she does here without you. And as for Debbie, why you'd think she was your own; the kid dotes on you.'

Helen felt embarrassed by his praise, little realising how pretty she looked with her flushed cheeks.

'Anyway,' Helen said, turning the subject away from herself, 'you talk to Gillian. If she thinks she can leave the place then forget you suggested it to me. And after all, what's the use of having a partner if he hardly steps inside the place? You'd think that before he goes off leaving her in the lurch he might suggest taking over so that she could have a break. Instead, they're looking for a stable hand to replace him. What sort of a partner does that make him? And that's really all he is, a stable hand with the good fortune to have had a windfall to invest. As for sharing the responsibility here, unless a guest is a rider he isn't interested. You've no idea, Stephen, how against their stupid plan I was. Hunters' Lodge was so lovely as it was before they brought all their horsey people in.' Wide-eyed, she looked at him. 'I've never told a single soul this before but horses frighten me.'

'And I'll let you into my secret, too, my pretty friend. They frighten me too – they're all teeth and hooves.'

She felt an unexpected glow of happiness. There could be nothing like a shared secret to set them apart from the rest of the party who, the hearse having disappeared, were following them back indoors.

Later on, the wedding guests gone, Stephen found Gillian checking that the tables were laid up for evening dinners.

'Hi, honey. Don't you ever stop working? This isn't much of a welcome to a love-starved husband.'

'Love-starved nothing,' she laughed. 'You enjoyed the party as much as anyone.'

'A week away and are you telling me you

221

haven't missed me?' It was worded like a question, but one that was asked in such a tone of confidence that quite clearly he knew the answer.

'You have enough self-conceit not to need me to tell you,' she answered with a laugh.

'That's better.' He moved to stand close behind her, slipping his arms around her and pulling her against him as he moved his hands in a way experience had taught him steered her where he guided. 'The tables look fine and Debbie has gone for a walk with Helen. Come on, Gill. How about you and me going out somewhere for dinner? I don't feel like watching you dish out drinks all the evening in that smoky bar.'

'What's the time?'

'Too early to think of dinner,' he laughed. 'It's ten past four; too early for you to be rushing off to change for the evening. Please, honey. This evening I deserve a treat.'

'Sarah might do the bar for me. I'll ask her. Room seven is vacant, I'll see if she'll stay the night.'

'That's my girl! Go and tell her now...'

'Ask her now, don't you mean? Looking after the bar isn't part of her job. She may have plans for the evening.'

The thought that the evening would be spent with Stephen was exciting, and yet mixed with that excitement was an emotion she couldn't – or wouldn't – analyze. She told herself it was the shadow of those years when they'd been

222

apart, when she had made herself accept that she felt nothing for him. But that had never been true, just one glance at him had told her she had never stopped loving him. And that was the thought she clung to now.

'Go and find the others while I talk to Sarah. They said they were going up the lane to the downs. I have to go to the stables. There's an applicant for the job coming at five o'clock.'

'That's nearly an hour way. Go and tell Sarah about this evening while I wait for you. You don't want to go to the stables. What do you keep that guy for if it's not to look after the animals?'

Ignoring his remark, she answered, hearing the chill in her tone, 'Mike and I are interviewing an applicant for the job. Not Mike's job – he isn't an employee, he's an equal partner.'

Stephen laughed. 'Equal my Aunt Fanny! When has looking after a few old nags been so important?'

She bit back her retort. Nothing must cloud her anticipation for their evening.

'I'll go and talk to Sarah. You can easily find the others if you don't want to hang around waiting. I shall be out at any rate until half past five.'

'OK. But if Sarah says she's got better things to do, remind Mike Trelawney the hotel isn't run just for the benefit of the horses and tell him to take the bar over for the evening. If he smartens up for once, surely he can pour a few drinks.' Gillian wished he hadn't said it. Each

223

time he spoke scathingly – and ignorantly – about Mike, it drove a wedge between them. 'Anyway, I'm off to find Debs. Gee though Gill, weren't you proud of her today? I know I was. She looked real pretty and behaved real pretty too. Off you go and fix things up with Sarah.' And with that he left her, seemingly having forgotten his veiled suggestions of how he'd meant them to spend the next half hour, and eager to join the walkers.

Sarah was more than agreeable. She liked nothing more than to be seen as essential in the running of the hotel, so she scribbled a note to her parents and took it to the kitchen where the early arrivals were already attacking the preparation of vegetables. Explaining that Mr and Mrs Sinclair wanted to go out for the evening but couldn't leave the hotel unless they were sure she was on hand, she asked that someone should take the note to her home in the village and bring back the overnight bag her mother would pack for her.

Gillian hurried to the stables. Like her, Mike had changed from his wedding attire and was looking comfortable in jodhpurs and with the sleeves of his checked shirt rolled above his elbows.

'It went well, Gilly,' he greeted her. 'Long may it continue that way for them. Those two have real guts.'

'They're both emphatic that they don't want help. And that makes it difficult. You know *me*, "tact" isn't my middle name.'

'You'd be a different person if it were.' Then, with a subtle change in his tone, 'Tact may not be, but "honesty" is.' He spoke quietly. Ordinary enough words and yet there was something in his manner that imprinted them on her to be remembered long after he'd gone. 'My dearest friend.'

What she saw in his eyes swept her mind clean of everything except the moment. Was she surprised by what she saw? Or was it what, in her heart, she had known?

'You'll find friends in Ireland,' she said harshly, frightened of something she didn't want to accept.

'Sure I will. I've found friends wherever I've been.' He gripped her shoulders, willing her to meet his gaze. 'Just once I have to say it: I love you Gillian, love you with everything that I am. My dearest friend, the person who gives meaning to my life.'

Her willpower had gone. She didn't even try to look away from him.

'No,' she breathed. 'No, Mike, don't. I have Stephen. He is my future. I never stopped loving him through all those years we were apart.' Then, that honesty he'd spoken of pushing everything else from her mind, 'But I can't bear it when you go away.' Immediately she was in control again. She stood a little straighter, raising her chin. 'We are friends, you and me. I've never had a friend like you. We mustn't confuse that with – with romantic love. But there can still be love between friends. Can't there? Can't there?' As she repeated the question she knew she moved her face closer to his, she knew it and had no power to stop herself.

His mouth covered hers. This wasn't the kiss of friends. He held her so close that she couldn't be sure if it was his heart she could feel beating or her own. Through the months as their friendship had grown deeper, even though in their behaviour they might have been brother and sister, she had sensed that he was a man capable of strong passion. These brief seconds were set apart, there was nothing outside themselves. Friendship, desire, passion, they shared all these things; the rest of the world didn't exist for them. Then reason returned.

'God forgive me,' he murmured, pulling away from her. 'Can you pretend it didn't happen?'

Did she want to pretend it hadn't happened? Yes, yes of course she did, she told herself.

'Wedding excitement.' She forced a laugh. 'Forget it, Mike. Mike, don't change. Don't let it spoil anything for us.'

'Wedding excitement, like you say. Gillian I'm a fool. You and me are buddies, *great* buddies. That's the way we'll go on being.'

'Sure we will, buddy.' She tried to mimic his Canadian voice. Then, resolved to look to the future, 'It must be nearly five o'clock. You liked what you saw of this fellow, didn't you?'

'I reckon he's a good guy. Add to that, he's had more experience in stables than I had when David took me on. I'd worked on the ranch

226

back home, so looking after horses was second nature. But Teddy Mitchell has been with a trainer in racing stables. He wants to get to Ockbury. His girlfriend is in the village. Do you hear a car? Yep, here he is.'

Gillian had come to the stables intending to be the one to ask most of the questions; after all it would be she who would work with whoever they engaged. But in the event, she left most of the talking to Mike simply because her mind refused to be held on course. Her head was filled with silent voices: "the only thing we share is sex" from Stephen; "the right stepfather is better than the wrong natural father" from Kathleen – and from Mike too. But of course Stephen wasn't the wrong father for Debbie, nor yet the wrong partner for her. Of course they shared more than sex, they shared Debbie, they shared ... what? He was proud of the success she was making at the hotel, think how charming and friendly he always was to the guests. Yes, and she was interested in and proud of his work too. And as the years went on, so those things would draw them ever closer.

'Are there any other questions you want to ask Teddy, Gillian?' Mike's voice cut across her thoughts.

She pulled herself together, turning a friendly smile on the interviewee and looking at him closely, concentrating for the first time. A very presentable young man, probably in his mid-twenties, his dark curly hair, brown eyes and slim lithe build making her suspect that he would attract attention as a newcomer to the village.

'You have a girlfriend in Ockbury? Isn't that what Mike told me?'

'Yes, m'am. Me and Mavis have been planning to be married just as soon as we could find a place to rent. But you know how hard that is – finding a place to rent is like looking for gold dust. Mavis is working at the vicarage, living in. If I get this place I reckon we could be fine in the rooms over the new stable block when Mr Trelawney here moves out. That'll give us a real good start.'

'Mike seems to have found them comfortable. You must bring her – Mavis, did you call her? – to see the accommodation. Will she be able to go on working at the vicarage if she's living out?'

He looked worried. 'We're keeping our fingers crossed. Be a bit of a hard nut to crack if she isn't earning.'

'We'll have to see what happens.' Gillian prided herself on the fact that she never let her heart rule her head, yet she found herself saying, 'But if the vicar's wife needs someone living in, then I dare say there might be an opening in the hotel.'

'Crikey! That would be great,' Teddy answered, his smile seeming to stretch from ear to ear. 'If you would take her on in the hotel and me here in the stables, I promise you, you wouldn't regret it, we're real grafters.' His beaming pleasure made a boy of him. 'I'm seeing her for an

228

hour when I leave here. Just wait till I tell her!'

Gillian realized that what she had suggested as what David would have called a "belt and braces" answer to an emergency, was being met with such delight that come what may, there would be no drawing back.

As they watched Teddy Mitchell's pre-war Austin Seven disappear down the drive, she turned to Mike with the honesty he saw as so much part of her character.

'So that's it, Mike,' she said. 'We've found someone to take over the stables.' She gripped her bottom lip between her teeth, shaking her head as she looked at him. 'You won't be here. Can't imagine...'

'No. It's like looking through a fog. But, Gillian, if the fog is all around, there's only one thing do to. To move through it, biding our time, day by day.'

She nodded. 'Day by day ... so many days ... months ... even years. Another routine will replace the one we made.' Then, forcing herself to sound a hundred times brighter than she felt, 'But you'll come back and see Hunters' Lodge. Of course you will. You have a lot invested here. It's not as though you are moving on and leaving a job.'

'Sure. It won't be goodbye, Gillian, my dear friend Gillian.'

It was another fortnight before he left. During the first of those two weeks, with Gillian's blessing, Stephen, Debbie and Helen were away from Monday until Thursday. Together Gillian and Mike exercised the horses that during the summer spent the days in the cool of the stables and were put out in the paddock overnight. With no Debbie and no Stephen, Gillian was free to start her day as early as she liked, so soon after six o'clock she and Mike were already out. Neither of them referred to those few moments on Ella's wedding day; they behaved as though none of it had happened. These days were precious – both of them aware that by the following Monday Teddy would be working in the stables, learning the ropes, ready to take responsibility just one short week later.

There was great excitement when Stephen's car drew up at the side door of the hotel in the late afternoon of Thursday. Purposely Gillian had dressed early, ready for the evening, partly so that she could concentrate on the returning travellers and partly so that she would be looking her best when they arrived. Perhaps she didn't make a conscious comparison between herself and Helen, but instinct led her to make herself coolly elegant in a way that was quite different from the ethereally beautiful Helen, who was utterly feminine in her summer pastels.

'We're home, Mum. We stopped for lunch on the way. It was gorgeous. Where was it Daddy?' Then, without waiting for an answer, 'We had our lunch outside on the terrace by the river. We had nice things: smoked salmon, then something with a funny name – they said it was

French – but it tasted scrummy. Then I had an enormous ice cream and strawberries. Where was it Dad?'

'By the Thames, in Sonning.'

'They must serve jolly late lunches,' Gillian laughed. 'That's only just beyond Reading. An hour's drive.'

Stephen scowled and Helen looked uncomfortable.

'Time was our own,' he answered. 'We went for a walk by the river, fed the swans, did all the tourist things. Had a great time, didn't we kiddo?' to Debbie.

'We sure did, Pa,' she answered in an exaggerated American accent, then fell about laughing.

'The trip went well, then? You found enough to fill your column?'

'Surely,' came Stephen's ever-confident reply. 'Anyway, if the events had been rained off, I would have got around it. My remit is to conjure up an image of John Bull and the quaint customs of Olde England. I hear that last week's effort went down well. Remember it Gill, about that couple of white-haired ladies selling raffle tickets at the church fête in some vicarage garden, blotting their notebook with an old towel so the ink didn't run in the drizzling rain, while the stoic locals lined up with their sixpences to buy, all hoping for the lucky number and the prize of a bottle of bath salts or some such. Back home they go for it hook, line and sinker. Say honey, how about you giving that bar of yours a miss and let's go and eat some place else? I've taken a fancy to dining out with company these last few days.'

'You know I can't do that again so soon. Anyway, Sarah is going to the pictures this evening and the waitresses are under-age for bar work. We're not full this evening, so I daresay I'll be able to join you when you come in after dinner.'

'Heck, why don't you take someone else on? You cling on to being necessary in this place as if your life depends on it.'

Was that true? She refused to look for the answer.

'If you don't want to eat here, then that's up to you.' Even as she heard the snap in her answer, she was honest enough to know she was hiding behind an instinctive defence mechanism.

'How about it, Helen? We could drive over to Oxford. What say?'

'Debbie has had too many late nights, staying up to eat with us. No. We're home now and back to routine. Anyway, it would be unkind to go off and leave Gillian.'

He didn't answer; he seemed to be lost in thought.

And so they did as Helen said and got back to routine.

The main change over the next ten days was that Mike's time at Hunters' Lodge was drawing nearer its close. Almost as if the past they had shared was already over, he and Gillian

spent less time together than they had previously. Teddy was proving as knowledgeable
and capable as they had hoped and on the
Wednesday afternoon he collected Mavis to see
the accommodation. David had originally pro-
vided a sort of makeshift accommodation over
the original stables, and that was where Teddy
was living until Mike moved away. There was
nothing makeshift about the accommodation in
the new block, built as it had been for Mike's
use. Although there was no more than a single
living room with "kitchen" at one end, one
bedroom and a bathroom, everything in it was
new and modern and they had had the foresight
to see there was plenty of storage space.
Naturally, Mavis fell in love with all she saw –
or was it that she was sufficiently in love with
Teddy to view everything in their life together
through rose-tinted spectacles?

'We had the Banns called last Sunday for
the first time, so we reckon to be married in
not much more than a fortnight,' she told Gillian. 'We don't want a big "do". Teddy's aunt
brought him up so she will come over from
Newbury; an early train to Reading and then
she'll get the bus to Ockbury.'

'Don't you have a family?' Gillian asked,
more out of a wish to be friendly than curiosity.

'Direct hit did for *them*: Mum, Dad and my
brother Bob. He was home on leave from the
Merchant Navy. All those ships being lost to U-
boats, then he copped it when he was on leave.
It was one of those rotten rockets that got the

house. If I'd been a month younger I reckon I'd have gone with the others, but I'd just gone off into the Land Army. So, there we are. It's Teddy's Aunt Flo and us.'

Later, when Gillian repeated the story to Stephen, she could see he took more than his usual interest in the happenings of the hotel – and the stables in particular.

'Say, how about you and I go along to see them tie the knot? Quite a story to send home, eh? All the bride's family wiped out. A new start for the only survivor, all that sort of thing. Makes a great read.'

She wished he hadn't said it, even though logic told her he was no more than wanting to do his job well.

That was on the Wednesday evening. On both Thursday and Friday she and Mike rode together on the downs, neither of them wanting to admit that the old camaraderie had been tarnished. She tried not to hear the echo of those words 'I love you with everything that I am...' and yet she didn't want ever to forget. And Mike? Surely he had nowhere to hide from the truth of what he'd said. So, as they rode, they talked not in the old, natural way, but aware that the friendship mustn't be soiled.

Just after eight o'clock on the Saturday morning, they stood together in the stable yard. Bella was already in her trailer ready for the long drive to the Welsh coast and the ferry crossing. On that morning, Mike didn't wear his comfortable jodhpurs, but in corduroy trousers and

234

a tweed sports coat he looked every bit the English countryman.

'Guess this is it, Gilly. A good move, eh? The lad is capable and Mavis will fit in well.'

'I know.' A million things they wanted to say, but in those moments they could think of nothing. It was as if that fog that lay ahead was already closing in on them.

'Tell you something...' The words tumbled out as if he couldn't hold them back. 'These last two years will be with me as long as I live. David, this place – you – what we've done together.'

'Mike, it's not the end. Hunters' Lodge is partly yours. I shall see you around every corner here in the stables. When I ride on the downs...' Her voice faded to near silence.

'Sure, sure.' He turned away from her, looking back at the new stable block. 'Jeez, but this is hard.' Then, making a supreme effort to keep their parting on a light note, 'Hey, Gilly, I wrote down the address of Dalgooney and the telephone number on a bit of paper here. We'll be in touch, eh? Let's not say goodbye.'

She nodded. 'Cheerio, partner. Safe journey.'

He got into his car and slammed the door. 'Cheerio,' he answered, the unexpected sound of his over-the-top English voice a feeble attempt at humour as he started the engine and, looking straight ahead, drove away. His willpower failed though and his glance went to the driver's mirror. There she was, one hand raised in farewell. No one but *he* knew his thoughts as his mind turned to Stephen, the errant husband for whom she must have carried a torch for so many years.

The remainder of that summer of 1950 passed uneventfully in the village on the Berkshire Downs. Mavis and Teddy were married, a ceremony that caused no local interest except for the vicar's wife and the party from Hunters' Lodge. They drove to the village, with Stephen and Gillian in the front and Debbie on her mother's knee so that there was room in the back for Helen and the Crosbie sisters.

'Two weddings in one summer,' Jane twittered excitedly. 'And such a nice young man he seems. Well, I'm sure the bride is nice too. So far we don't really know her, but we walk across to the stables sometimes and have a word with Teddy. Poor boy, fancy having no one but an aunt there to see him married.'

'We must all be his family now, Miss Jane,' came Helen's ever-caring answer.

Afterwards, at Gillian's invitation, the party returned to the hotel. This time the restaurant remained open, but a long table was laid up for the wedding party. Apart from the six who lived there and the bridal couple, there were the vicar and his wife and Teddy's Aunt Flo, who might have stepped straight out of the 1930s with her straw hat adorned with a new floral trimming she'd sewn on for the occasion and wearing her best kid gloves, normally kept in a box. To her – and from years of knowing her, to Teddy too

– the fact they were brought into use proclaimed this to be a most Special Occasion. Stephen was enjoying himself hugely; this week his column was being presented to him on a plate.

That was the only highlight in the remaining weeks of summer. Although Stephen was European representative, he seldom went abroad during the summer months. His word pictures of England were finding a place in the hearts of the American readers and he was left very much to his own devices. Scanning local papers, he could always find something worthy of his attention during the season from June until October: regattas, gymkhanas, garden parties with tea served in steamy marquees where locals demolished homemade and often diabolical scones coated with a scraping of margarine and a smear of homemade jam. Gillian was irritated by the way he wrote; indeed she was ashamed that, although he probably didn't mean it unkindly, he could mock the efforts made by women who volunteered their time and even shared their meagre rations so that local customs should survive. If the English were looked on as quaint and behind-the-times by their cousins in the New World, Stephen's column certainly brought its weekly grist to the mill of their opinion.

For the remainder of Debbie's school holiday, wherever he went, she and Helen went with him.

'We don't stay with him all the time,' Helen

237

told Gillian as she checked that Debbie's hair ribbon was secure and that she had her clean handkerchief in her pocket. 'No, when we get to the show, Stephen prowls about on his own. He's so good at meeting up with total strangers. They all warm to him. That's how he gets his notes together while Debbie and I look around the show. Today there will be lots of animals, Debbie: cows, pigs and sheep, and I think traction engines too. Then there are stalls.'

'And ice cream, Mum. There's always ice cream.'

Gillian saw them off with no thoughts of envy. Had Hunters' Lodge had this effect on David, she wondered? Each day brought its routine, but each day brought some fresh challenge, and each day it dug deeper into her heart. It had to. This was her life. But Gillian was nothing if not honest and it was that honesty that wouldn't be denied as she went back down the passage into her own rooms.

Would she feel like this if she were the only owner of the hotel – just she and the mortgagor? Closing her eyes, she tried to shut out her surroundings, to will herself back to the time when Mike had been still there. All she had to do would be to give the operator his telephone number and within minutes she would hear his voice. But she couldn't do that. Everything was going smoothly; there was no decision needing a discussion with a business partner. And he could have called her if he had wanted. Perhaps when he had said those things to her it really had been the result of wedding excitement. And, if none of that had happened, would she still be missing him as she did? The honest answer to that was "yes". He was her dearest friend; he knew her better than any living person.

Her mind took another turn, one she had been trying to avoid. Through all the years she had been alone, when every sex-starved nerve in her body had driven her to find her own salvation, always in those final seconds it had been Stephen's presence she had felt before she dropped from the heights to new depths of loneliness. Now that Stephen was a reality, sex was as important in their lives as ever it had been. Oh yes, she was totally fulfilled, never was she left on the edge of the precipice while he turned away, satisfied. So when had her thoughts started to take a journey of their own? Had it been before Ella and Derek's wedding day? Or perhaps not even until after Mike had gone? She didn't know the answer. Perhaps over the last two years as he'd become so much a part of her life it had happened gradually.

Opening her eyes, she seemed to give herself a mental shake. She and Stephen were gloriously happy. Did they ever quarrel? No. They were drawn closer by their shared love for Debbie, Debbie who seemed to grow more like her father with each passing day. What was she doing wasting time with idle thoughts when she had the daily shopping run waiting? And she ought to go upstairs to the bedrooms to make sure Mavis was coping with her new job. For the first few weeks after the wedding, the new bride had cycled each morning to the vicarage, working her notice while a new girl was found. But from this week she was part of the team at Hunters' Lodge. Daydreaming over, Gillian started on her morning round of tasks, first a few friendly words with Mavis, then a drive to the local farm shop and on to the village in the unchanging way that had become second nature to her. Not once did she wonder about the three who had gone off to a late agricultural show in Dorset, not expecting to be home until well into the evening.

So the days went by. Mavis settled in; Debbie's jaunts came to an end as Michaelmas term started, and therefore so too did Helen's. Gillian continued to hunt on Saturdays just as she and Mike had done the previous two seasons. That winter, though, although she still enjoyed the unpredictability of the chase, it was a constant reminder of the gap in her life now that Mike had gone. Stephen pretended to resent her being out so long on a Saturday, but in fact many a weekend he was away himself, and when he was at home she was sure he enjoyed the opportunity of having Debbie to himself.

When the accountant gave her his annual report, she looked at the figure with pride. For more than two years she had been in charge of Hunters' Lodge and the business David had started had steadily grown under her hand. A copy of the figures would have been sent to

Mike. Perhaps he would speak to her; she needed his praise. Whether the telephone in reception or her own private number on which
Stephen was normally the only caller, each time
she heard the shrill bell she hoped. But no call
came. Temptation and willpower fought. Twice
she picked up the receiver, and then put it down
again. If he'd wanted to speak to her there had
been nothing to stop him. Wherever he went
he made friends, hadn't he said so? Perhaps
already he had met some local woman, someone with a love of horses, someone to help him
organize the restoration work he wanted to do at
Dalgooney, someone who had come to rely on
his friendship ... That time willpower won.

Then as she stood gazing at the instrument,
the silence was shattered by its shrill bell.

'Ockbury 382,' she said, scarcely able to
breathe, so sure was she of the voice she would
hear.

'Gillian, have the children been in yet?'
Kathleen's voice came over the line.

'I saw them yesterday, but not today. Why?
Did they say they were coming round?'

'Hark at me, calling them children. No, they
said they were going home. But I wondered if
the excitement of it made them change their
minds. They'd come from the doctor's surgery.
Gillian, Ella is expecting. Please God, oh please
God, she'll be all right.'

'But that's wonderful, Kathleen. She's so fit
in herself, and she is managing beautifully in
the bungalow.' Gillian hoped her delight sound-

241

ed natural; Kathleen needed to be pulled back from the fears that plagued her. 'She's never given a hint that she thought she might be pregnant. There's seldom a day goes by when I don't see her, either over at the stables or at the bungalow and she always looks a picture of health. It must be very early days. Is she sure?'

'She waited until she was a week past two months late, then they saw Dr Fleming and he sent tests away just to be certain. They went today for the result. She doesn't look a scrap different and says she hasn't felt sick even once. They worked it out that the baby will be due the first week in May. It's almost a honeymoon baby.'

'We'll all support her, Kathleen. I know how independent they are, but with a baby to consider they might be prepared to have some help. We'll play it as it comes.' But how were they managing financially? Even though she asked the question silently, perhaps her thought waves travelled through the ether, or perhaps Kathleen's mind had been going in the same direction.

'He's getting a collection together; he must have told you. He's planning to have an exhibition in Brindley in the run-up to Christmas, but whether that's a good time in a small town I don't know. Around Christmas-time folk haven't spare cash for pictures; that would have been my thought. He paints extraordinarily well, you know. Before that dreadful accident he had an exhibition and Ella showed me the newspaper cuttings, the things quite important art critics had written. He's worth something better than that little hall at the end of Franley Road.'

'But think how his confidence has grown. Ella has done that for him. When he first came to the bungalow he was too self-conscious even to walk through the village and now he's planning an exhibition and hoping for crowds of people.'

'Indeed, yes. They do wonders for each other. Please God the exhibition won't be a let down. Brindley is hardly a cultural centre.'

'And just before Christmas not the best of times, when people have to stretch their money in so many ways,' Gillian agreed.

They talked on for a few minutes while Gillian's mind was going in another direction. Now, here was a piece of news worthy of telling Mike. He had been Derek's first (and almost his only) friend. So, as the call came to an end, almost as Gillian replaced the receiver, she picked it up again and asked for Mike's number.

He might have been on the other side of the globe instead of only just across the Irish Sea, the operator had such trouble in getting a connection. Then at last came the voice, 'You're through to the number, it's ringing for you.' It rang and it rang. Long after it was clear there was to be no answer, Gillian still held on. Perhaps he was in the stables; perhaps he was at this moment hurrying back having just heard the bell, perhaps...

'Hello Mum, we're home,' came Debbie's shout as she and Helen appeared after walking from school. 'Oh sorry, I didn't know you were on the phone.'

'I'm not. I was just putting it down. I've been talking to Mrs Harriday.'

That evening seemed long and the guests tedious.

'Are you feeling quite well, dear? You look tired this evening,' Margaret Crosbie said, speaking quietly as if in confidence and innocent of the fact that no woman likes to be told she looks tired.

'Imagination Margaret,' from her sister. 'Mrs Sinclair always looks very nice.'

More to put poor Margaret at her ease than anything, Gillian laughed 'Nothing to worry about, but I have a bit of a headache,' she lied.

'I expect you're missing that husband of yours. He's been gone two days this time. Helen tells us he's in Paris. My word, but he does get around. She said he should be home tomorrow – but I got the impression she suspected he might even get the late train tonight. So cheer up, Mrs Sinclair dear.'

'Come along, Margaret, do.' Jane, the elder, drew her sister towards the door to the corridor and their room. 'Here come more people from the dining room, we'll say goodnight.'

If Gillian had met the Crosbie sisters under different circumstances, it was unlikely that she would have felt anything for them other than a vague irritation. But they had come to her with

244

the hotel, part of David's legacy, and because he had been genuinely fond of them some of that sentiment had been passed on to her. As they went on their way, she turned her attention to the group who had come for a nightcap before going home. It was only when Stephen was with her that Helen came into the bar in the evening; normally she sat in the visitors' lounge after dinner and read her book or listened to the wireless. She had hinted to Gillian that in some of the hotels where she and Debbie had stayed with Stephen the visitors' lounges had had television sets.

Helen's suspicion that Stephen might get home that evening proved to be well-founded. It was a few minutes to midnight, and everyone had vacated the bar except one couple who were staying overnight and seemed in no hurry to go to bed, when the taxi from Brindley station pulled up at the door. Gillian heard it, and felt the usual rush of excitement.

'Surprise for you, honey. I'm home,' he shouted as he came through the front door, presumably addressing his greeting to Gillian, despite the fact that there was no sign of life in the front foyer. She came out to meet him, all sign of both tiredness and headache vanishing as she felt his bearlike hug. 'I could murder a Scotch – a large one with ice.' With his arm around her, he ushered her back to the bar, where she found that the two she had left had become three. Like her, Helen had heard the taxi.

'Hi, sweetie,' he beamed at her. 'I told you I might make it. The ferry was dead on time, which was lucky for me, or I should have got in too late for the train. What'll you have? The usual?' Then, to Gillian, 'This is her nightly tipple when we're away. A peach brandy, that's our Helen's idea of heaven, eh?' Certainly it came as a surprise to Gillian, for the only alcoholic drink she had ever known Helen take was a small sweet sherry. Those summer jaunts must have broadened her horizons.

With Gillian still behind the bar, the other two went to their usual table in the far corner.

'Can I get either of you anything more, or shall I close up?' Gillian asked the wideawake guests with more hope than expectation.

'The sound of peach brandy is nice; I've never tasted it. Get me one of those, Bert, will you.' With a toothy smile and a clearly wide-awake expression, Mrs Bentall, as Gillian knew from the visitors' book, answered.

Bert, her rotund and rosy husband, beamed his delight.

'Make it a large one. It's our anniversary, y'know. Ten years ago today we waltzed down that aisle. Just the two of us there are, no kids. Yes, give her a good big one and I'll have a Scotch.'

'No fear you won't,' came his wife's quick retort. 'Can't have you coming near me with whisky on your breath. You stick to the G and T.'

'Ah well,' he laughed, shrugging his

shoulders. 'All things being equal maybe I'll do as m'lady says. Sounds like I've been promised. No, on second thoughts, I'll give another drink a miss after all. Come on, my love, get that down you and we'll get up them stairs.'

These were the moments when Gillian hated running the bar. Surely a wedding anniversary ought to have been something private, something precious. She took their empty glasses and bid them goodnight, her manner frostier than she realized. Now only Helen and Stephen remained, sipping their drinks as if they had the night before them. As Gillian rinsed the last of the glasses and closed the grille at the front of the bar, she could hear Helen's unusually animated voice relating the fun she and Debbie had been having making a scrapbook of pictures of all the outings they'd been on with him during the summer. From behind the closed grille she felt caged and distant.

'I've finished here, so I'll go on to bed,' she called, knowing that what she ought to have done was to pour herself a drink and go and join them. Yet something stopped her.

'OK honey, I'll be along in five minutes.'

Going back through the foyer, Gillian felt very alone. She honestly cared about Hunters' Lodge; willingly she gave it her whole attention. But was that right? Oughtn't she to have wanted to join Stephen and Helen, add anecdotes of Debbie's doings? Perhaps Margaret Crosbie had been right, perhaps she was tired. She opened the front door and went outside into the night air, breathing deeply, thankful to be out of the smoky atmosphere of the bar. Uninvited came the thought of Mike; she seemed to feel his presence. Like her, he had loved this place. Did he love it still? Did he love her still? Wedding excitement ... but that hadn't been true. Deep in her soul she must have known for a long time how he felt.

Above her the bedside light still burned in Room 6, that occupied by the anniversary couple. So they don't belong to the lights out and under the bedclothes brigade, she thought in some surprise. And yet why should other people be different? She shivered; the night air was cold. The light in the bar went out, but still she stood where she was, letting her thoughts take her on a journey of their own. This time last year there had been no thought of Stephen coming back, no thought of anything except the satisfaction of those first weeks when so many of their guests were coming for the sake of the riding. It had been like living a great adventure, she and Mike each as thrilled as the other.

With a sigh, she turned back into the building.

'Where were you?' Stephen greeted her as she reached their own sitting room. 'I thought that fat guy and his talk of promises had turned your thoughts the right way. I expected you'd have got the bed warm for me. Or what about staying a while out here? Hey, honey, you're cold. Come here.' From where he sat on the sofa, he reached to pull her down to his side.

The guest's remark, then Stephen's repetition

248

of it, seemed to besmirch Gillian's certainty of what was ahead. Often enough, they'd locked the sitting room door and rejoiced in indulging their carnal appetites on the sheepskin rug covering the hard floor. Tonight she yearned for love that was tender, love that reached beyond the boundary of animal satisfaction.

'Let's go to bed,' she answered.

He frowned. 'You're not welcoming me home with a headache or some such.'

'No to the headache, and the some such too. But yes to the welcoming you home part.'

Some time later, lying side by side with the light finally turned out, she took his hand in hers, refusing to admit to an empty feeling of disappointment. Sex never failed for them, but on that night she was reminded of what he'd said so long ago: that a marriage needs more. Perhaps that was what made her want to talk.

'Don't go to sleep, Stephen. Let's talk. We've hardly spoken since you got home.'

'Not much chance, with you always behind that bar. Any other wife would want to know how her husband had got on, would want to hear about the trip.'

'So now you can tell me,' she said with a soft laugh.

'It all went OK. I got a good account and managed to draft it out on the ferry. Helen was telling me about Debs and the scrapbook. Helen is really impressed with the way the kid writes – puts her words together well. What do you reckon? Think it's in the genes?'

'Maybe. But right since she was a baby, she's always been quick to grasp things. Not just *your* genes, my darling.' This was good; this was the sort of friendship she had sensed their love making had lacked. Wriggling closer, she went on, 'You know what I was told today?'

'About Debbie?'

'No. About Ella and Derek. She's pregnant. They're over the moon.'

'Bloody hell! Will she be all right? I never thought of her as having a proper married life, kids and all. The way he takes care of her – well, it was all a bit beyond me. I thought there must be something odd about the guy.'

'So now you know how wrong you were. The only thing different about Ella is that her legs don't work. Something damaged in her spine, right from birth. But otherwise she is in working order the same as any other woman. They are a perfectly normal couple except that they have both had troubles.'

'Umph...' He seemed to be mulling over what he'd heard before he spoke again. 'We'll have to do something to help them. But what?'

'I've been trying to think, but I've come up with nothing. They're so stubborn, absolutely determined they can manage on their own. I was wondering if they might let Mavis go round and work for an hour or two each day – pretending she wasn't busy in the hotel and could spare the time.'

'Not clever,' was his opinion and she admitted

he was right.

'He's been working hard getting pictures together for an exhibition. He's hired a hall in Brindley for a week in the run-up to Christmas.'

A pause so long that she thought he must have lost interest and then he said, 'Leave it with me. I'll have a talk with him – not about the hotel paying for a woman to clean their house. No, what I have in mind will mean that the money earned is Derek's.'

'Tell me.'

'All in good time. Turn around and go to sleep.'

'Not tired,' she whispered, an invitation in her voice as she rubbed her face against his.

'Go to sleep, you witch. If you're not tired, I certainly am. Even a guy of my prowess has limits.'

She wished he hadn't said it. It seemed to draw a line between the joy of loving and the ease of friendship. She did as he said, turned around, plumped up her pillow and closed her eyes. Such clear pictures were waiting for her behind her eyelids, pictures of shared moments riding with Mike, pictures of the two of them working together on their plan for the stables, echoes of laughter, echoes of his voice telling her – no! She opened her eyes wide in an attempt to banish the ghosts, then she consciously turned her thoughts to Stephen's concern for Ella and Derek. From the village in the stillness of the night she heard the single distant chime of the church clock. Would Stephen sleep so contentedly if he knew how much she needed him to help her, to reassure her? He was her future. That's what she had told Mike, and it was true. Through all those years she had wanted no man but him; he was her future, he was her life. If only he would wake, if only he would love her with the tenderness she craved.

'Are you awake?' she whispered, but Stephen slept. Only Gillian lay awake, haunted by memories.

Eight

Sometimes when Gillian went on her daily round to the village and the farm shop she called to collect Ella. Not only did Derek have to do many of the chores normally undertaken by a housewife, but he was working all the hours sent to have his pictures ready for the exhibition. Although it was still five weeks away, he was haunted by the thought that he'd not be ready. Most of his earlier work had been lost in the gas explosion; only three landscapes remained, all of them New Forest scenes painted by knife when he had been staying there the summer before the accident and which he had wrapped carefully for protection and stored in the garage of his parents' home. If the exhibition were to be in that area he was sure they would have sold, but it was unlikely that any householder in Brindley would want one on the wall. So he worked, driving himself as if his life depended on it. And in a way it did – his, Ella's and the baby's too.

On that morning after the news of the coming event had broken, he carried Ella to Gillian's car and deposited her on the front passenger seat.

'Kay,' he said, using his own name for Kathleen, avoiding calling her "Mother" so soon after his own mother's death, 'Kay says she's told you our news.' He beamed with pride as he said it. 'I'll have to build up my sinews as the months go on.'

Gillian said all the right things and managed to hide her anxiety for the young couple. Since Ella had been at the bungalow they had formed a very relaxed friendship and often, instead of trundling herself only as far as the stables as she had when Mike was there, she came that bit further to the hotel itself. The side door, leading straight into Gillian's living quarters, had a step, so she usually tapped on the window and one or the other would come to wheel her in. For her to look back at her life even a single year ago was to look at a different era. She had always been made welcome at Hunters' Lodge, but now she was a neighbour and a married woman too. Her confidence had grown a hundredfold.

Gillian cast an affectionate glance at her as they drove, reminded of a little girl playing at being grown up.

'You never guessed, Gillian? I've been burning to tell you – and Mumsie too – for weeks but I made myself wait until the doctor confirmed it. I was afraid that I couldn't really be pregnant, I haven't once felt sick,' spoken with something like disappointment as if she had been deprived of some of the thrill of this life-changing experience, 'and I don't show yet, do I? Except perhaps for here.' She puffed out her small chest hopefully.

'Being sick isn't obligatory,' Gillian laughed. 'I was well all the time too. And who wants to rush into putting on weight? I certainly didn't. But then of course I was working and wanted to keep on working as long as I could for the sake of the money.'

'How rotten,' Ella said with more sympathy than Gillian felt the situation had merited. The state of pregnancy had held no appeal for her. 'I look in the glass every morning when Derek gets me out of the bath. I expect it will all happen suddenly.' Then with a giggle, 'Perhaps I'll outgrow my chair! Poor Derek, what a lump I shall be – or I suppose it's me and the baby, so I should say what a lump *we* shall be.'

Gillian's listened to the childish chatter and managed to give encouraging answers, but her mind was flitting from that to Stephen's unexpected concern for the young couple, then on to the shopping she had to do – only to be interrupted by the sight of a pair of riders on their way to the open downs. Shopping, Stephen, her own concern for the future awaiting the confident young girl at her side, all these things were blown away. Was his life good at Dalgooney? Did he think of her? Did the sight of a pair of riders do to him what it did to her?

When they arrived back at the bungalow, Derek came out to carry Ella indoors, and behind him, standing in the doorway, was Stephen.

'Oh dear,' Ella whispered to Derek, none too tactfully. 'Haven't you been able to get any work done?'

'Better than that. Arms around my neck. Comfy? Wait till I get you indoors and you'll hear all about it. Are you coming in to listen to what Stephen has suggested, Gillian?'

'He'll have to tell me when I get home. I must get the vegetables delivered.' Then, shouting to Stephen, 'Can't stop. Tell me when you get home.'

She saw his tight-lipped expression and as she let out the clutch his answer was clear. 'If you can spare the time.'

Helen was in the garden hunting for some greenery to add to the table flowers she knew Gillian would have collected from the village florist. She did very little in the hotel but prided herself that she had a gift for flower arranging.

'You've been to the bungalow?' she greeted Gillian as she made towards the kitchen door with her bundles of shopping. 'Isn't he a...' She cut the sentence short before the word "darling" escaped. 'Isn't he what he'd call "a honey"? He has so many contacts, it'll make an enormous difference to them.'

'I only dropped Ella off. I'm running late.'

'There, that's enough greenery I think.' Helen picked up her trug and shears, then turned back to Gillian. 'If he's still over there – and he will be, he'll want to tell Ella himself – I'll tell you while I see to the foyer flowers. Get rid of the shopping and I'll be in the washroom.' It was unlike Helen to be so positive – and perhaps unlike Gillian to meekly do as she was told, too. But a minute or two later she came into the washroom where Helen had the table vases washed and lined up ready for refilling.

'So?' Gillian prompted. 'You said Stephen has contacts. Yes, I know he has, he knows art critics from some of the national papers. But, being practical, they are hardly likely to give time and space to an exhibition in the hall of a small town in the middle of nowhere. Those sort of people work on a national or even international scale.'

Helen smiled – a secret, confident smile. 'Stephen can work miracles. You see if he doesn't. He's been at the bungalow nearly all the time you've been out. I told him a bit about Derek's background and, of course, he knew much of it already. But it was as if it sort of made a chord chime in him. I could see how touched he was with the story.'

And hearing what she said, Gillian too was touched, touched with pride in him that he was prepared to move heaven and earth to help the

256

plight of the young couple. Even so, her hopes didn't ride as high as Helen's.

Just in time for lunch, he arrived back from the bungalow, and one look at him told her he was in high spirits. As always, Helen took her meal in the restaurant, more often than not sharing a table with Margaret and Jane Crosbie, while Gillian's – and Stephen's too when he was home – was brought to their own living room.

'This is a crazy idea, Gill. Why can't we eat like civilized people in the restaurant?'

'Because this is our own space. I should have thought you would be glad to be away from the hotel.'

'Sure, sure I am, honey. It's just that out there Helen would have been with us to hear how I got on with Derek. She gets easily hurt, you know, if she feels she isn't looked on as one of us. Anyway, about Derek – he showed me the cuttings from the reviews of his last exhibition. Great write-ups and from top-notch critics too. I don't understand what's so-called "good"; I only know what attracts me. But it seems he was all set for glory. Things could have been so different for him now if it hadn't been for that ghastly injury. Poor young devil. Jeez, though, Gill, you'd think some plastic surgeon could do something better with his face than that. Yet, you know, from the way Ella gazes at him you'd think he was perfect. I don't reckon she even sees the mess he is.'

'That's what love does.' Then, shying away

257

from anything emotional, 'Young love ... new love.'

'You mean you see me differently now from back in the beginning?'

'I see you warts and all – just as you do me. But warts or no, I really am so – so proud of the help you are giving them. Their independence is so precious to them, but this way anything that comes out of it will be through Derek's undoubted ability.'

'Sure, honey. Hey, what are you doing leaving that second lamb chop not eaten? If it's going spare, pass your plate over and I'll put paid to it. All this do-gooding makes a man hungry.'

If the years had taken some of the gloss from her early starry-eyed love for him, in that moment she looked at him with very real affection.

The day followed its usual pattern: on her own, Gillian rode for an hour or so on Brutus before writing the order for the wine merchants, then spending a while on the hotel accounts. She was just putting her papers away when Helen looked in to say Stephen was driving her to meet Debbie because it was so cold, and that when they'd collected her they were going into Reading because he wanted to mail an urgent letter from the General Post Office.

Still in the same mood of affection for him that he was going so far out of his way to help Derek, Gillian watched the car disappear down the drive, stopped in the foyer to greet two guests who had just unhitched their horse trailer at the stables and were checking in, then checked that the restaurant was ready for the evening and went back to her own quarters.

It was unusual for Stephen to leave his work around. He must have decided on the spur of the moment to take Helen and Debbie with him to Reading. And it was unusual too for Gillian to have enough curiosity about what he'd been writing to look at it. But the letter to his critic friend was very different from his weekly report for the American newspaper, so she opened the folder he'd left lying on the table and took up the carbon copy. She frowned as she read his brief but accurate account of the follow-up to the accident but then she told herself that there could be no disguising the truth. If this acquaintance of Stephen's was prepared to come to Brindley to the exhibition there would be no way of Derek hiding the disfigurement that still played such a big part in the way he lived. So her frown lifted and by the time she finished reading and opened the file to replace the carbon copy her mouth had softened almost into a smile.

Then she saw the headline for his weekly report: *Like Phoenix from the Ashes*. All trace of a smile vanished. The shock she felt was physical.

The original three sheets had gone, only the copies remained. Sitting in a chair where probably no more than an hour previously Stephen had sat as he worded his weekly missive, she started to read. But this was ridiculous! How

259

dare he do this! The Derek Denvers character he described bore little relationship to reality; he was portrayed as a young man downtrodden by the cruel blow Fate had struck. It was a wicked lie! It was a blatant cry for sympathy, and worse it was a cry steeped in the sort of emotionalism that Derek would have hated. And that all in the first eye-catching paragraph.

Then the article turned the clock back and carried the reader on a descriptive journey, giving an over-colourful exaggeration of the facts. It told of a young man gifted with a rare talent, which even at his first exhibition had been acclaimed by the foremost critics in the country. Gillian conceded that at least *that* part was based on the truth. Then, in a changed scene, the same young man staying with his elderly and infirm parents, parents he adored and protected. Gillian bristled with anger. Sometimes Derek had talked of his parents and had shown her a few photographs he had salvaged from the family home. Elderly? Infirm? What utter nonsense. His father had been senior clerk of the local bank, his mother had been a stalwart worker for the WVS, and neither of them more than in their early fifties. The relationship between parents and son had been one of loving friendship. But this article was aimed at drama, and elderly and infirm gave the heart strings a firmer tug.

So she read on. It was Derek's love for the frail old couple that led to his present tragic plight. Then, briefly, was a scene based on truth as Stephen described the explosion, the flying debris, his parents being knocked to the ground and trapped as the outside wall caved in on them, then the blaze as the escaping gas ignited. Stephen's young hero, sobbing in his fear, fought valiantly to free his beloved parents, but the flames overcame him. His clothes were alight, his hair was alight, the flesh on his face too; he was being cremated alive. Then, and mercifully, he lost consciousness as the rest of the dislodged ceiling fell on him. A neighbour had raised the alarm and the firefighters arrived, but talking of it now, Derek Denvers remembers none of that. He knew nothing until long hours later he regained consciousness in hospital where he remained for months. His beloved parents were dead and his promising career had been knocked off course.

Gillian read on, horrified, ashamed, furious – and in those moments filled with disgust that Stephen could use the young couple as a means of feeding his readers' insatiable love for emotional drama.

The scene changed to an isolated spot deep in the heart of the country where the young artist lived like a hermit, hideously scared, frightened to go out in daylight, finding solace only in his solitary painting. Then – ah, now here comes romance – then one day as he looked out from the window of his hermit's cottage, he saw a cripple girl in her wheelchair. She was quite alone, her beautiful face filled with sadness. His heart reached out to her and some force greater than his own led him to emerge from hiding and go out to speak to her. Is there, indeed, some force of destiny that guides us? Stephen led his readers to consider:

That meeting was to change their lives. Love is the strength they drew on, drew on not to cure what ails them, for nothing can do that, but to give them the courage they lacked. They have been married for nearly two months now, and Derek Denvers, the young man who had previously been proclaimed to have the future of a great artist, has harnessed his courage and faced the world. As he carries his fragile and beautiful wife to her wheelchair, does he see her as a cripple? My belief is that he sees her simply as the centre of his universe, the human soul so closely entwined with his own that they are almost as one person. And does she cringe with horror when she looks at his disfigurement? If she does, she has learnt not to show it; but my feeling is that in her eyes he is the handsome young god he was before that fateful event.

Sadly, though, as the crowds flock into the hall where his work is to hang, their vision won't be charged with love. He will need all his courage to stand amongst a throng of strangers, to see the way they flinch at first sight of him. As his story spreads in the small country town perhaps there will be those who will come out of curiosity; there will be others who appreciate his sensitivity and will shun the exhibition altogether. And then what? Will his genius flower unappreciated? Will the power of his beautiful, paralyzed wife's love give him the courage he will need to fight back yet again? Before the tragic event that changed his life, the critics thought highly of him. We can but hope they will come once more to see his work and his life might move forward.

I shall be in the hall to watch events. And I will let you know.

Gillian read the whole thing through twice, the second time without the original sense of shock but with the same fury. Then, her face expressionless, she put the papers back in the folder and went to shower and dress for the evening. She was just ready when she heard the car door slam and knew Stephen and the others were home.

Her mind was alive with the things she wanted to say to Stephen, but she couldn't talk in front of Helen and Debbie. So she waited in her bedroom.

'Hi, honey. We're home.' Bursting with his usual self-confidence, he came to find her. 'Helen bought Debs some plasticine and they've gone to the kid's bedroom to make models.' Gillian had never felt like this before. It was like listening to a stranger. 'Hey, what's up? You OK?'

'You can't send it, Stephen. I read the rubbish you'd written. How could you do it to him – to *them*?'

Sitting on the bed and pulling her down to his side, he kept his arm around her.

'Hey, hey, honey. Didn't we say we wanted to help them?'

'And you call that help? That creature you wrote about wasn't Derek, neither was the cripple girl, as you called her, Ella. They're *strong*. They want a chance to prove themselves, but they don't want the sort of maudlin sympathy you're trying to unleash. You can't send it. You mustn't.'

'Too late. It's on its way to the London office and they'll rush it through. You call it maudlin. Oh no. It's ... it's powerful. That's what writing a word picture is all about.' Then, to her ears the excitement in this voice completely out of keeping with the situation, 'Hey, listen. Forget Derek and Ella for a moment, just think of the appeal of the plot. Jeez, if I were anything but a newspaper hack I'd write such a script. Think of the film it would make. Can't you just picture the two of them, the cripple girl and the hero with the face like some disfigured devil? Then see what love can do. On the screen you could do the theme real justice so folk would see the girl through *his* yes, see her standing tall and glorious – and see him through *her* eyes, as handsome as he probably was at one time. All through the eyes of love.' He tightened his hold on her and with the other hand tilted her face towards his.

'Don't!' She wriggled free. 'That's probably how they do see each other, but if so it's not for the entertainment of emotion-seeking viewers – or readers for that matter. How could you do it, Stephen?'

'I don't get you, honey. Honest to God, I don't. This is a big story. Listen, I sent a copy to a buddy of mine back home, he's a script writer in the movie industry. If they take it up, have you any idea what it would do to the young-sters' future? Why, he'd never have to lift a paint brush again.'

She stood up and walked towards the door.

'You honestly don't know, do you?' she said. In all the years they'd been apart, no matter how often she had told herself he was out of her mind and out of her life, she had never felt as distant from him as she did at that moment. No, he honestly didn't understand. 'I take it you didn't give Derek a copy to read?'

'Of course I didn't. I couldn't raise the poor bastard's hopes until there is something concrete to offer.'

'And what about your art critic friend? Did you supply him with a copy too?'

Stephen laughed, glad the conversation had taken a different turn.

'What sort of an idiot do you think I am? I don't even know how much he knew of Derek's family background. Anyway, he wouldn't be into what you term over-emotionalism. I got Derek talking this morning, he gave me a brief outline of how far his career had got and I managed to fill in the gaps. But I told you what I intended to do – I wrote to Miles Summerton like I said I would and filled him in without elaborating, truthfully or otherwise,' he added, with a mischievous twinkle, 'and told him about Derek trying to make a comeback. Whether anything will come out of my letter I don't know. But honey, I told you; I just want to give them a break. What I'm supposed to have done wrong is beyond me. Helen read it, and she – well, she was moved, truly moved. And would you call Helen an emotion-seeker? Of course you wouldn't; she's just a normal tender-hearted girl. Anyway, she actually shed tears. That's what gave me such a boost.'

Gillian turned and left him. An evening in the bar and restaurant held no appeal. She was conscious above all else of the yawning gap between herself and Stephen. And yet, was she being fair to him? Was she letting her affection for Ella and Derek blind her to the fact that he was using the best means he had of helping them build an independent future? He had tried to help them in the only way he knew, so ought she not to be grateful? She reminded herself that the young couple would never read Stephen's weekly column, so what harm could it do? She reminded herself that he had kept his word and written to his art critic friend – and for that she most certainly was grateful. So forget the rest, just hang on to the thought that his intention was to help. So she told herself over and over again, each time with more determination than the last. If there was any lack of understanding, surely it must be hers. Stephen

266

was kind, he was generous – and above all he was the man she loved. Those were the thoughts she clung to.

Automatically she smiled at the hotel guests; automatically she took orders for their food while they sat in the bar with their pre-dinner drinks; automatically she made polite and cheerful conversation with complete strangers who were staying in the hotel for the first time. All that had become second nature to her. Their dinner over, Stephen and Helen had their coffee brought to the bar lounge, the waitress knowing just where they would be sitting, as always at the table in the far corner of the room. From out of nowhere into Gillian's head came the echo of those words she had spoken to Mike: 'Stephen is my future.' Turning her back on the bar counter, she made pretence of arranging the array of bottles, gripped by a longing for privacy. Her thoughts were her own, no one could guess at the aching void she felt. "Loneliness of the soul" – the words came to her uninvited, words she immediately pushed away. Then, with no one waiting to be served at the bar, her smile was back in place as she went to join Stephen and Helen.

'He says you read his account,' Helen said quietly. 'Didn't he write it beautifully, with such gentle understanding?'

'They are gentle people,' Gillian answered. 'Yes, he is trying hard to help them.' She made herself say it, just as she made herself smile in his direction. What was done was done, and as long as Ella and Derek never read the article they couldn't be hurt by it. The most important thing was that he had written to Miles Summerton.

Excitement grew as the week for the exhibition drew closer. Building on his involvement, Stephen regularly called at the bungalow and when he came back to the hotel cook-a-hoop with the news that not only had Miles Summerton written to Derek saying he was looking forward to the event, but so had Dominic Faulkner, a critic of even greater stature. Gillian had almost managed to forget the incident of that other letter, that addressed to a film scriptwriter.

'Derek and I went into the village this morning,' Ella told her one afternoon during the week leading up to the exhibition. They were on their way to Brindley, where Gillian wanted to do some Christmas shopping before life got too hectic.

'I saw you were both out when I called to see if you were coming on my round. I wonder we didn't bump into each other in the village.'

But Ella wasn't listening.

'He left the car by the park and we took the chair after that. It was lovely walking through the park, cold and crisp.' She giggled as if she were more Debbie's age than her own. 'We sang carols. If anyone had heard us they would have thought we were batty; it's almost a month until Christmas. But no one was there except us, so we sang at the tops of our voices. Gillian, isn't life simply gorgeous? Our first Christmas together, Derek and me – and our last for just the two of us.' Before Gillian had a chance to answer, if indeed an answer were needed, Ella held her hands across her growing stomach. 'You know how long I was before I started to get fat. But now he – or she – is really getting going. My shape is quite different.'

Gillian laughed. 'Was ever a woman so keen to expand?'

A light remark, but Ella took it as a serious question. 'You know what I suppose? I think I want to get huge, the sort of huge that if I could walk would turn a walk into a waddle, just to show that ... to show that ... well ... that I'm the same as other people.'

Stopping behind two waiting cars at the traffic lights recently installed to create one-way traffic across the ancient and narrow bridge on the edge of the small town, Gillian looked affectionately at her passenger.

'The same as other people?' she repeated. 'There are no two people the same, Ella. We all have our own ghosts, our own hidden secret selves.'

'Hidden from most people, yes, I guess we do. But honestly – really honestly – I don't have anything hidden from Derek. That's what's so wonderful. You know what, Gillian? Some-times it's so wonderful that I'm scared. I never thought, never expected anyone's life could be so good. But it can't last like that, can it? I mean, it wouldn't be fair for one person to have a sort of special right to such happiness.'

'I would guess that you and Derek are due for some happiness. But Ella, no one gets through life unscathed.'

'That's what I mean. Even you. For you everything must be wonderful now, but think of all those years when you and Stephen lost each other. And then there was David. You lost David.'

'I'm not sure that I have lost David. Don't ask me to explain. I'm not sure I could.'

Ella seemed to wriggle more comfortably into her seat. All she said was, 'I so like coming out with you like this, Gillian. You talk to me as though I'm ... sort of ... well, just an ordinary grown-up woman.'

'You, my dear Ella, will never be swept aside as being ordinary. You have gifts most us more mundane ones can't even dream about. You and Derek too. How are the paintings coming on for the exhibition?'

'He's done so well. Some people might say that because he has to work at such a pace to get things ready the work can't be as good. But that's not true. It's as if having the exhibition looming so close inspires him. He hardly sleeps and yet he doesn't seem tired.' Then, like the sun disappearing behind a black cloud, her expression changed. 'He's so keyed up, so full of hope and confidence. But suppose, just suppose, the critics don't turn up, or suppose they don't like what they see? But they *must*. I'd sell

270

my soul to make things go well for him. Mumsie tries so hard to be tactful, she offers help in hidden sorts of ways – "Can you use this joint? I bought it because it looked so good, but I'll never get around to eating it all by myself," or "If you have any extras to fill the washing machine, it might just as well all go in together." She means to be so kind and I'd love to accept what she offers, but I can feel his hurt every time. Stephen's help is different. If Derek can make some money on his pictures that will be wonderful.'

There was but a thin veil between her confidence that the exhibition would make a new beginning and Ella's fear that Derek's dreams would crash. Gillian heard the fear in her voice and answered with more certainty than she felt in order to chase it away.

'I'm no artist. I don't know a good painting from a bad one, I just know what I like. But those critics who gave him such praise before the accident can't all have been wrong. Miles Summerton and Dominic Faulkner say they're coming, and their reviews are sure to be good.' Again Ella wriggled in her seat. 'Are you OK? Not getting cramp or anything?'

'No. Just a funny feeling. A sort of bubbly feeling. Flickery. I don't know how to describe it.' There was no hiding the fear in Ella's voice.

Gillian drew into a lay-by and gave Ella her full attention as the girl's eyes shot wide open and she said. 'There it is again. I don't feel ill, it's not wind or anything. Is something wrong?'

'Can't you guess? That, Ella, is your baby trying to move for the very first time.'

Whatever reaction she expected to her words it certainly wasn't the one they brought forth. Half laughing and half crying, Ella cradled the stomach that over recent weeks had given her such pride.

'Our baby. It's really going to happen.' Tears overcame laughter – tears of joy grown out of years of frustrated dreams. 'I've been so scared, Gillian. Wasn't sick even once, and then I took so long to start to get even a bit fat. I couldn't tell anyone how frightened I was, not even Derek. If I said it aloud it would have been like accepting that I wasn't going to be able to have a baby like an ordinary person.'

Cool, reserved, practical, Gillian was all of those things, but in that moment as she turned and drew Ella into her arms she ached with pity. Her mind went back to the months she had been pregnant with Debbie, a working woman facing motherhood alone. There had been moments when it had taken all her courage to stamp on the self-pity that would threaten her without warning, but looking back to those distant days she knew that her own fears melted to nothingness compared with the shadow that lay across Ella's life.

'Never be frightened to talk, Ella. If you keep things to yourself they magnify out of proportion. There are thousands of women who turn into baby elephants by the time they are three or four months and they'd think you have all the luck in the world to have progressed more slowly. Most of it is excess water and fat anyway. If things weren't going well with you, do you think you would look so *blooming*? Come on, love, wipe your eyes and blow your nose. You have to go home and tell Derek his heir is making its – his? her? – presence felt.'

As they neared home Ella told her, 'Derek is letting me show four of my paintings too. The critics won't be interested; in fact I hope they don't even bother to look at them, but he is giving me that little niche at the end of the hall and putting a notice up that the pictures have been painted by me.'

'But that's splendid. He must think they are worth it or he wouldn't suggest it.'

'Perhaps. But I shall have my chair by them so that no one imagines they are his work. And you know what I really hope? I hope they will all sell. I look at my work and then at his and I haven't any illusions, but what I want is for people to buy them even if it's out of sympathy. That's why I shall sit right by them. That's what I meant when I said I would sell my soul if it would help. And you know before I met Derek, before I began to know about loving someone, it really would have been selling my soul to know that anyone bought my painting out of sympathy. But now none of that is important – it doesn't matter a jot. All that matters is that somehow we make enough so that we don't have to be helped out of a financial hole. We'll fight our own battles – and we have to use

273

whatever weapons we have. And if people see me as someone to be pitied, why should I care? I know it's not true.'

'Is that how Derek looks on it too?' For Gillian was sure it wasn't.

'Probably not. You know what I think? I think men aren't as practical as women. Belonging together like Derek and I do, having the baby coming, it's all made me see things quite differently. I know now what really matters and what is a sort of puffed up pride, something we wrap around ourselves for protection.'

Gillian weighed up her words, temporarily lost for an answer.

'Listening to you, Ella, I feel – it sounds crazy – but I feel humble. We all do it, you know, let that devil Pride defend us from facing the truth. All right, most of us are much luckier than you have been, we have two good legs to prop us up...'

Ella cut her short. 'But there's more to being a whole proper person than whether we can walk. I used to let being stuck in my chair get magnified into the thing that ruled my life. But it's not really so vitally important. I don't think Derek thinks "Poor Ella"; in fact I know he doesn't. I'm just *me* and I wouldn't change places with a living soul.'

The exhibition opened on the first Saturday in December, and true to his word Miles Summerton arrived in the middle of the afternoon. Of all the weekends of the year, that first one in

December was probably the busiest in Brindley. Another fortnight, or probably even another week, and Saturday would see people queuing for the buses to Reading or Oxford, looking forward to the buzz of excitement as Christmas drew nearer.

Stephen was in the hall to help pull back the bolt and open the double doors. He even took it upon himself to be the one to hang the notice on the railings to attract people. Admission was free and the afternoon was cold, so most people passing stopped to read the notice and "just pop inside to take a peek, out of the wind". Derek's previous exhibition had been in the more affluent area of the New Forest, where people had been eager to buy oil paintings of the views they knew and loved. In Brindley, Derek was uncomfortably aware that many of those who came in were there to look at *him* rather than at his work.

Then Miles Summerton arrived. For Derek that was a difficult moment.

'How good of you to come.' He moved towards the door as he saw Miles enter, his hand extended in greeting. Perhaps only Ella knew just how difficult the moment was for him.

'I wouldn't have missed it. But it's thanks to Stephen here that I knew you were painting again. So things are better?'

Derek gave a slight shrug of his shoulders.

'Better than a few months ago. I now have a wife. Come and meet her before you cast your eye over what I've been doing.'

Ella watched them approach, prepared to fight with any weapon she could find. It occurred to her that before Derek loved her, she had never thought of herself as beautiful. Now though she took great pains with her appearance and she was aware that she had been blessed with good looks, with delicately beautiful hands (not surprising, since they did very little to roughen them) and with a figure that had at last started to blossom into fruitfulness. These were her tools and she meant to use them to her advantage.

'Mrs Denvers,' Miles bent down and took her hand. 'This is a pleasure.'

'And for us too, Mr Summerton. Oh look Derek, there is someone looking interested in your picture of the paddock.' Then, smiling her satisfaction as Derek left them. 'When Stephen said he had written to you about the exhibition, I just prayed and prayed you would come.' She gave an involuntary and barely audible 'Ooh' as she moved her hands to cradle her growing bump.

'Are you all right?'

She nodded. 'Yes, it's nothing, just sudden tummy cramp. It's always having to sit in one position, I think the baby wants me to be up and doing. They say, don't they, one should take normal healthy exercise. As if the discomfort of cramp matters, though. The only thing that matters is that we have a healthy baby.' Her smile was cheerful and yet the solicitous Miles was aware of her bravery.

Variations on the theme were played out when Dominic Faulkner met her. Gillian, who had driven out to Brindley as soon as she had settled Brutus back in his stable after the hunt, watched from a distance and knew exactly the role Ella was playing. Could Derek see it too? she wondered. Poor Derek, the courage he was showing was heartbreakingly real. Looking across the crowded hall she suspected that the number of viewers interested in the paintings could be counted on the fingers of one hand. Ockbury villagers had become used to the sight of him, but in Brindley he was a stranger and a curiosity. The local paper had printed an anonymous article – in fact produced by Stephen – not only giving an account of Derek's original expectations but also briefly outlining the injuries that had kept him so long in hospital and left him scarred beyond recognition. Ella had read the article, but her instinctive wish to shield him had prompted her to throw the paper away before he saw it.

So passed the opening afternoon of the exhibition, to be followed by a week when for hours at a time Derek and Ella had the hall to themselves. Certainly Miles Summerton and Dominic Faulkner wrote favourably of the talent of the young artist, but words of praise did nothing to fill the coffers. One picture was sold, a view of the downs with a distant group of riders, bought by a guest from Hunters' Lodge as a memento of his stay.

* * *

Ever since the hotel opened it had catered for Christmas breaks and that year was no different – at least, on the surface it was no different. Before the end of October they were fully booked, in the main with riders who had come for the first time the previous year. Gillian tried to throw herself heart and soul into the preparations and surely it should have helped her that Teddy and Mavis Mitchell were so enthusiastic. This would be their first Christmas together; their first Christmas not only belonging to each other but being part of the determined effort to make the event something very special for the guests. Add to all that was the fact that through the weeks of December hardly a day passed when there wasn't a special booking for a lunch or dinner party, leaving the restaurant fully booked throughout. Wasn't this what Gillian had strived for, just as David had before her? She might have found satisfaction in the way things had shaped up if it hadn't been for the ghost of last year. Mike's shadow seemed everywhere. Watching Teddy and a group of riders disappearing down the drive she only had to close her eyes and Mike's image was before her, his voice echoing in her head.

'Mum! Mum, come and see!' Debbie's voice broke into her all-too-frequent reverie. 'I 'spect you wondered why Auntie Helen and I were so late back from school. Come and see, then you'll guess where we've been.'

In the car park Stephen was untying a fir tree, which had been anchored to the roof rack on

278

his car.

'Another tree?' Gillian tried to sound pleased, and indeed she was both pleased and surprised that he should have shown enough interest to want to add to the decorations that already transformed the restaurant into Santa's grotto, and the bar and lounge – both with their swathes of greenery, open fireplaces and huge log fires – into scenes depicted on many a Christmas card and conjuring up the atmosphere of Olde England. 'The bar gets so crowded. We'd better put it in the corner in the visitors' lounge, don't you think?'

'Jeez, Gillian, what about your own family?'

'I've ordered a wreath for our door and an arrangement of Christmas roses.'

'Come on, Gilly, this is *Christmas,* a time for fun and excitement. A wreath and Christmas roses! This tree is just the start for our own sitting room. You should see the lights we've bought. Hey, but honey, don't you realize? This is the first time Debs has had a family for Christmas and, boy oh boy, is it going to be just great, eh, Debs?'

Debbie's head nodded as though it were on a spring, her eyes shining with excitement she could find no words to express.

'I'll take the boxes of lights and all this stuff straight in, shall I?' Helen said, holding a large cardboard packing case containing what looked like enough baubles and glistening streamers to decorate a family house.

'Yep, good girl,' Stephen answered. 'I'll go

and dig young Teddy out and get him to fill a tub of some sort with soil and stones. How about it, then Debs?' If his excitement was aimed at boosting hers, he was doing a grand job. She was beyond standing still; first she hopped on one foot, then the other, then she jumped around in a circle. There was no way of containing her joy, so she burst forth with what they had been singing at school, 'Ding dong merrily on high...'

Gillian wanted to be part of it all, but she felt her smile to be forced.

'Run to the stables, Debbie,' she said, 'and ask Teddy if he can come and give us a hand for a few minutes.'

'Yep, good idea,' Stephen agreed. 'Tell him to bring a shovel and to find a tub, an old bin or something. Tell him to buck up. I'll wait for him to give me a hand lifting the tree off the car.'

'Debbie!' Gillian called as the child sped off. 'It's not for you to *tell* him to do things. Make sure you *ask* him very politely.'

''Course I will, Mum. Me and Teddy are good mates.'

''Struth, Gillian. You sound like some hatchet-faced schoolmarm. The kid's just excited.'

'And not the only one, if loss of good manners is anything to go by.'

Turning on her heel, Gillian left him, but not before she saw his crestfallen expression and felt a pang of guilt. She was honest enough to admit that her behaviour stemmed from that remark: 'This is the first time Debbie has had a family for Christmas.' The first time she has had a father perhaps, but she and Debbie had been their own family. Did he believe the years without him had counted for nothing? Or had she failed Debbie? Ought she to have turned their flat into something resembling Father Christmas's grotto?

Retreating to the bathroom, she concentrated on getting bathed and dressed for the evening, telling herself that the only thing that mattered was that he was with them, that they would celebrate Christmas together.

'Gillian.' A light tap on the bedroom door accompanied Helen's voice a quarter of an hour or so later. 'Gillian, are you dressed? May I come in a second? I don't want to shout.'

'Of course you can. I'm just about ready. There's a big party this evening.'

'It's just that I wanted to make sure you don't think I'm butting in. I mean, it's really you who ought to be helping Stephen and Debbie with the tree and all the decorations. But I know you can't, you'll be busy. You don't mind if I give them a hand, do you?'

'Since when have I minded?' Gillian was surprised at the rush of affection she felt for the never-to-be-sister-in-law who so often irritated her. 'Quite honestly, Helen, I don't know how Debbie and I would manage if you weren't here for her. I've had more than enough of clambering up ladders in the hotel without having another dose of it, but Debbie will love it. I'll
281

tell her she can have a late-to-bed pass.'

Just for a second, Helen looked doubtful. 'Stephen didn't suggest she should stay up to help.' The words escaped before she realized their lack of tact, but she soon had herself in hand. 'Still, I expect he took it for granted that that was what you'd say. We'll have our meal sent through to the sitting room, shall we? Then Debbie can be part of all the fun.'

Gillian didn't let herself dig into her mind to find out why it was she was glad to turn her back on the chaos of boxes, lights, tinsel, shining stars and all the other paraphernalia of the sort she considered to be tastelessly over-gilding the lily. The sitting room had been her sanctuary, just as it had been David's. On that evening, twelve days before Christmas, she felt herself to be a stranger. Once in the surroundings of the hotel, she immersed herself in what she knew would be a busy evening, finding time for only a fleeting return to the hive of industry in her own quarters to say goodnight to Debbie.

That evening set the scene for the run-up to the festival. The "house party" guests arrived the day before Christmas Eve. Some of them had booked when they left, the day after Boxing Day a year ago; some were there for the first time. Everywhere Gillian seemed to see the ghost of that other year, the first she and Mike had organized together. If she had hopes that he would telephone her, they were dashed by the arrival of his greetings card bearing the message: "Last year was a success, and I'm confident this one will be even better. Every good wish to you for the coming year and always. Mike." Why should she feel hurt and rejected? Was his card any different from the one she had sent to him with, "Greetings and happy memories from Gillian and everyone at Hunters' Lodge"?

Wearing her pregnancy like a badge of honour, Ella was as excited as Debbie by the wonder of those few days. At the Manor, Kathleen had never turned their environment into such a wonderland; for her, Christmas meant a display of lilies for the hall and Christmas roses for the drawing room. The idea of lights that flicked on and off, of chiming bells and a tree so over-decorated that the branches were lost in a maze of tinsel, had nothing to do with the festival and everything to do with the commercialism that was gradually gaining footage. After years of shortages, any form of luxury was clutched at and even though rationing was still tight, the shops were managing to display plenty of extravagant extras.

'What are you doing that for?' Stephen asked Gillian late on Christmas Eve, when he found her filling one of her stockings to tie to the end of Debbie's bed.

'If she wakes and finds it not there she'll think Santa's forgotten her.' With the customary orange pushed to the toe, she was following it with a rolled up comic.

'Hey there Gilly, *me*, I'm Santa now. And she

won't be disappointed. You wait till she finds the sack on the end of her bed in the morning. I brought it back from London yesterday and a whole load of things to be in it. I ought to have told you, but I had to keep the trunk of the car locked in case Debs saw any of it. What have you got there? Anything worth adding to the tree or is it just junk? I got her a pair of roller skates, a smashing painting outfit, nurse's gear for dressing up and a couple of games to ring the changes when Helen plays with her in the evenings.'

'But those are proper presents, Stephen. As if Santa could take those to children everywhere.'

'Ho! Ho! Ho!' he laughed, mimicking the saint, and then he pulled Gillian into a bearlike hug. 'Hey, but think of it Gilly, her first Christmas with a proper dad. And you know what else I brought back for her – for her proper present? It's locked away in the summer house but I'll go down and get it in before we go to bed. A bicycle. Her first bicycle. Did you get her something too – or just these bits and pieces?'

'I bought her a new riding crop.'

'Bet you one thing: once she gets pedalling that bike she'll forget riding. What kid wouldn't? It takes her all her time to groom the creature and see to her tack when she gets home after a ride. A bike you just prop against the wall and you're done. Agree?'

She recognized the laughter behind his words. That, and the boyish eagerness as he looked around him at this flickering grotto of man-made celebration, drove away her resentment. All this was for Debbie, the love they felt for her was surely something that bound them close.

'It's gone midnight,' he whispered, rubbing his chin against her always-groomed and elegant pageboy hairstyle. 'Happy Christmas, Mrs Sinclair. And don't you think I've been on approval long enough? Don't you think it's time we re-tied the knot? See what I've bought for your present?' He passed her a ring case, and inside she found an eternity ring.

'It's beautiful. But no, Stephen. We're OK as we are. I don't know why ... I can't explain ... but re-marrying would be like putting the clock back. We're OK as we are,' she repeated. 'And happy Christmas to you, too. It's not much, but I thought you might like it.'

He unwrapped the cherry wood pipe and put it in his mouth.

'Sure I like it. Pipes are a sign of contentment in a man. And you know what? Just at present I find life pretty much the way I like it.'

For a moment they remained where they were, the empty pipe in his mouth, the ring glistening on her finger, his arm around her holding her in a loose embrace. It was already nearly one o'clock in the morning, Christmas morning, not the time one would expect a telephone call. When the shrill bell shattered the silence they sprang apart, each reaching to pick up the receiver before it woke Debbie. Gillian's immediate thought was of Mike.

Perhaps he was calling because, like her, he was haunted by memories of last year. But even as the thought came to her, she knew there was no logic in it. If he thought of her at all, it would be to imagine her in bed with Stephen.

'Hold the line please, I have a trans-Atlantic call for you.' It was Stephen who held the receiver to his ear, but the clear tone of the operator was audible to both of them.

Nine

'They're putting me through to New York. Sounds like they're having fun back there; they must have forgotten we're five hours forward on them. Go and get the bed warm, I'll be with you as soon as I've brought Debs's bike up from the summer house.' He meant to keep the atmosphere of the last minute or two unchanged, that was clear from the way he half-closed one eye in a lingering and telling wink. It may be late and tomorrow a hectic day, but neither the evening that was gone nor the day that was ahead would be allowed to intrude on the time that was their own.

When, some minutes later, he joined her in the bedroom, all he said about the phone call was that it was great to have spoken to friends

286

back home. His mind was on other things, something for which she took the credit. There were nights when, after a busy day culminating in hours in a full and noisy bar, she would come to bed longing just for silence and darkness. When he was away, within minutes she would be asleep. When he was home, no matter what her mood, he knew exactly how to steer her in the direction he wanted.

So it was in those small hours of Christmas morning and willingly, eagerly she let herself be led. This was their first Christmas as a family; along the corridor Debbie was asleep with the bulging sack attached to her bedpost. Stephen had entered heart and soul into making everything what, in his eyes, the festival should be. With her thumb, Gillian twisted the new eternity ring on her finger as if by touching it she would find reassurance. Yet, even in moments like this, perhaps especially in moments like this, she was haunted by the sound of a voice, the touch of a hand, the joy of being with that one person ... Mike. She wanted to forget; she longed to be free of the hold that never let her go. And yet without the comfort of those memories, how empty her life would be. No! She pulled her thoughts up short. That was a wicked thing to believe, for how could it be empty when she had Stephen, Stephen who had held her heart for so long? He hadn't changed; he was still as fun-loving, still as handsome, still as sex-driven; nothing was different about him except his devotion to Debbie. He and

287

Debbie were her future, the future she wanted. She was happy, gloriously happy. So could it have been the never-failing wonder of satisfying her body that heightened her emotion and made a hot tear spill? True to character, she brushed it aside and settled for sleep, reminding herself that already the night was half gone.

Through the next two days Stephen was constantly aware of Debbie's need of him, just as he was increasingly angry that Gillian had kept from him the knowledge of his daughter's existence. With the pride and patience of many a fond father, he ran beside the new bicycle holding the back of the saddle while, well wrapped up against the cold, Helen applauded from the sidelines. Gillian's time was taken elsewhere: on Christmas Day she turned herself into the perfect hostess, ready with a tray of sherries to welcome home the morning church-goers and walkers alike. Arrangements had been made to see that the afternoon hours were filled: a conjuror, followed by a pianist with a relaxed and pleasant singing voice, all of it aimed at breaking down any remaining barriers. Even the Crosbie sisters joined in the fun, enjoying the fuss made of them by visitors of another generation. Just as for Sunday lunches which brought the weekend breaks to an end, the dining tables were arranged so that every-one sat together, and for Christmas this includ-ed the two elderly residents. It was years since they'd enjoyed themselves so much.

When Gillian went through to her own rooms

to dress for the evening, she was pleasantly surprised to find Ella and Derek there.

'Horrid hotel, Mum,' Debbie greeted her. 'We are having a lovely time. It's not fair you being in there with all those horrid people.'

'It wouldn't be fair if I weren't, Debbie.' Then, to the room at large, 'It's gone off splendidly. Last year was good, but I think they've all enjoyed this one even more.'

'Christmas was always good in the hotel. David used to make sure it was,' Helen said, earning a look of something akin to affection from Gillian.

'Yes, I remember. And he would have loved it this time. They're *his* sort of people.'

'Horrid people,' from Debbie, although in truth she had been having such a great time that she'd not really noticed her mother's absence.

The rest of the day followed much the same pattern as any other evening, the only difference being that the bar was even busier than usual. Fortunately it ended fairly early, as the riders all wanted to be breakfasted and ready to set off by eight on Boxing Day morning. The meet was at Changford Hall, some five miles away and, many of them strangers to the area, they would follow the Hunters' Lodge horse-box.

Sometimes Gillian took Teddy as a guest, but on that day, a morning that had turned much milder after a night's rain, she drove the horse-box herself and went alone. Last year had been so different: the ground had been hard and dry,

289

the air crisp, and she and Mike had led the procession from the hotel. As she drove, she let her left hand rest on the empty passenger seat. Would he be remembering? The day ahead had lost its magic. She just wanted it to be over. But, never a person to allow her innermost feelings to show, she gave every impression of being as exhilarated as the next one. The fact that the effort she made was for Hunters' Lodge helped her and when they at last arrived home tired, hungry and satisfied, even though the fox had gone to ground, she stayed in the stables to help Teddy. This was his Boxing Day as well as hers, his first one with a wife waiting indoors for him.

With a feeling of thankfulness, she waved the last of the guests on their way the next morning and turned back to the house. Even in the restaurant the magic had gone from the decorations and, as for her own sitting room, to her eye it looked pathetic on this dreary post-Christmas morning. But running a hotel allowed no time for rest and recovery. Upstairs Mavis and a girl from the village were stripping beds and preparing the rooms for the next intake; in the kitchen, supplies needed replenishing. So started the daily round.

Blowing her horn outside the neighbouring bungalow, she waited while Derek pushed Ella to the car then, taking a deep breath, lifted her to the front passenger seat.

'Have you room for me too?' he suggested. 'If I fold the chair and put it in the boot, you could dump us off when you start shopping and we'll walk home. No exhibition to prepare for, so here I am with time on my hands.'

'Have you had any follow-up from those good reviews?' she asked, detecting a note of dejection in his voice.

'No. I doubt if anyone in this neck of the woods will have read the reviews, and Brindley is hardly the place to find folk with spare cash for paintings. I was crazy to imagine it might have worked.'

'Rubbish. I agree about Brindley, but you have something to build on. Next time maybe you could get your pictures exhibited in Oxford.'

'I sold all mine,' Ella put in with a ring of pride. 'And you know why? I got the sympathy vote. I've been telling Derek – we talked about it half the night – I've been telling him, what Fate dishes out to you is like a hand of cards. It may not be all trumps and aces, but it's what you've got. So the skill is in playing it right.'

Gillian laughed. 'You make it sound so easy,' she said.

'And so it will be. Stephen is confident. However did you manage to keep it to yourself, Gillian? I suppose he told you not to say anything until he'd talked to us. And of course we've hardly seen you over Christmas, you've been so busy."

'Keep what to myself?'

'About the phone call Stephen had from his friend in America. How this scriptwriter fellow was so excited he couldn't wait until morning and rang in what was almost the middle of the night here.'

'But ... yes, I know he had a call...'

Derek leant forward from the rear seat. 'There,' he said to Ella, 'didn't I bet you Gillian didn't know what he'd been doing? Not that I'm not grateful, Gillian, but ... but...'

'"But" nothing,' Ella cut in. 'Are you suggesting we ought to hide ourselves away because people who don't know us consider us handicapped, disabled, without the same opportunities as ordinary people? They may think we're sub-standard, but they're wrong. It's just a matter of accepting what Fate has given us and making it work for us.'

Listening to them, Gillian felt uneasy.

'You've talked about this to Stephen?' she asked, still uncertain exactly what "this" was.

'Of course we have,' Ella answered, 'and this friend of his is dead keen. They both say it could be a real box office buster.'

From the recesses of Gillian's mind she recalled the remark Stephen had made about the story of the cripple girl, the hideously scarred artist and the overriding power of love. She remembered her angry disappointment in him that he couldn't understand how such a suggestion would hurt their pride. But had she been wrong? She pulled the car into that same lay-by where less than a month previously she had stopped to try and comfort weeping Ella.

'Are you saying Stephen has discussed his

idea with his friend? You're right, Derek, I didn't know. When he first hinted at the idea I thought it was all a flight of fancy on his part. I don't know what he's trying to arrange.'

'There!' Derek said again. 'He means to be helpful – please don't think I don't appreciate what he suggests. But we can manage. Tell her we can manage, Ella. I'll try and arrange an exhibition in Oxford – and if that goes well perhaps in London. We don't need people going out of their way to make things easy for us.'

Ella wriggled round in her seat so that she could look directly at him.

'With just the two of us I expect we could muddle along. But Derek, how many artists make a fortune? And there are going to be three of us – and maybe more babies later on. If this friend of Stephen's is going to write our story as a screenplay, if he can persuade one of the big film companies to bring it out, don't you see how splendid it would be? It would bring us proper money, and even better it would stir people's interest in the real Derek Denvers. It would help sell your pictures. He'll make it a really great love story, that's the whole point of it.' There was something about Ella's expression that made Gillian uncomfortable; her smile held triumph rather than happiness. 'We'd have enough money to live much better – and we'd have it not because of Mumsie trying to be tactful and bring us things, but because we are who we are, we are what we are.'

'We'll have money, Ella. I'll make money, I

293

swear I will.'

'Yes, of course you will. I know your work is good. But just wait until our story is on the cinema screens, everyone will know your name, *everyone*, not just highbrow people who read what the art critics write. And they won't look at us with sympathy either. Oh no! They'll see us as special, *romantic*, two beautiful people in each other's eyes. That's the whole point of the story.'

'And it's true,' Derek said, resting his hand on her shoulder. 'But what's that got to do with the World and his Wife?'

'You can understand, can't you Gillian?' Ella turned to her for support.

'I can understand from both angles. I was furious with Stephen when he suggested it. It seemed like exposing something personal and beautiful and turning it into over-emotional entertainment.'

'Yes, that's about right,' Derek said.

'But then there is the other angle,' Gillian went on, thoughtfully. 'Think how proud this baby of yours will be in a few years time to know that its parents have the sort of love that sets them apart. Forget the temptation of making easy money from it, just think of it as ... as...'

'As a gift from the gods,' Ella chuckled.

Gillian wished she hadn't said it. As long as she had known her, Ella had been uncomplaining, seeming to accept, hiding her frustration and, until she met Derek, living on dreams.

Perhaps her maternal instinct, developing in line with her advancing pregnancy, was making her realize no one can live on dreams. Hadn't she felt the same herself when she had been expecting Debbie? If Derek had been happy to go along with the idea, Gillian could have accepted it; but, glancing in the driver's mirror, she saw the hurt expression in his eyes and her heart ached for him.

'Anyway,' she said as she restarted the car, 'don't count your chickens. The fact that some chap is prepared to exaggerate your situation and try and sell his work to a film company doesn't mean he'll be successful. If I were you, Derek, I'd work hard on preparing an exhibition in Oxford, something you can be sure of.'

'Silly, of course one of the big producers will see what a wonderful film it could be,' Ella answered, speaking with excited assurance. 'It'll be the greatest love story since Romeo and Juliet.'

Gillian dropped them off by the park gate and left them to walk home as Derek had suggested. It was uphill most of the way and she had intended to try to persuade them to stay in the car, but instinct told her they needed time by themselves. Perhaps Ella would put her excitement to one side long enough to tell him the things she had said on that drive home a few weeks before, to make him realize that it was because of the love they had for each other that neither her own disability nor his disfigurement cast a shadow on their happiness.

Except for the weekend parties of "horsey people" as Helen still referred to them, and a few business people who had used Hunters' Lodge even in David's time, the hotel was fairly quiet during the first two months of the year.

'It's ages and ages since Dad took me and Helen with him,' Debbie complained. 'There's no fun at all. It's even too rainy for me to ride in the lane on my bike.'

'Never mind, sweetie,' Helen answered, speaking before Gillian had a chance to tell her erstwhile cheerful daughter to stop grizzling and find something to do. 'I'll tell you what we'll do – if your mummy says it's all right for me to take you – I'll take my car and drive us to Brindley. I still have my whole month's sweet coupons. We'll buy a bag of sweets and we'll ask the baker if he has any stale bread or buns or something, then we'll walk to the lake in the park and feed the swans. Is that all right, Gillian?'

'It sounds a good idea. But whether Debbie deserves a treat is another matter,' Gillian answered. Then, seeing the way Debbie scowled, 'Put your bottom lip in Debbie, before you step on it.' Just for a second the scowl lingered, then it vanished as the little girl giggled and in a rush of affection put her arms around Gillian's waist and hugged her.

'Will you be OK if I go out, Mum?'

'I'll manage. Run and get ready – see your hands are clean, go to the loo, get a fresh hanky and bring your hat and coat.'

'OK. Quick as a flash, Auntie Helen.' And she was gone.

'Thanks, Helen. It's even been too wet for her to go out on Lyndy. I'll see to the table flowers and when I get the fresh ones for the bar I'll put them in a vase. Not my strong point, but you can tweak them up when you get back if they need it.'

Helen nodded. 'I changed the water in the table vases and don't worry too much about the bar. Just dump them in water and I'll do them properly later. Poor Debs, she really is out of sorts today. She misses Stephen. Usually he tries to take her somewhere on a Saturday. When you're little a week seems a long time.'

The relationship between the two women had definitely improved since they'd first been thrown together after David's death. Gillian had long since ceased to expect that Helen should want to do something with her life instead of wasting her days and contributing nothing to the running of the hotel other than being charming to the guests and using her artistic skill on the flower arrangements. She was honest enough to acknowledge that without Helen, her own challenge would have been much more difficult. Somehow they had each slotted into place as comfortably as pieces of a well cut jigsaw puzzle and, especially after Stephen's return, Helen's role had become ever more important. If she hadn't been there for Debbie, Gillian had no doubt he would have resented her commitment to Hunters' Lodge. And without Helen, it would have been impossible for him to take Debbie with him as he had so often during the summer months.

Already they were half-way through the school term. By the time the Easter holidays came there might be events for him to cover where Debbie – and so Helen too – could accompany him. For the last five days he had been travelling in Germany, sending back to his own country reports on the rebuilding work, writing about the American Army bases he visited and, for good measure, throwing in a touch of romance when he talked to a soldier who had lost his heart to the daughter of the local baker. Mostly, though, in the early days of the year, Stephen had chased after news items, telling his story always from the personal angle of the people affected. There had been an explosion in a factory which took one short paragraph to describe, to be followed by the human angle: a man who lay unconscious with a distraught wife only too pleased to bare her soul; a blazing house and the heroism of a neighbour who'd rescued the puppy who'd been shut inside. Dig the surface of any incident and there would be a story waiting to be written and elaborated.

The one thing that made the start of that year different from any other was the enthusiasm shown by Stephen's scriptwriter friend for Ella and Derek's story, or rather of Stephen's slant on it. Gillian tried to believe his confidence in it was good news. Derek appeared to have accepted the idea, so she liked to believe that Ella must have opened her heart to him and made him understand that for her the story angle was no more than the simple truth: she saw his face, and indeed the scars on his body too, as nothing that set him apart; to her he was, and always would be, perfect.

The school term had only a week and a half to run when Stephen presented his idea to Gillian. Driving back from an assignment on the south coast where he had attended the launching of a new lifeboat, he had arrived in Ockbury and seen Helen waiting at the school gate with a group of mothers. A toot on his horn, an unusual horn that played three notes and immediately attracted her attention, and she rushed across the road to where he had drawn up. If some of the waiting women looked knowingly at each other, no one voiced their thoughts, thoughts that Helen didn't suspect.

After she'd spoken to him for a moment, she left Stephen and returned to the school gate.

'Debbie will be over the moon. She loves it when her daddy meets her,' she told the group she looked on as her friends. Probably there were those amongst them who were disappointed as they acknowledged this wasn't a woman with designs on someone else's husband. Then they forgot the incident as in a clamour of voices the children rushed towards the gate.

'Now listen, girls,' Stephen said as greetings over, he started the engine. 'Driving home I've been having a think. And this is the idea. I have some work to do in Paris; I shall go over on the ferry at the end of the week. You have only three days of school after that, Debs, and who can complain if you bunk off just for that little while? Schools don't do any work as near the end of term as that. Then I'm due for a break. I've been talking to the New York office and I've got things fixed. We'll all go across at the weekend. You two girls can kick your heels just while I'm doing what I have to do, then we'll take a break over there.'

'And Mum? But Dad, that's Easter and I heard her say that they were booked right up.'

'So I believe. It'll be just the three of us. Same as always, Debs. It's no use suggesting Gillian comes. I reckon she thinks she's indispensable.'

Debbie frowned. She felt uncomfortable. Even though she didn't really understand what he was saying, she knew from his tone that he was cross about her mother and that made her feel funny inside. She just wished grown-ups didn't make things difficult; why couldn't they all just enjoy doing nice things?

'Did Mum say it's OK for me to go? I mean, did she say I could stay off school before the end of term?'

'Oh, don't you worry your pretty head on that account. I'll fix her. She doesn't know anything about any of it yet awhile, I only heard myself when I called the office back home in New York.' Then, to Helen, 'What about you, Helen? How does Paris in springtime appeal, eh?'

'It sounds like paradise.' There was something in the way she said it that momentarily made him take his eyes off the road and glance at her.

'I guess if that's what we look for in it, that's what we shall find. Paradise is right out there waiting for us to grasp.'

Debbie didn't like what she thought of as "silly talk". She didn't know how to join in.

'Can I be the one to tell Mum, Dad?' she asked, standing so that she poked her head between the two in the front seats.

'Best you leave it to me, Kiddo. Best not to let her know we've got it all set up before she even hears about it. And that goes for you too, Helen. Maybe I ought to have talked to Gillian about it before we got it all cut and dried. I know she'll agree just like she always has, but tact can be my middle name. Not a word about it from any of us for the present. I'll pick my moment.'

'That would be kinder,' Helen agreed. 'It might hurt her feelings if she thought we were making plans without her knowing.'

Debbie clutched at the word "kinder" and felt satisfied. Auntie Helen was always kind. Now, with that nasty uncertain feeling gone, she felt warm and excited. The three of them always had such a good time together.

On that occasion, Stephen had only been away for one night, but even one night made his homecoming something of an event. Gillian consciously took special care as she dressed for the evening, although in truth the end result was

301

the same, for never was she anything but perfectly groomed and made-up. The only difference was that on the evenings when he had been away, she dressed with him in mind, knowing she meant to look her best. If, buried deep in her mind was the knowledge that in the beauty stakes she couldn't hold a candle to Helen, she wasn't going to admit it. The evening was fairly quiet and she was able to join them with her drink. There was a comfortable, friendly atmosphere and, not for the first time, it struck her that Helen seemed happier. Was she getting over losing David? No, Gillian was sure she wasn't. It was as if she had come to terms with what life had to offer. And at that thought, Gillian's mind turned to Ella.

'There have been no phone calls or messages for you,' she told Stephen as she drew up a third chair at their table in the otherwise empty bar. 'I wonder how your friend – Dick Troughton is it? – I wonder how he's getting on with that script.'

'I might give him a call tomorrow. It'll keep the youngsters buoyed up to hear how things are coming along.'

All in all it was a comfortable, friendly, relaxed atmosphere, one that disproved the adage that two's company and three's a crowd.

Later, three became two.

'Good to be home,' Stephen said, just as he might if he'd been away for a month instead of one night. Their love making always left him not merely satisfied physically, but on a broader basis satisfied in the knowledge that he had carried Gillian with him. He felt at peace with himself and even though he would have liked to have drifted into sleep, he knew this was the right moment to talk to her about Easter.

'The week running up to Easter I have a mission in Paris. Before I leave I need to go into the London office, so I thought I'd take the train in the morning. And I want a day in town for another reason. I've been thinking, thinking about Easter and the school holiday coming up. What do you say to Debs coming with me to Paris? It would be a great experience for her. Helen would look after her while I'm working.'

'You can't just take her abroad like that. She hasn't a passport.'

He smiled in the darkness, his plan coming nearer fruition by the second.

'Why do you imagine I said I was glad to be going to London? Make sure I have all the details: your details, her birth certificate, anything I'll need. Remember the photograph I had taken of her back last summer so that I could carry it in my wallet? I guess I must have known this would crop up at some stage, she's plenty old enough to appreciate overseas travel. I guess that's what I had in mind when I got extra copies and made sure they were passport size, the guy who took them told me they'd be OK. Just one thing, though, Gilly: to be on the safe side it might be as well if you wrote a note for me to take her abroad, just something to the effect that I am applying for a passport for our daughter named so-and-so. They may be sniffy if both parents aren't in agreement. It probably won't be necessary but I don't want little Kiddo to be disappointed at the last moment. I'll go and collect her passport there and then, no messing about waiting for the post.'

If he thought he was home and dry, he found he was mistaken.

'I'll talk to Miss Aldridge, Debbie's head-mistress. But if the school objects, then you'll have to go on ahead of the others.'

'Better still,' Stephen answered and she could tell from his tone that he was smiling, 'I'll take her to school in the morning and have a talk to this Miss Aldridge. Trust me, Gillie. I have a winning way when I need it.'

And she couldn't argue with *that*. Wasn't that exactly why everything always fell neatly into his lap? As she turned to settle for sleep, some of Gillian's euphoria had vanished. She was left with an all too familiar sense of emptiness.

True to his word, Stephen worked his charm on Miss Aldridge and it was agreed that for Debbie the term would end on the coming Friday. From her first day there she had made playground friends but, once word spread that her father was taking her abroad, friendship developed into something akin to hero worship. She was in her element. So too was Helen. Never before had she applied for a passport and she could see now why Stephen had insisted she too be photographed the previous summer. After his phone call to the New York office, on his way home from the launching of the RNLI boat he had collected two application forms.

Perhaps Gillian was naïve in not realizing the forward planning that had been going on, but when he returned from London with two new passports in their blue booklets it didn't occur to her to wonder how he had managed to have one issued for Helen, who would have been responsible for completing her own application, as well as Debbie's, for which she had given him all the necessary documentation.

'You know what I think?' Ella said when Gillian told her about the trip. 'I think you ought to keep your eyes open.'

'What am I missing that I ought to be seeing?' Gillian laughed, silently putting Ella's unsmiling countenance down to the fact that she was probably getting weary and finding her days long and uncomfortable. Her body had more than made up for its slow start; at not even eight months she was enormous and was plagued with cramp.

'You're years older than me, and much more experienced – about men and that sort of thing. But Gill, there's more to being married than going to bed together. How often do you and Stephen go out together and have any fun? Never. Just look at the hours *she* spends with him – Helen, I mean. I bet he tells her all about his work, probably talks about where he comes from, listens to her too. And then there's Debbie.'

'Debbie's fine. Of course she loves having

him, she was years enough with no father.'

'Oh well, you know best.' And that seemed to be the end of the matter until she threw in, 'I've never liked her, never trusted her. When David died, she seemed to think she was the only one to be hurt. She wears her heart on her sleeve. I suppose that's what I hate.'

'In that case you are barking up the wrong tree, Ella. If Helen had designs on Stephen as anything but a friend and Debbie's father, she wouldn't have the guile to disguise it. Now what about you? Did you get a better night last night?'

'Me? The cramp is horrid, but it won't be for much longer now. I just want to get on with things. And one really good thing: Derek has accepted what's going to happen once the script gets accepted.'

'*If* it gets accepted. They turn down more than they accept, you may be sure.'

'But not this one. I just *know* it will be accepted. To start with I could tell he hated the idea, it was a sort of blow to his ability. But I think I've made him understand. I'm just proud, so proud I could burst, that no matter how weepy and mushy they make the film, it really will tell our story. You know what? No more than a year ago I lived on dreams, but no dream can come near to touching reality. We had a letter from the writer this morning. He is coming to England and wants to meet us. I expect he wants to make sure they get the right sort of people to play our parts, when the time comes.

306

We're so lucky, Derek and me too. Sometimes I get frightened it can't last.'

'Then don't. You both deserve your luck. And your mother sees you are managing well on your own; that was something you were both determined to show her. If she didn't think you were managing she wouldn't spend so much time in Devon with Paul. She goes so much more often than she used to.'

'When Dad was alive she had her hands full, with him and then me too.' Yet Ella seemed to find no satisfaction in Kathleen's new freedom.

'Is she staying down there for Easter? I had a card this morning but it was only one of those "having a good time" sort, she didn't mention coming back.'

For a moment Ella seemed to hesitate, then she answered, 'At her age it's ... it's ... I was going to say it's disgusting. And if it were anyone but Mumsie that's what I would say. She is seventy-one, for goodness sake. There's this man she's met. Paul told me when I telephoned from the village call box. I wanted to know which day she was coming back so that Derek could light the Aga and get the place warm. But she was out and Paul seemed tickled pink about what she's up to. Major someone-or-other, a widower as old as she is herself, that's what's keeping her down there. Paul says they are smitten with each other. But he said he was giving me warning because she intends to come back – she and "Major Blimp" – and tell me herself. He guessed I'd not be pleased, I suppose.'

The idea of Kathleen finding romance seemed as unlikely to Gillian as it did to Ella, but in her view it was anything but disgusting.

'If it's serious, can't you be glad for her, Ella? She must be very lonely at the Manor by herself. She had you to care for when your father died, and when you fell in love with Derek I bet you didn't give it a thought that she would be losing such an important part of her life.'

'Of course I didn't. Mothers expect their daughters to marry and have lives of their own. Anyway Derek and I are young. Love – and all that – is for young people. At her age it's horrid – yes, like I said, it is disgusting. They are old, both of them. I know it's not right to think about your parents that way and I never did with Mumsie and Daddy, but imagine these two on their honeymoon. It's revolting. Paul was pleased as punch.'

Gillian smiled at her young friend. 'And quite right too,' she said. 'Didn't you just say to me that there is more to being married than sleeping in the same bed? Be happy for her Ella. Anyway, very likely they are like Helen and Stephen – easy companions.'

'Humph,' was the only reply.

When Stephen returned from a long day in London, Gillian was busy in the bar and Helen had already seen Debbie to bed. Despite Helen's recent more relaxed manner, without

Stephen's company she still went straight to the visitors' lounge after dinner. And that's how it was that she didn't hear him arrive home.

'I'm back, honey,' he greeted Gillian, just as he always did, and waited for her to pour his whisky and soda.

'Did you collect the passports?' she asked, passing him his glass. 'Was Miss Aldridge agreeable about Debbie missing school?'

'Sure, she was. More than agreeable, she was keen. Said it would do more for her education than end-of-term frolics in the classroom. The Kiddo's asleep I suppose?'

'Hours ago. I haven't seen Helen, though.'

'I guess she'll be keeping the old Crosbie ladies company. I'll take my drink into the lounge and give her her passport.' Briefly, Ella's warning came back to Gillian, only to be pushed out of her mind as nonsense. Without Debbie to bring them together and give them common interests, he and Helen wouldn't have given each other a thought. Even now their relationship was as easy as might be between brother and sister.

He didn't come back to the bar, and she was already in bed by the time she heard him coming along the passage of their own quarters. A gentle click of Debbie's door as he looked in on the sleeping child, then she heard water in the shower. He was a long time coming to bed, but she was wide awake when he threw off his bathrobe and climbed in by her side.

'No spanners thrown in the works from the

London office? You are still off to Paris at the weekend?' she asked as she wriggled closer to him.

'Yep. Then I've fixed a bit of leave to follow on after Easter. I've got one or two columns held over, nothing topical, just word pictures. They'll fill the gap.'

'So how long will you be away?' She had thought four days of work, then the long Easter weekend, but it seemed he had plans for another week after that.

'I shall take the car, then we'll make the most of the time. I'll be able to show Debs something of the world. It's been quite a day. Reckon we'll head straight off to sleep tonight.' A rare thing for Stephen.

Lying in the darkness, she suspected that, like her, he was wide awake.

'Ella and Derek had a letter from your friend this morning, about the script he's working on. He is coming over to England and wants to meet them. I suppose he wants to make sure he has portrayed them as they really are. Just imagine being in their position. Suppose a film were to be made about us...'

'Us? Why should it be?'

'That's what I mean,' she tried to explain. 'We are just ordinary people, and that's what they are too. She can't walk, he's been in an accident, but none of that makes them different characters. It won't spoil things for them, Stephen?'

'It will make life a heck of a lot easier, I'd say.

Imagine the repercussions once the ordinary public knows their names. All this high-flown talk about selling his paintings – what sort of a living could they hope for on that? What he needs is to sell prints of the originals; they don't need fine frames, just something to sit comfortably on the wall of the sort of two bedrooms and a box room house. That way instead of selling *one*, he could sell thousands and if he only made a few shillings on each one it would give them something to raise a family on.'

'A sad way for dreams to end,' she answered. If only he would agree, or give some sign that he understood.

'Just wait till we see Debs' face when I show her her passport,' he said, his mind already moving on as he turned his back on her and prepared to give the impression of going to sleep.

The travellers were to leave home very early on Saturday morning, so while Gillian was busy in the bar on Friday evening, Stephen and Helen carried the luggage out to the car. The week-enders had arrived in time for dinner, so the evening was busy. There was nothing new in Gillian being grateful to Helen; the thought cropped up at regular intervals during each day but never more than on that Friday.

'Here comes the first horse trailer,' Helen said, coming through the front door of the hotel with a bunch of daffodils she'd collected from the far end of the garden.

'They're early. I thought I'd have time to sort Debbie's things before anyone came.'

'Leave her packing to me, Gillian. I thought it would be fun for her to help with it when we get back from school. Half the excitement of going away is getting ready.'

Gillian's gratitude was warm. 'You're a saint. And you'll have more idea of what you'll be doing. Will she need her party dress, for instance?'

'I don't know, but I bet she'll want to take it. Gillian,' she spoke hesitantly, as if she couldn't find the words for what she wanted to say, 'I'm *not* a saint – you shouldn't have said that. The guests will be here in a few moments – and we've both got a lot to do – but going away like this, going abroad where I've never been before, everything new and hopeful ... I don't know what I'm trying to say. Only that it's not right that you thank *me* for things I do for Debbie. Looking after her has helped me to see that life isn't over. I wanted it to be; after David died I just wanted to die too. But, even though I don't love him any less, I love being alive too. Is that wrong? Does it mean I'm shallow and selfish? I mean, is it right that while you're left here that I can feel so ... so ... so *eager?*'

Gillian had never heard her speak like it, never heard her speak at such length. But the minute or two while the guests were taking their trailer to the stable block and handing it over to Teddy was no time to start an in-depth analysis of Helen's innermost feelings.

'Of one thing I'm absolutely certain,' Gillian replied. 'If David is watching us, he will be relieved and happy that you're eager for life again. You're ready now to enjoy a holiday. A change of surroundings is probably the best thing in the world for making you look to the future.'

'You mean my future ought to be different?'

At that, Gillian's laugh was genuine. 'Well, I hope it will be. You're young, you're pretty, you deserve something better than being at the beck and call of someone else's child.'

Some of Helen's new hopefulness evaporated. 'When you put it like that it sounds useless – it sounds *ugly*. I never look on Debbie as someone else's child. I mean, I couldn't love her more if I were her real mother. Honestly, Gillian.'

'I know. And it's mutual – she looks on you as her special property. Oh here they come. You're sure you don't mind seeing to the luggage?'

'Debbie and I will do it together.'

And that's what they did, Helen not having the heart to refuse anything special the child considered ought to go with her, whether it was her party frock or her favourite play clothes, her teddy bear or even the roller skates Stephen – in the guise of Santa Claus – had put in the sack at the end of her bed.

Amidst great excitement they said their good-byes just after seven o'clock the next morning.

'You'll be all right, Mum? I wish you were

313

coming too, then it would be perfect. But you'd only be thinking about here all the time. You'll be all right, though?'

'Yes, sweetie, I'll be fine. You have a really wonderful holiday and be sure to send me a postcard – in your best writing so I can show it off.'

'Silly Mum,' Debbie giggled. On a different occasion she might have scowled at her mother's remark, seeing her as a killjoy. But on that early spring morning nothing could kill the joy that seemed to be bubbling inside her as she settled on to the back seat of the car. Stephen checked the luggage was all in, and then came over to Gillian. As she raised her face he kissed her, a light kiss on the forehead, but even then he didn't move away.

'Wish us well, Gillian.'

She laughed. 'Oh I do. But wishing doesn't come into it, I *know* you'll have a wonderful time.'

'And Gilly, you know we'll take care of her.'

'Of course you will. Get on your way, Stephen. Being serious first thing in the morning doesn't agree with you.'

Again he kissed her, this time on the cheek, and moved to get into the car. But even then they didn't go, for this time it was Helen who climbed out and almost ran to Gillian, giving her a bearlike hug that was so out of character Gillian drew back in surprise.

'Gillian, this means everything to me. Everything.'

'Then hop back in the car and get started,' came Gillian's cheery reply, aimed at disguising her discomfort at Helen's sudden burst of emotion.

'Yes, yes, I will. So much I want to say...'

'Say it when you get home. Off you go.' Gillian's words were almost drowned in the sound of the car horn and Stephen's, 'Hey there, are you with us, Helen?'

Then, the car door slammed, the engine started, they were off with cries of 'Bye Mum', from Debbie who was kneeling on the back seat to wave through the rear window, 'We'll keep in touch,' from Stephen and, 'Feel awful, leaving you like this,' from kind and gentle Helen. That was the last thing Gillian heard as she turned towards the stables ready to help Teddy get the horses saddled up for the pre-breakfast riders. She was thankful the hotel was busy for the weekend, and she was even more thankful that the days leading up to Easter would be buzzing with preparation. She kept her mind firmly on what she had to do, refusing to acknowledge the aching void in her life. Yet there was no way she could escape the echo that had haunted her through the years on her own, 'We share nothing except sex.' Her heart hadn't let her believe him. But what else did they share now? There was no denying that he adored Debbie. Easy for *him*, came her silent retort. He had discovered an adorable seven-year-old, grown up for her years – and what was he doing? Buying her everything she decided she wanted, destroying her ability to accept life as it came. That pout had become all too frequent recently and yet when he'd first come back there could have been no happier child anywhere than she had been.

'Morning, Mrs Sinclair,' Teddy greeted her. 'I hear Debbie's gone off. She came rushing over to say goodbye.'

'She's over the moon with excitement. Oh well, Teddy, here at Hunters' Lodge it's business as usual, I fear.'

The young groom gave her a quick look, surprised at her unusual tone.

'I guess you would like to have gone off to foreign lands with them. But I tell you one thing: for me, there's no place I'd rather be than this. Me and Mavis, well, we're doing just fine, both of us sharing being part of Hunters' Lodge.'

'I know just what you mean,' she answered, a thousand memories crowding in on her, memories she tried to escape and yet dreaded ever losing. Sharing being part of Hunters' Lodge ... oh yes, she knew just what he meant.

The days went by and no word came from the travellers, despite Stephen's promise to keep in touch and Debbie's to send a card in her best handwriting. At Hunters' Lodge, through Easter weekend the rooms were fully booked and the restaurant bursting at the seams; then gradually during the following week the visitors departed and life slowed down. The following weekend was quiet, then a week of unchanging days – but still there was no word.

'No post for us this morning Mrs Sinclair, dear?' Margaret Crosbie asked, standing timidly in the open doorway of the office where Gillian was scanning through the mail. That was on the following Wednesday; by Friday they would have been gone for three weeks.

'Nothing I'm afraid,' Gillian answered, knowing without asking that what Jane and Margaret Crosbie waited for was a letter or card from Helen. 'Not for me either. Perhaps there's a hold-up in the postal service in France.'

'Yes, that'll probably be what's making their cards take so long. At this rate they'll get home first themselves. What day is it they arrive?'

'I don't think Stephen actually said. I just know that originally they were to be there while he was working and then for the Easter break. After that he was taking some leave and driving. But they must be back by the end of this week at the latest. Anyway Debbie starts school again on Tuesday.'

'One blessing, dear: you have no need to worry about little Debbie with Helen there to care for her. Not that her father wouldn't, of course,' she added quickly, frightened Gillian might take offence. 'Dear Helen, we used to worry so much about her. If ever a girl had a broken heart it was she when she lost dear David. Many a tear we shed for her. But, between ourselves, your Debbie was her salvation.'

'And she was certainly Debbie's. The poor mite would have had short shrift if she'd had to rely on *me* when I was learning about running this place.'

'Time is the greatest healer. Now, here you are as efficient as dear David, and Helen seeming to have got back in step again.' She leant forward so that her head was just inside the doorway, then looked around to make sure no one would hear, 'Prayers are private things, between us and our Maker, but because I'm sure you care for her and understand what a struggle she had when she lost him, I'll tell you. Each night Jane and I would kneel by our bedside and beg she would find consolation. So we knew that in the end she would come through and learn to be happy again. Such a dear, jolly girl she was before that dreadful accident.'

'Hark! There's a car coming up the drive.' Perhaps they were home. Perhaps they'd crossed on a night ferry. Both she and Margaret moved expectantly to the foyer window. But the car drove on towards the stables.

'The horse dentist,' she told Margaret. 'He'll be here working for some time; he has to file all their teeth. If you've nothing more interesting to do you might like to wander round and see how he does it.'

'Perhaps we will. There's a real feeling of spring in the air today. And I expect poor little Mrs Denvers will wheel herself round in her chair. Oh dear, oh dear, as Jane and I say, here we are old and with good healthy lives behind us, and that poor little soul and her nice hubby have everything stacked against them.'

'She wouldn't like to hear you say that, Miss Crosbie. Ella is tough. No one is ever going to tread over her.'

'It is to be hoped you're right. Well, Mrs Sinclair dear, I really have enjoyed our little chat. Jane will wonder where I am. And she'll be so disappointed the card hasn't come yet. But I'll tell her what you say – that there is probably a hold-up in France. And then of course there was Easter. Be sure we shall get a whole batch tomorrow.'

But tomorrow came, followed by Friday, then Saturday, and still there was no word.

It was then that Gillian decided it was time to make enquiries of the ferry company. If she gave them details of the outbound crossing, they would be able to check their records and see what date Stephen had booked for the return. In her mind it was easy, but in reality they could tell her nothing. That's when she did something she had never before contemplated doing: she felt in the pockets of the clothes Stephen had left hanging in his wardrobe. By nature he was a tidy man and she found nothing. By Monday, the day before the start of term, she was envisaging every possible disaster: a fire in their hotel, a motor car accident, a trip on the Seine and someone – Debbie – falling overboard.

It would be no use telephoning the village

constable. She must go to a higher source.

'Will you put me through to Brindley 370,' she instructed the operator. It was like living through a nightmare, but what else could she do?

Ten

There was no escaping the images of disaster. It took no more than the shrill sound of the telephone bell to turn Gillian's legs to jelly and tie her stomach in knots. And this was the woman who had lived through a broken marriage, as a single parent worked to make a life for herself and Debbie, felt as if a part of herself had been stripped away with David's death and made herself pick up the gauntlet of running Hunters' Lodge. She realized now that for months she had blinded herself to what deep in her heart she had known but refused to acknowledge: just as Stephen had said years ago, all they shared was sex. An important part of any marriage, that's what her subconscious had made her believe. But how could it ever be enough?

Now she had nowhere to hide from the truth that, just as Mike and Kathleen had both warned her, no happiness could come from making a new beginning for Debbie's sake. "The right stepfather would be better for her than the wrong natural father." And here her mind baulked away from facing that other truth: the rightness of being with Mike, the rightness of the relationship that had developed naturally between Debbie and him. If only she could talk to him now. The silent telephone tempted her just as it had so often. He'd been gone for more than half a year and in that time his only contact with Hunters' Lodge had been through their accountant.

In her mind's eye she imagined him riding over the glorious countryside with a pretty Irish colleen; she even looked back with shame to that first ride she had had with him when all her hard-fought-for restraint had snapped. And yet ... and yet ... she knew he had meant what he said on the day of Ella and Derek's wedding, when her stupidly unbelievable remark about it being "wedding excitement" had been no more than a lifeline to help them both. "Stephen is my future." And so he was, then and now, he had to be. Debbie may have appeared happy enough in her early years, but there could be no going back now that she had had known what it was like to have two parents.

But where was she? What could possibly have happened that neither Stephen nor Helen had been able to telephone? In the hotel she worked like an automaton; she smiled at guests, she cared for their welfare, she gave the same appearance of perfect grooming that she always had. Most of the staff had been there in David's day and out of affection for him they had stayed long enough to "give her a chance". Their respect for her had grown out of that trial period and, although she never lowered that barrier that held her aloof from them, they were content to stay, finding her to be a fair employer.

'She's a cold fish,' Sarah Wright told her parents. 'Never gives a hint what's going on in her mind. Mrs Sinclair ... one of these days I'll call her Gill like we always called him David and see whether she even notices.'

'Poor woman,' Mrs Wright said. 'Whatever can have happened to them?'

The police in England contacted their French counterparts, giving details of the missing trio and the registration number of Stephen's car. That same day at the end of the BBC early evening news bulletin, as so often, there followed an announcement concerning missing persons and asking for anyone with knowledge of Stephen Sinclair, an American, who was travelling with his young daughter and with Miss Helen Murdock, to please contact the police on Brindley 370. Gillian heard it and felt sick with fright.

'We just listened to the news,' Jane Crosbie whispered as she and her sister looked into the bar before going to the restaurant.

'News?' One word was all her sandpaper dry mouth could manage.

'They gave it like a little story, you know how they do. Your husband missing with little Debbie and Helen. Dear Helen, it wasn't what they said about her, not in so many words, but the inference was unkind. It seemed to hint that she had come between you and your husband. I do wish people wouldn't always look for such – such nasty underhand ways to explain things.'

'I expect it's on the wireless in France too if they have announcements like that, so someone is sure to know if anything is wrong. Even now it may just be the post. Stephen may have had a sudden job crop up out there. There must be a good reason they're so long.' She tried to put conviction into her voice even while her mind was racing in another direction. On the wireless ... insinuating Helen had been the cause of their going. She remembered Ella's warnings. She remembered her own certainty. But suppose Ella had been right, how much did she care? Not at all. The stark reply was the honest truth. Only now could she let herself admit how hard she had tried to make it work for Stephen and her, and yet in the year he'd been with her they had grown no closer. No, if he had transferred his affection (affection? How deep had it ever been?) to Helen, she felt no grief, she felt nothing. But Debbie is *mine*. Damn him, damn, damn, *damn* him. Don't let Debbie be hurt. Give her back to me. I don't give a damn about the others. I don't care if I never see them again. But Debbie is *my baby*. We managed without him before and so we can again.

Somehow she got through the evening, hoping with every minute for a call from Brindley to say that they had news and there was a good explanation for the silence. But no call came. It was after ten o'clock, and except for a few stragglers who liked to sit long over their coffee and seemed impervious to the watching eyes of the staff who were waiting to lay up for breakfast, everyone had gone when the door of the bar opened and holding it back with his foot, Derek pushed the wheelchair in.

'No news?' He asked too quietly for the one or two residents to hear.

Gillian shook her head. 'Not yet,' she answered. 'They'd phone from Brindley if anything came through. Let me get you a drink. Ella, what would you like?'

'Not for me. I've already had my milky cocoa. Derek's speciality. You're not busy, come and sit over there at the table.' Then, as Derek pushed her close to the table in the far corner – Stephen and Helen's corner – she gave Gillian what could only be described as "a knowing look", one out of keeping with her innocent and uncomplaining youthfulness. 'You wouldn't let yourself listen to what I was trying to tell you. She's as selfish as she is pretty, she knows just how to wheedle folk to give her what she wants. And she wanted a man, someone to fuss over her and protect her.'

'No. You're not right, Ella. She drives me insane sometimes – or she used to when she was so full of self-pity. But there's nothing like that between Stephen and her. And they both love Debbie.'

'So do you, but Helen doesn't hang around

you like she does around him.'

Derek looked uncomfortable. 'We mustn't jump to conclusions. Perhaps there has been an accident, a minor accident, just enough to put them in hospital. Debbie will be looked after.' What a dear he was. Gillian's expression softened as she looked at him. He who not many months ago would have hidden behind the pulled down wide brim of his hat and the turned up collar of his coat, now he pushed Ella into the hotel, prepared for the embarrassed stares of total strangers.

'Gillian, I've had a telegram from Dick Troughton – you know, the scriptwriter. We had expected him to visit us at the bungalow but he has asked us to go to London tomorrow instead.'

Ella beamed with self-importance as she took up the story.

'He doesn't know how soon the baby's due. But look at me! I get more enormous every day. Think of poor Derek having to haul me on and off trains. So we've come to say, may I please spend tomorrow here?'

'I'm going up in the morning.' Derek took up the story. 'But I imagine I'll be back in time for dinner. Can you keep us a table? I shan't leave home until Ella's sorted out and ready to bring herself across here.'

Willingly Gillian agreed and by the time the young couple took their departure, the residents still sitting in the bar decided to move up to their rooms. At last the long-sitting diners went home and the dining room was laid up for morning. Hunters' Lodge was ready for the night. And so another day came to an end, another day with no news and with fear tightening its hold.

The next morning Gillian heard Derek's "hearse" depart for the railway station, then a few minutes later Ella tapped at the window. It seemed the day was set to follow its usual pattern, the only difference that there was no Derek to lift her to and from her chair at the start and finish of the morning shopping trip. Somehow the two of them managed, Ella trying to guide herself by hanging on to the frame of the car while Gillian "lifted" and heaved her in and out.

Each time the telephone rang they waited, Gillian half expecting and half dreading what the call might be. But by the end of the afternoon, the only personal one concerned them both, for it was Kathleen.

'Gillian, my dear. I've had a letter from Ella. Is there news?'

'Not yet. Someone must have seen them. But Kathleen, there can't have been an accident,' Gillian's voice defied argument. 'The police would have been notified and I should have heard. And what about you? Are you enjoying yourself?'

'More than that. Gillian, I am coming back to the Manor, and a friend – a very dear friend, Edward Masters – is coming with me. He had

326

an appointment in Exeter this afternoon but as soon as he arrives we shall start back. I can't speak to Ella on the phone, so will you tell her? And Gillian, a lot to ask of you I dare say, but please try to help her accept it.'

Nothing could have taken Gillian's mind off herself more instantly.

'How nice he's coming with you, Kathleen. Ella will be delighted to meet him. We have talked about how pleased we are for you. But let her tell you for herself, she's right here by my side.' Then, her hand over the mouthpiece, 'Be kind, Ella. Make it easy for her,' in an urgent whisper as she passed the phone.

Ella was surprisingly cooperative, a sign perhaps that her own mind was centred firmly on her own affairs these days.

The second call was from Derek. He would try and get back that evening, but not until a later train, so could Gillian give Ella a double room for the night and he'd get there as soon as he could.

That led to a trip to see Miss Henderson to arrange for her to come to help Ella to bed just as she used to before she was married. She was to have her usual room, Number 14, over the visitors' lounge from which there was a door leading to a straight flight of stairs and no other accommodation but the one double bedroom and shower.

And so the day finally came to an end. Ella was safely in bed; the diners had gone and the last of the guests had vacated the bar. There was still no sign of Derek so Gillian was prepared to get up and unlock the door when he arrived.

With her make-up creamed off and her hair brushed, each of her nightly preparations automatically carried out in her habitual methodical way, Gillian was about to start to undress when she was pulled up short, all power of her limbs seeming to leave her, by the bell of the telephone in her sitting room. This must be *it*! No one else would call at midnight. Just as her strength seemed to have gone, so it returned and she rushed along the corridor and almost threw herself at the instrument.

'Yes, hello,' she shouted into the mouthpiece.

'Hold the line please. I have a call for you from the United States.' Her heart sank. A call from the United States must be for Stephen, and hard on the heels of that thought came another: it must be his newspaper expecting him to be at home. No wonder her heart was banging.

Then a distant ringing tone and another wait. Seconds seemed like minutes.

'Hello! Hello!' she said anxiously, as if that would hurry things.

'Gillian? Is that you Gillian?' Could it be Stephen? No, of course not. They must all sound the same. 'Gillian, are you there? Can you hear me?'

'Stephen? But they said the call was from America. Where are you? Where's Debbie?'

'Sure it's me, and that's right, I'm back home in New York.'

New York or anywhere else, it wasn't where

328

he was that mattered.

'You left Debbie with Helen? But they haven't come home. What's happened? Why didn't you phone and tell me? You had no business to leave them, Helen had never been abroad and Deb...'

'Stop talking, why can't you, and listen for a minute.' It took a lot to ruffle Stephen and, although she believed it must be an illusion, he sounded not only calm but speaking with exaggerated patience, as if he might be humouring a frightened child. 'What kind of a father do you take me for? As if I'd have left them in France without me. You mustn't worry about Debs; she is absolutely fine.'

'You should have let me know. When are you coming back? I must go and see Miss Aldridge and explain why she'll be late starting term.'

'Why in heck's name can't you stop talking and just listen? My job in Europe is over. I've been brought back home. They told me when I was in London getting the passports.'

Gillian pulled a chair near to the phone and sat down, gripping the receiver hard to try to stop her hand shaking. She had heard exactly what he'd said, but surely she must have misunderstood him. What he meant was that he'd taken Debbie for a holiday and would be bringing – no, not bringing, he'd finished in England – *sending* her home in Helen's care. She made herself think that way. She blocked her mind to anything else. 'You knew when you left here? You lied to me.' And when he didn't answer immediately, 'Stephen? Are you there?'

'Sure I'm here. Just stop talking a minute and listen to what I have to say. For more than seven years after we split up you deceived me. You kept it from me that I had a daughter. She's the most important thing that's ever happened to me. And I can give her a great life. What sort of time has she had with you? Always she's been pushed aside and looked after by someone else. It won't be like that any more...'

'Oh no?' she sneered, feeling she could score a point and clutching at the chance. 'Are you going to give up work so that you can be with her?'

'Don't be ridiculous. If you'd been interested in anything except running that bloody little hotel or galloping around the countryside on some nag, you might have realized what was happening. The one thing you did right was refusing to remarry. Now I don't have to wait for a divorce; I'm free to take a wife. As long as Debs is with Helen she'll have as much care and love as any mother can give her, and a lot more than she ever had from you.'

Gillian opened her mouth to speak but the words didn't come. It couldn't be happening ... he had no right ... but he did, he had the right of a father ... they'd been divorced before Debbie was born so the court hadn't decided that she had sole custody ... his name was on Debbie's birth certificate ... he could provide a good life for her ... Helen was like a mother to her ... In the second that she seemed devoid of speech these things crowded her mind.

Then her voice came back to her and she shouted, 'You can't just take her away from me. She's *my* baby, my little girl.'

'Calm down, Gilly. Remember what you said to me the day I arrived at Hunters' Lodge, the day I met her? I told you she belonged to me as much as to you – and what did you answer? That she *belonged* to no one.'

'Why the hell did you come back? We were all right as we were. She was happy. You can't do this.' She felt trapped. 'I'll see a solicitor, I'll take it to court.'

'No, you won't. We can't do that to her. If you could have seen her over these last weeks, you would understand. In France she had a wonderful time, we both saw to it that she did. We sailed out from Cherbourg and you'd have thought heaven had fallen at her feet. She played games on deck, and oh boy! Didn't she just love the food on board! It was a US ship and the poor kid had never seen food like it. We only docked early this morning. But we haven't wasted any time. There's an apartment to fix, and arrangements for Helen and me to tie the knot.'

'You can't do it ... Please...' Hardly more than a whisper, reality taking an ever firmer grip on her.

'Hey, hey, honey, that's no way to talk. I offered marriage to you and you turned it down. Can't you see things from Debs' angle? She needs two parents and she needs them to be a proper Mr and Mrs, not just hanging on to the name after a divorce. We can give her a new start. And, like I was telling you, I've never known the kid so happy.'

'What time is it there? Is she in bed or can she talk to me?'

'Helen's kept her watching the dancing till I signal. Promise not to upset her. Listen Gilly, I'm not doing this to try and knock you, and I swear to God I've done what I've done because I know it's right for the Kiddo.' A pause so slight it was hardly a pause at all before he added, 'I never knew I could love anyone like I do Debs.'

Gillian knew the battle was lost. 'I won't upset her. But I must hear her speak.'

'Sure, sure, honey. First there's Helen, she wants to talk to you too. I'll wait with Debbie.'

'Gillian,' Helen's voice sounded timid. 'I don't know what to say to you. You've been kind to me and I've done this to you. But I love him more than you do, I'm sure of that. I really care about his work and I want to know his friends and just be part of his life.'

'You don't have to explain. Honestly, *honestly*, I'm not even interested in where he is or what he does – except for Debbie. Helen, how can I do what he wants? How can I let her go?' Suddenly they were just two women, both loving Debbie, both understanding the pain.

'I'm so sorry.' Helen was crying. 'Hearing you miserable is awful. But Gillian, he *is* her father, and he lost all her baby days. It's so

332

awful when parents fight over their children. All any of us want is that she should be happy and have a good life filled with love. And we can give it to her, I promise you.'

'Let me talk to her.' It was worse than any nightmare, for after a nightmare comes the relief of waking.

'Mum?' As if she were right there in the room, came Debbie's young voice. 'Oh Mum, I wish you could just see it all. This hotel is huge. D'you know Mum, there's a *gigantic* arrangement of flowers, it's almost as big as ... as big as the table in the sitting room. Auntie Helen can't stop looking at it. Everything's big – and sort of different ... brighter, um, er, shinier. You should see the things they bring us to eat! Wish you could see it all, Mum. And the ship too, you would have loved it on the ship. We've been having such a great time. And Mum, this afternoon Dad and Auntie Helen and me went to look at apartments. We found one that was really super. Dad says that's the one we're going to have – well, if you say I can stay – but Mum,' and here the first note of doubt crept in, and her voice lost some of it's certainty, 'if you're going to be all alone, well I ought to come home, oughtn't I? But if Auntie Helen's staying over here, it would be hard for you with me and the hotel too.'

'Debbie, darling Debbie...' She mustn't cry, she *mustn't.*

'Silly Mum,' Debbie was clearly embarrassed by such an unusual show of affection from her mother. 'But Mum, you are all right if I'm not there aren't you? And what about Lyndy? You'll look after Lyndy?'

'You know I will. Anyway, when you come back you'll want to ride her.'

'You bet I will. And Dad says that if I live out here, go to school and all that ... if you say I can do that, then I can still see you. He says sometimes I can have holidays with you. Auntie Helen will come too, then you won't be worried if you have to be busy.'

It was that last sentence that was Gillian's final undoing as the tears spilled. In that moment she hated Hunters' Lodge and all it had done to her life. Keeping her mouth rigid in an effort to control her voice she said, 'I'll take some time off when you come. Promise.'

Debbie giggled, a giggle that didn't hold as much mirth as embarrassment, covering the fact that she was floundering out of her depth. Despite Gillian's effort to keep her voice free of emotion, Debbie was uncomfortable.

'Debbie, tell me the cross your heart honest truth: do you want to stay in New York with your daddy?'

'Of course I do. But I want to be with you too.'

Gillian nodded, frightened to speak.

'Mum? Can you hear me Mum?'

'Clear as a bell!' Ah, that sounded better. 'I know you'd like to be with us both. But we can't do that, Debs, your dad is going to be married to Helen.'

334

'Most of anything what I wish is that we could all live together here. Then you wouldn't have to always be in the hotel and ... oh Mum, it's just gorgeous here, so bright and you should just see the things you can buy.'

Gillian knew Stephen had won.

'Write me a long letter and tell me all about it – your new room, your school...' She bit hard on the corners of her mouth.

''Course I will. And you write to me too. And I want a picture of Lyndy for my room. They said I could have the bedroom that looks straight out over a huge park.' Stephen must have come back, probably to tell the child it was time to end the phone call. 'She says I can stay, Dad. I've got to go, Mum. I'll write, I promise I'll write.'

Then the voice was Stephen's. 'I'm sorry we had to do it this way, Gill honey. I just didn't want any scenes.'

'I don't make scenes,' she answered coldly, untouched by his words. 'I want to know where Debbie is living, so send me the address. Thank God I had the sense not to be persuaded into our remarrying.'

'Sure, it makes things a heck of a lot easier now that Helen and I will be tying the knot. I guess there's a lot of our stuff left behind at Hunters' Lodge, so I'll send the address and get you to have it shipped across. And Gillian – thanks for taking it well. But at least you know now that the Kiddo will have a proper home that's her own and she won't have to play second fiddle to things you find so important in the ho–'

Cutting him off mid-sentence, Gillian slammed down the receiver and with more strength than she knew she possessed she pulled the wire from its socket. Reason should have told her that that would leave the hotel with no outside communication, but reason was lost to her. Alone in the night-time silence, the broken cord in her hand, misery descended on her like a blanket of hopelessness. How long she sat, she didn't consider. Minutes? Hours? It seemed like eternity and yet something held her back from going to bed. It was as if just to shut herself in her bedroom as she did every ordinary night would be like drawing a line under a past that had been snatched away from her.

In fact, after a few minutes she stood up and, like a sleepwalker, went out of the room, turning the light off behind her. Then in the dark she walked along the corridor to Debbie's room. Last thing each night she'd always looked in at the little girl, enough light from the passage falling across the bed for her to see she was covered. Now she switched on the light in the room. Gone ... yet how could she be gone when her presence filled this tiny room? Blinded by tears, Gillian looked at the unslept-in bed. Her body was weary but her mind couldn't relax. Sitting on the edge of the bed, she closed her eyes and let herself be enveloped in memories. The sweet smell of the baby, the way she used to open her mouth wide, showing her first milk teeth in a beam that held too much joy for an ordinary smile; the way she used to jump with excitement she hadn't the words to express when, home from work, Gillian collected her from Sally Bryant; her pride as she sat astride Lyndy; the feeling of her warm arms when she'd been frightened by the storm on the night David had died ... on and on the pictures came into Gillian's mind. At what point she drew up her legs so that she could lay on the bed she could never be sure, nor yet at what point memories turned into a dream: they were riding together on the downs, she could hear Debbie's laughter, then another voice – Mike's. Joy, perfect joy, enveloped her. But the chill of night woke her, a chill that even in the first seconds reached her soul. The moon was casting enough light into the room for her to be aware of every inch of it; was it because she was still not fully awake that she could so clearly hear Debbie's voice and her happy laughter?

Tears choked her and she made no attempt to stop them. There was no logic in her need to escape, for where was there to escape to? Kicking off her shoes with their four-inch heels, she fetched her coat, thrust her feet into walking shoes and went out into the car park. Instead of taking the car, she turned towards the stables, then went out through the small gate into the lane. Just for a moment, as she passed the bungalow, her thoughts turned to Ella. We have to play the hand life deals us, wasn't that what Ella had said? But Ella lived the only way she'd ever known. Debbie ... Debbie gone. An echo of her own voice came to Gillian, telling Mike that Stephen was her future. Thank God at least that wasn't true. Damn him, from the bottom of her soul, damn him. But to take Debbie ... to spoil her with gifts ... had he been buying her affection right from the start? Or was it something much, much deeper? Was it a blood tie between them that made *her* the outsider?

As she strode along the lane the only sounds were of her footsteps and her choking and uncharacteristic sobs. There in the empty countryside there was no one to hear her, no one to care. Usually when any of them walked to the downs they took the footpath through the wood on the brow of the hill, but in the dark she automatically took the longer route, keeping to the lane as they did when they rode. Once on the open downs, she skirted the edge of the wood and started down the hill. It was about a mile to the stream where she had so often come with David and where she and Mike had ridden together that first time. Mike, if only Mike were here now. Stephen is my future, she'd told him; what a fool she'd been. In her heart she had known how right it was for her to be with Mike. But Debbie had so loved Stephen that she had known she couldn't destroy her happiness.

Mike ... she must talk to Mike ... she must hear his voice and even though he was hundreds of miles away, she would feel his love.

Then she remembered what she'd done to the telephone. She had never needed Mike more than she did in those moments. Sitting hunched on the fallen tree trunk by the stream, the place that had always been special to her, her heart and soul reached out to him. She would go back to the hotel and fetch some coins, then take the car to the telephone kiosk in the village. If it were the middle of the night, Mike would understand. In her mind she could already hear his voice, gentle, strong, calm and, above all, loving.

If the night had been warmer she might have been less aware of the passing of time. As it was, emotionally exhausted, she stood up for the long walk back to the hotel. Surely that couldn't be dawn lighting the sky? It was too dark to see her watch, and for a moment that was what she supposed until she realized the east wasn't in that direction. Blundering on the uneven ground she started to run. Despite the darkness, she took the short cut through the wood, stumbling, her clothes catching on rough wood. As she emerged at the other end, she could hear the unfamiliar sound of voices shouting and surely the clanging of a bell, and now that she had climbed to the height of the downs the smell of smoke was evident. There were only two properties in that lane, Derek and Ella's bungalow and Hunters' Lodge. As she pounded along the lane, she knew even before the two buildings came into view, just which one it was.

At Hunters' Lodge, where she had believed the guests had all gone to their rooms, one man had been sitting alone in the visitors' lounge. Despairing and morose, he'd been there all the evening, his only company a bottle of whisky he'd brought with him and a letter from his solicitor. If he'd intended the neat whisky to boost his spirit, he was sadly disappointed – just as he'd been disappointed by everything else over these last months as he'd seen his world destroyed. Even the solicitor's letter became harder to read – the words indistinct – as the evening progressed and the bottle was steadily emptied. His wife had left him, he had lost his job, his house was to be repossessed; which ever way his mind turned – and in truth he had difficulty in steering it in any direction – the outlook was worse than hopeless.

In the hotel bedrooms, the lights were turned off, and he was surrounded by silence. He shivered. He'd put another log on the fire, that would cheer the place up. He tried to stand but he really felt most strange; was the room swaying or was something wrong with him that he felt he was going to fall? Down he sat again. But he ought to do something about the fire. Best if he did it on his hands and knees, yes that was the way. That nice long thin log, that's the one he'd use. He pulled it from the basket and pushed one end of it into the dying embers, rewarded by the flames that licked at it. Moving back to the chair meant turning around, but first he'd just lie on the fireside rug a minute and get warm. Warmth, that's what he needed. In a minute he'd go back to the chair and have a drink. In a minute ... there, in front of the fire, he slept.

Coming towards the small gate into the stable yard, Gillian met Teddy leading two horses towards the field where they grazed.

'Trying to get them in the clear before they take fright,' he greeted her, the urgency of the moment in his tone, 'these are the last two. Mavis has given me a hand.'

'Where is it? What's happened?' Even as she heard herself ask, Gillian knew it was a silly question. Where else could it be except Hunters' Lodge?

'I heard the fire alarm in the hotel.' Anxious to get the horses well clear he was walking on towards the paddock as he called to her. 'Don't know how it started. I got in to call 999 but the phone was dead so I drove down to the village. Reckon everyone's out OK; they looked to be outside by the time I drove back. I heard the bell on the engine, so the men'll soon get it under control.'

By that time he was some way away, but she thought what he said was, 'Seems to have started in the lounge beyond the bar.'

'Oh God! Ella!' Gillian imagined that narrow staircase. 'Let Derek be there, please let Derek have got her out. No one else would even know she was there. Please, let Derek have got her down.'

The volunteer firemen from Ockbury were already taking control. The guests, wrapped in blankets over their night clothes, had been moved away from the building and the hose was already unfurled and connected to the hydrant in the lane. Derek's "hearse" was parked by the stable block, but there was no sign of either him or Ella.

'Is anyone hurt?' she shouted as she came near to the huddled group. 'Have you seen Ella?' The thought came to her that perhaps he had taken her home.

'Some chap just rushed in, haven't seen him come out,' someone called to her.

That's when Teddy arrived, satisfied the horses were safe. He didn't need to have it spelled out to him. Ella and Derek were his friends and she had told him that if Derek were late home he would ask for her to stay the night.

'Must be Derek, he'll need help,' he yelled at Gillian. 'Where...?'

'Up the stairs from the bar. Tell the firemen. They'll get her.'

But Teddy didn't stop to speak to the firemen, who were still busy with the hose. Instead he rushed in just as Derek had a few minutes earlier. As he opened the front door the smoke poured out, then the draught fanned the flames that were already gaining a hold. It was Gillian who alerted the firemen and told them where Ella was.

Minutes seemed more like hours before Ella

was brought out, carried by a fireman with the frame of a giant. On the waiting stretcher, she was lifted to one of the two ambulances parked half way down the drive, whilst at that same moment a third trundled up the hill. Derek and Teddy appeared, both supported by two more fire fighters. In fact they had managed to get Ella half way down the narrow stairs when help had come. Once outside the firemen more or less dragged them to a safe distance and then left them. With everyone out, their attention was on the building that minute by minute was giving itself up to the flames.

'Wait!' Gillian called to the stretcher bearers as they lifted Ella aboard. 'Her husband's here. Can't he come with her to the hospital?'

'Next trip for him. This one is to the maternity hospital, and from the look of it we shall be delivering the baby before we get there...' His last words were lost in a scream from Ella, Ella the stoic who never complained.

Derek lurched towards the ambulance, coughing and choking, his lungs full of smoke, but his strength gave out and he collapsed in a heap on the edge of the grass.

So the night went on: Derek and Teddy were taken to Brindley Cottage Hospital; the charred remains of the guest whose body had been found on the floor of the lounge were brought out, covered with a blanket and, later, removed in a police van; the hotel guests, of which there were fortunately few on that particular night, were taken to the village hall where, as if by some miracle, beds had already been made up on the floor and two local members of the WVS had teapots and boiling water ready to greet them. And through it all Gillian and Mavis watched as Hunters' Lodge burned.

'My dear,' Kathleen's familiar voice broke into Gillian's horror as the thatch ignited, the smoke, which had been seeping through it, giving way to flames. Sparks flew upwards, the forecourt and garden illuminated by the blaze. 'Oh my dear. Is everyone safe? Where have they taken Ella?' The words carried conviction that Kathleen had no doubt her daughter was safe; the over-confident tone told Gillian just how frightened she really was.

'She has been taken to the maternity hospital. The baby has started.'

'Oh, dear God.' Then making an effort to pull herself together, 'Edward, this is Gillian. But ... this ... *this* ... how did it happen?' Then, without waiting even for an answer (an answer which Gillian couldn't have given), 'Edward, I'll direct you. We must get to the hospital. Is Derek there?'

As briefly as she could, Gillian explained, but Kathleen hardly listened.

'Ella was an eight month baby.' She spoke her thoughts aloud, her voice full of fear. 'Suppose, oh God no, don't let it happen again.'

Edward, a man of about seventy but still with the same straight, military bearing of his youth, put his arm around her shoulder and turned her towards the drive; but not without a quick

344

glance at Gillian, a glance in which, even in the eerier light of disaster, she could read sympathy and a plea for understanding. Then her own tragedy overtook all else. There was room in her thoughts for nothing but what she had allowed to happen to David's dream. Just as Kathleen's mind had focused solely on Ella, so Gillian's did on Hunters' Lodge. If she thought about Ella at all it was to suppose that, like any other woman, she was going through the throes of childbirth. She even supposed that Derek would be released from hospital and, perhaps by daybreak, would bring news of either a son or a daughter. Had she been able to know what was happening at the Maternity Hospital, it might have put her own troubles into perspective. What are bricks and mortar compared with the gift of life?

At last the eastern sky took on the hues of morning. Once fire engines from further afield had arrived, the fire had been overcome and the remains of the building were no more than a wet, smoke-blackened ruin. Alone in the summer house Gillian had watched, helpless and defeated.

'Best you come indoors to our place, Mrs Sinclair,' Mavis said, coming to find her where she sat in the summer house gazing at her collapsed world. 'I've got the kettle boiling. We'll have a pot of tea and some boiled eggs, how would that be?'

What a moment for Gillian to remember Helen and how the girl used to retreat alone to the summer house after David had been killed. She recalled her own irritation and knew she had been brought closer to understanding.

'It's what we both need, Mavis,' she answered, determined that neither self-pity nor the overwhelming sense of isolation that threatened her was going to beat her. 'Thanks. A thousand and one things I must do ... can't think where to start.' But that wasn't true. The first thing she would do would be to go to the telephone kiosk in the village and put a call through to Mike. Her possessions might all be gone, but his phone number was inscribed on her mind.

'Start by getting some breakfast inside you,' said practical Mavis who, in truth, was making herself sound confident to hide her own concern about what was happening to Teddy at Brindley Hospital and what would become of them now that Hunters' Lodge was gone. 'Then nothing will seem so bad. And Mrs Sinclair, don't they say there's always a silver lining in every cloud? We must be grateful Debbie was still away with her father when it happened.'

Gillian knew that that was the moment she ought to have made herself say it: Debbie was gone, she wasn't coming home. But she couldn't. Instead she repaid Mavis's attempt at cheerfulness with a smile, as she got up to take a detour around the firemen's remaining hoses and go to the rooms above the new stable block.

'I have a friend who says that life works to a pattern,' she answered. 'It's hard to see how last night could have weaved a necessary strand.

But we have to trust, we have to hope.'

'That's about it, Mrs Sinclair. I bet you were sorry when Mike Trelawney went off to Ireland, he was sort of part of Hunters' Lodge. Then you got lumbered with Teddy and me.'

'Not lumbered, Mavis. You and Teddy have become part of the place too. And I wish you'd call me Gillian.'

'That's nice. I don't mind telling you, between ourselves that's how Teddy and me always speak of you. It's rotten, all your nice clothes, all your make-up and things that make a girl feel she's worth tuppence, all lost. Tell you what, back at our place, you hop into the bath and spruce yourself up. You're welcome to use my things for your face.'

Gillian felt touched by the girl's natural kindness. Yet bathed, made up with cosmetics she found on the dressing table, and back in the living room to share a pot of tea, when Mavis said perhaps that would be the day there would be the news they'd waited for about Debbie, still Gillian couldn't bring herself to tell her.

'Debbie is safe. Stephen phoned late last night.'

'Thank God for that. If he'd waited until today he would have found no telephone. Funny the way things work out; I've thought so hundreds of times. Like when the house copped it with that Doodlebug, do you reckon Fate knew what it was up to that I was off in the Land Army just days before? At the time I felt sort of guilty that I had got off scot-free. But

347

then I met Teddy and I could see where it all fitted into place.'

Fitted into place: Debbie gone, Hunters' Lodge gone. Mike ... but Mike wasn't gone, he was at the other end of the telephone.

'I don't know, Mavis. At the moment I can see no reason. If I'd not gone walking before I got ready for bed last night, Hunters' Lodge would still have been standing. I had the telephone call and I just wanted to get out, to walk in the clear air.'

'I can understand that. Sounds sort of mushy and I don't usually talk that way, but somehow you feel nearer to – well, I suppose it's God – out in the country in the clear air. And I bet last night you wanted to say a *big* thank you. Good things or bad, that's where we turn. When I got the news about Mum and Dad and Bob, I walked for miles that night. But you must have been sort of bursting with thankfulness, 'cause, say what you will, you must have been out of your mind with worry about where they'd got to.' And where had they got to? She didn't ask but from the pause in her chatter, Gillian knew she hoped to be told.

'You've been a real friend, Mavis. Now I have a hundred things to do. I shall be out for most of the day: I have to go to Reading to the insurance company and I must see what's happening to the Crosbie sisters and anyone else in the village hall. And call in at the Maternity Hospital too and see whether it's a boy or a girl. I expect Derek and Teddy will be allowed home this morning, but tell him not to worry about the horses, I'll see to them later if he's not feeling up to it.'

Leaving Hunters' Lodge, she drove to the village telephone kiosk, where she put through two calls. The first was to Mike; just to hear his voice would give her the courage she needed to find her way along the unknown path ahead. But the message came back to her that there was no reply. Feeling empty and alone, as lost as a rudderless ship, she put through her second call. Ella had been well all through her pregnancy, so by this time the baby would be sure to have made an easy entrance into the world. But she was wrong. All she was told was that Mrs Denvers was in labour.

'Is it going well? How long do you think she'll be?'

'I'm sorry, I can't tell you anything more.'

So another telephone call, this time to the Manor, where she was answered by Clarry Higgins, the local postman's wife who worked for Kathleen each morning.

'I've not seen hair or hide of her. She rang last night and said she and a friend would be here when I arrived this morning, but the place was all locked up. I used my own key, you understand. Then the phone went and it was her to tell me Miss Ella was in the Maternity Hospital. She went in in the early hours, so I dare say it'll soon be over for the poor child.'

'Is that what she said – soon be over?'

'Well, Mrs Sinclair, truth to tell, she sounded

349

... well, not like herself. Hard on a mother when her daughter goes through the mill and Miss Ella of all folk, it can't be all beer and skittles. We'll have to keep our fingers crossed that it'll get itself born soon now.'

With a heavy heart, Gillian drove on to Reading. First she went to the insurance company, where she filled in forms and talked to the head of the claims department. Before a claim could be met, the assessor would have to see the state of the hotel, but she was able to arrange for an advance payment to be made to Jane and Margaret Crosbie, who possessed nothing but their nightwear and the blanket they had carried for added protection when they evacuated their room. After that she made another call to Mike, but still with no reply. There were so many things to organize: clothing coupons supplementary to those originally issued to replace what had been lost in the fire; whatever she made of the future had to be up to her, and with that in mind she drew money out of the bank and went to the cosmetic department of the large department store where she spent freely believing, as she always had, that if life throws you off balance it's easier to fight back with a well made-up face and manicured nails. Then came another abortive attempt to contact Mike. He was her rock, he always had been, and she hadn't the courage to imagine that his own life might have pushed her into the background. In need of at least a ray of hope, she phoned the Maternity Hospital.

'It's not in my remit to discuss the patients,' came the starchy reply from the secretary.

'Perhaps you'd be good enough to find someone who can.' Gillian spoke in a voice that defied argument. Then, fearing she might have spoilt what chance she had of getting news, 'You see, she was staying in my hotel when she was brought out from the fire last night. Her husband was taken to Brindley Hospital. I feel responsible.'

'Well, that's different. He's in the waiting room now, I'll fetch him to speak to you.'

Gillian fed two more shillings into the slot and waited to press Button A when she heard the pips telling her that her time was up.

'Gillian?' It was Derek's voice, and perhaps it was the after-effect of the smoke that made him sound so husky. 'Gillian, it's been awful. They're letting me wait, but even her mother hasn't been allowed. Ella's must be so frightened – and they won't let me see her. Hour after hour and it seems no nearer. Sister says it's not Ella's fault, she has pushed and pushed, but the baby is no nearer getting born. They think they will have to operate and take the baby that way. Cut her open, Gillian...' His voice broke and he gave up the battle as he wept. 'I've prayed and prayed. Gillian, what if she...'

'No, Derek! Don't even *think* it. Some women have their babies by Caesarean operation. Just pray for Ella that that is what they'll do and the pain will stop.' She made herself sound more optimistic than she felt. Ella had had no fear of

351

going into labour, she had just wanted to prove she was the same as other women. But what had he said? That she had pushed and pushed and the baby was no nearer getting born. Then came the memory of Kathleen's premonition of disaster. Ella had been an eight month baby. Was history repeating itself?

So the day went on, and the afternoon was well on by the time Gillian arrived at the Village Hall. The other few of the hotel's residents had been collected by relatives or friends, dressed in clothes brought for them, either their own or borrowed. Just Margaret and Jane remained, both wearing ill-fitting garments loaned to them by members of the WVS.

'You've come Mrs Sinclair dear.' Jane greeted her with relief. 'We've been sitting here worrying. How will Mr Sinclair get in touch with you now? Or are they home? Oh dear, what a mess it all is.'

'And us,' Margaret put in. 'The ladies here have been so kind. But we must look to the future. We've been so comfy at the hotel, we don't know anything about the sort of residential places for the old.'

Gillian felt a wave of compassion for them. Old was exactly what they both looked.

'Stephen telephoned me last night. There has been no accident. They are fine, all three of them.'

'Thank God for that,' from Jane. 'That makes our own troubles seem paltry.'

'I will help you look for somewhere. I wonder

352

about Brindley House, on the edge of town. The matron used to come to the hotel for dinner sometimes. You remember Mrs Wells and her jolly husband?'

'Yes, we remember them.' Margaret spoke for them both. 'David introduced us to them. He liked them.' And, for them, that was recommendation enough. 'Would they have us, do you think? We would share a room.' It was pitiful to hear them. Could David know what had happened? He had loved them as though they were family.

'I'll drive straight over there.' The old ladies looked at each other in relief. Someone was going to see to things for them. 'Now about the others: Stephen telephoned from New York.' And so she told them.

'The naughty, wicked girl. How could she do it when you and your husband had come together again? She doesn't deserve happiness! I hope she gets her just desserts.' Margaret spoke for both of them, while Jane nodded in agreement.

'No,' Gillian answered. 'Let's hope they will have a long and happy marriage. I truly hope so. I just want Debbie to be secure and happy. They both love her.'

'Oh dear, it's so cruel. Your little girl.'

Gillian stood up, anxious to put an end to the conversation while she still held on to her control. Over the time she had run the hotel, the sisters had felt they had come close to knowing what went on under that cold exterior. Looking

353

at her now, they saw no further than the woman they had first met.

'I'll drive straight to Brindley House and then come back to tell you how I get on.'

In fact she did better than that. Within an hour she was back, Frances Wells with her. And that night Jane and Margaret settled into their new home, sharing a large bedroom overlooking the garden of Brindley House.

They had no luggage, so seeing them settled took no time at all. Arranging to collect them to go shopping the next day, Gillian went back to Hunters' Lodge. The acrid smell of the fire filled the air, the forecourt was a quagmire and now that the remaining fire tender had gone, the enormity of what had happened seemed even greater than it had through the activity of the previous night. Teddy was home from the hospital and the horses had been brought back to the stables.

'Derek's in the bungalow,' he greeted Gillian. 'He keeps going off to phone, but they don't tell him anything except that she's in labour. A long time, isn't it?'

'First babies don't always hurry.' Gillian tried to sound more optimistic than she felt. 'I'll go and see him.'

She found him sitting at the kitchen table and one glance told her that it would take more than forced cheerfulness to help him.

'I've done this to her,' he said as without knocking on the door, Gillian let herself in. 'How can she stand it?'

'She's proud to have her baby the same as any other woman. Derek, for her sake, you've got to be strong.'

'They don't tell me anything, and yet they don't hide from me that they are worried. Something is wrong, I know it is. This morning when I got there they said it would soon be over. They said something about contractions being almost continuous. And that's how it's been ever since.'

'Perhaps by now they are giving her a Caesarean. The pain will be over.'

'I phoned the Manor. I could tell her mother was frightened. She said something about having a premonition. She said, "Even if the baby is born like she was herself, don't let us lose Ella, please God don't take Ella."' He had his head buried in his hands and Gillian wasn't sure how much he'd repeated Kathleen's words and how much was his own plea.

Time ticked on. Derek again went to the village to phone but was told nothing, just as Gillian's further call to Mike brought no reply. Kathleen arrived at the bungalow, this time without Edward. Perhaps they each drew strength from the presence of the other two, but if they did they weren't aware of it. At about eleven o'clock, having eaten nothing more than toasted stale bread and a piece of cheese while Derek played with that on his plate and Kathleen refused food altogether, Gillian left them and went to the spartan accommodation that at one time had been Mike's in the original stable

355

block. With a put-u-up bed in a living room furnished with a table and two chairs, a cooker and a sink, even when it had been permanently occupied no one would have seen it as comfortable. A small adjoining room held a toilet and a bath with a temperamental geyser fed by the same gas container as the cooker. It had been empty all through the winter and was cold and unwelcoming, but by that time Gillian was too tired to care. Not attempting to undress she lay down on the sofa without bothering to open it into a bed and, despite her mind being in a confusion of anxiety, immediately fell asleep.

When Derek climbed the wooden steps to the stable loft the next morning she was still sound asleep, so he scribbled a note on the back of an envelope he found in his pocket: "We have a daughter. Ella conscious and proud. Derek." Then he crept away, careful not to wake Gillian.

Hours later, with consciousness on the brink of return, first she was aware of sunshine streaming through the window at the far end of the converted hayloft then, like a wave sweeping her into a slough of despair, the realization of the events of recent days came back to her. She closed her eyes as if to escape. In seconds – or was it minutes, she had no idea – came the feeling that she wasn't alone. That's when she saw him, just as she had so often imagined. Had she opened her eyes, or was this just another dream?

'Mike,' she mouthed silently, as if she were scared the image would vanish. Then as he bent closer she suddenly sat bolt upright, reaching out to touch him. 'Mike, you're real. I thought I was dreaming. Kept phoning you...'

Sitting on the edge of the sofa, he took her hand in his.

'I had a call from Nicolas Messer,' he said, naming the accountant. 'That was in the early hours of yesterday. He'd driven up from the village and seen the blaze. Gilly why didn't you tell me – about Stephen and Debbie I mean? Nick had heard it on the wireless.' As if the sound of his voice fascinated her, she gazed at him. 'If there has been an accident...'

'There was no accident. Mike, Debbie's gone.' And so she told him. For all her misery for what had happened, she clung on to what she tried to see as one bright strand in the pattern of events: from the day Debbie and Stephen had found each other, they had grown closer. If ever he loved *anyone* with pure, un-selfish love then it was Debbie. 'Better the right stepfather than the wrong natural father, that's what Kathleen said – and you too in different words. But, Mike, best of all for her is the *right* natural father.'

'And mother,' he added. 'Tell me, Gilly, when you took him back into your life, was it for love?'

She considered the question, determined to find the honest truth.

'I'd never even imagined myself in love until I met Stephen, and when he'd gone I tried to believe that Debbie and I were sufficient for

357

each other. Perhaps I thought I was still in love with him when he came back – yes, I must have – but I soon knew it had been a mistake. For Debbie's sake I tried, *honestly* I tried, to make it work and to make myself believe it was right for us to be together. But Mike, you can't be happy married to one man when with all your heart and soul you love another.'

Just for a moment they looked at each other, everyone else forgotten, the blackened remains of the hotel forgotten, then he took her in his arms and she clung to him as if her life depended on nothing ever coming between them.

That day they faced the tasks ahead of them with new resolve. Nicholas Messer had realized it would take many hours for Mike to get back to Ockbury, and because as partners in the business there were things that would need to be organized by both Mike and Gillian, he had telephoned him in the middle of the night as the hotel blazed. On that morning – or what remained of the morning – a future that had seemed desolate and without purpose found a new meaning.

When late in the afternoon they returned from a meeting with Stuart Gregory, the senior partner of Gregory and Tufnell, they found Kathleen and Edward waiting.

'Kathleen, I had Derek's note. Wonderful news.'

Kathleen nodded, for a moment frightened to trust her voice.

'A Caesarean birth. Why they had to let the poor child suffer all those hours, I don't know. But Gillian, my dear, they say the baby is well. All my fears...' She turned her head away. 'And today,' she went on, 'I told Ella that I am marrying again. I've dreaded telling her.' Then with a sudden smile, 'But today she has ... has grown up ... grown wise ... she understands.'

Of course there were handshakes and hugs. Emotion was running high as they stood there in front of the acrid-smelling ruin.

'Now it's my turn,' Mike said, his arm around Gillian. 'I'm afraid you're going to lose a good neighbour. Gillian is coming back to Ireland with me. I guess you're not the only ones to be getting wed.'

'And about time too!' Kathleen was laughing and crying at the same time, the emotion she had held in check for so many hours finding release. 'Silly fool I am. But bless you both. If ever I saw a couple tailor-made for each other it's you two. So what are your plans?'

'As soon as at least on paper things are cleared up here, we are going to Dalgooney,' Gillian told her.

'There's a lot to do there.' Mike took up the story. 'But the stables are ready, so we shall have the horses brought over and we'll start again there. Another Hunters' Lodge.'

'A hotel?'

Gillian shook her head. 'Not really. We think of it more as having house parties; house parties with a theme. But before we get to that stage there will be a lot of work to do. It's a new beginning, a new life, Kathleen. It has to be.' At her words, Mike tightened his hold on her shoulder. A new life without Debbie. He, who had felt instant dislike for Stephen, had never been as filled with hatred for him as he was at that moment. Yet surely he should have simply been thankful that Gillian had fallen out of love with the man who had haunted her for so many years. Indeed he was thankful, but the image of the little girl he had come to love seemed to be there amongst them. A new life, a life without her.

'We don't design the pattern we weave.' Kathleen's voice cut into his thoughts. 'A new beginning, as you say, Gillian. How much harder it would have been for you to take up the challenge of Dalgooney if Hunters' Lodge had still been here. A time for change, all round. Paul is selling up in Devon and coming to live at the Manor, where he intends to offer space to Ella and Derek – but they will make their own decision. I am moving to Devon with Edward. You have made a great sacrifice in agreeing that Debbie should stay with her father, for you may be sure if you fought him in the courts you would be able to force him to bring her back. But my dear, the greater love is to let her go. There is something between them that is too strong to be broken. I disliked the man,' she said with her usual honesty, 'but the tie between them was obvious. And as for Helen, she has faults aplenty but if there is one golden strand she might add to the pattern it's that in her care a child will be given genuine love.' She seemed suddenly to become aware of her long speech and looked around at them in something akin to embarrassment. 'Just hark at me!'

'We do, and we shall remember what you said,' Mike told her. He had no illusions. He knew there would be times when Gillian would be overcome by misery because Debbie was gone.

'Now I'm off to the hospital to meet my new granddaughter,' Kathleen said. 'They told me that I could see her early this evening. Is there any message for Ella?'

'Give her my love, tell her we shall come and see her tomorrow...' Gillian started, when Mike interrupted with, 'We want to talk to them both, Ella and Derek too.'

It was only after Kathleen and Edward had gone that he told Gillian of the plan that had been forming in his head. She listened, the future taking shape in her mind and with it the birth of new hope.

'If only David could know and be part of it,' Mike said as he waited for her to express her reaction with anything more than a sequence of nods of approval as she'd listened, her eyes bright with hope.

'He does know, Mike. David will always be part of it.'

It took another month before the convoy of vehicles set off at the start of their journey to

Ireland. Mike and Gillian were at the head of the procession, he driving her car; next came the converted hearse, Derek at the wheel with Ella by his side, the Moses basket on the floor at the rear next to the tightly secured wheel-chair; behind that came the horsebox driven by Teddy with Mavis by his side. All the horses were being taken by a firm dealing with animal transportation, so on that occasion all the available space was taken by their own few possessions and Derek's canvasses.

To all of them, this was the start of a great adventure. There was work to be carried out in the house before they could take visitors, but work held no fear for any of them. They were a team. And when the house was ready they would market Dalgooney not just for riding holidays but for painting courses too.

'Here we go, Gilly. This is really it,' Mike said as they turned out of the drive and started down the hill to the village, reaching to take her hand. 'The first day of the rest of our lives.'

She nodded, raising their linked hands and holding his to her cheek. Turning in her seat, she caught a last glimpse of David's dream. In her handbag she had a letter from Helen, enclosing one from Debbie. School was "great"; her new bedroom was "fantastick".

A month before, when Mike had come from Ireland, she had known she loved him. She had known he was her dearest friend and the man she wanted to be with for the rest of her life. But knowing it then seemed a poor thing compared with what had developed between them through those last weeks.

'Yep,' she answered him, 'here we go, Mike. You know what I think? Dreams aren't for dreaming, they are for building. And we six, we're going to do just that.'

'Six?' he laughed. 'Don't forget little Kate. Dalgooney is a great place for youngsters.'